TALON

Janet Lee Carey grew up surrounded by redwood trees in northern California. The sea was only a short, winding road ride away. It was in this magic place that she first dreamed of writing children's books.

Janet is the author of four previous children's novels, including *The Beast of Noor*, and *Wenny Has Wings*, which received the Mark Twain award. She lives with her family near Seattle, Washington.

Visit her website at www.janetleecarey.com

by the same author
WENNY HAS WINGS
THE BEAST OF NOOR

TALON

JANET LEE CAREY

ff

faber and faber

First published in 2007
by Faber and Faber Limited
3 Queen Square London WCIN 3AU

Typeset by Faber and Faber Ltd
Printed in England by Clays, St Ives Plc

A CIP record for this book
is available from the British Library

ISBN 978-0-571-23311-3
ISBN 0-571-23311-2

2 4 6 8 10 9 7 5 3 1

To Heidi Pettit who helped me find the dragon's cave
below the waterfall.

TALON

Prologue

OR SIX HUNDRED YEARS PENDRAGON KINGS AND queens ruled Wilde Island, though none in England recognized their lineage. King Arthur's younger sister, Evaine, was the first queen of the isle. Banished from England in AD 520, she lived and died in exile. And if there is no record of her birth or lineage in history or legend, the blame rests with her father King Uther.

The night he learned his youngest child had ridden to the wildwood to wed the outlaw Kaydon Mallory, King Uther spat upon a candle. In the dark he swore never to speak Evaine's name again. And though Queen Ygraine wept and pleaded with him, Uther would not be moved. Eschewing jail or burning he cursed Evaine and banished her.

That night as Ygraine wept and King Uther paced the halls, Evaine packed her chests for the long voyage. She filled the trunks with gowns, jewels, and her princess crown. Last, she packed the royal Pendragon sceptre, taken in stealth from her father's strongroom. With these things she planned to rule her own kingdom without the blessing of her father.

She heard Merlin slip into her room, knowing he'd passed the guards invisibly and entered without a key, but she kept packing.

'A storm comes,' said Merlin.

'It does not matter,' said Evaine. 'I set sail with Kaydon at dawn.'

Merlin eyed the chests now spilling over with castle bounty. 'You take more than Kaydon with you.'

Ignoring the remark, Evaine peered out of the window and heard an owl's cry in the trees. She shivered. Not for the owl or for her good man waiting in the woods, but for the fearsome journey ahead. None had ever returned from Wilde Island once they'd been sent to rot there.

'You shall live,' said Merlin, 'and the child within you.'

Evaine turned to face the wizard. 'Have you read my destiny in the stars?'

'Not your destiny, Evaine, but one that will come long after.'

'What shall her name be?'

Merlin shook his head. 'Names are not written in the stars, but destinies. The signs all point to the twenty-first queen of Wilde Island.' He stepped to the window and peered into the night. 'Three things the stars say of this queen. She shall redeem the name Pendragon. End war with the wave of her hand. And restore the glory of Wilde Island.'

He tilted his head. 'And yet I see darkly in the stars . . . a beast.'

Evaine heard Merlin breathing hard, as if the starry vision had him by the throat. So there was a dark side to this prophecy. She didn't want to hear it. It was enough to know her offspring would endure centuries of banishment. 'The twenty-first queen?' said Evaine, a slow heat rising up her spine. 'Do you think this vision pleases me? By the gods, Merlin! This prophecy could take six hundred years!'

PART ONE

Wormwood and Poppy

I

The Queen's Knife

MOTHER PULLED OUT HER KNIFE. WE WERE ALONE in her solar.

'It's time,' she said. 'Give me your hand.'

I drew back. 'It's not yet Sunday eve.'

'We're together, Rosalind, and the door's well locked.'

'Tomorrow.'

'Tonight.' Then softening her voice, she said, 'Come, Rosie, take off your gloves.'

Her blade flashed in the firelight, which sent a russet glow across the room. She was ready for the ritual. I dreaded it.

'Take yours off first.'

Mother placed her knife on the table and bared her hands. Queen Gweneth's fingers were finely tapered as candles, her skin milky as the moon. It was a shame for her

9

to wear golden gloves, but she'd donned them at my birth to protect me, and had worn them ever since.

'Now you, Rosie.'

I bit my lip as she removed my right glove. Pretty hand that never saw the sun with soft and creamy skin not unlike her own. Mother kissed it. Then taking my other hand in hers, she peeled away the left glove.

My throat tightened as we looked at my fourth finger. The horny flesh. Blue-green and scaly as a lizard's hide. Claw of the beast with a black curving talon at the end.

I rubbed the scar at the base of my claw. A wound I'd made myself the night of Nell's witch burning. With her cunning craft Nell had lured folk into the woods and fed them to the dragon. Of this she was accused and, too, she had a devil's mark on her back. I'd seen the mark myself before they burned her – it was nothing compared to mine. None but Mother and myself knew what hid under my glove lest I be burned for a witch.

With Cook's sharp knife, I'd stolen to my room to cut off my cursed part. The wound was deep and the blood had drenched my kirtle before Mother caught me.

The queen was peering at my claw now, working her face to hold back a sickened sneer but with all her trying, her lip still tightened. 'The sorrow of it,' she whispered. 'That it should be your wedding finger.'

'No man would marry me unless he were a leper.'

'Rosie. Don't say such things.'

'Then say it isn't true.'

Mother took out her silver vial, sipped the poppy potion and closed her eyes. The fire crackled. When the lines around her eyes and mouth grew smooth she corked the bottle and set her jaw. 'Now.'

I hid my hand behind my back. 'It will hurt.'

'I'll cut with care.' Tugging my wrist close, she started peeling the black talon as a fletcher sharpens an arrow.

Curled bits of hard black nail fell to the floor, clickety-click. Sparks flew and a trail of smoke rose as she trimmed. It was a wonder we'd shaken our heads at. For what kind of talon hides a spark?

Scrape. Scrape. I closed my eyes and smelled the odour of ground bone and, stranger still, a smell of rusted metal. The stench filled me with shame.

I waited for her to finish, breathing slow to calm myself. Then I felt a sharp prick.

'Too close to the quick!' I drew back and blinked away the tears.

'Done,' said Mother, sweeping the broken bits of nail in her hands and tossing them in the fire.

Gently now, she slid my golden gloves back on and put her cool hand on my cheek. 'This secret is heavy between us,' she said. 'But do not weep, Rosie. I'll find a way to cure your cursed part. Well and whole you'll wed. I swear it on my life.'

2

The Sacred Finger Bone

QUEEN GWENETH TOLD ME THE STORY OF MY BIRTH once, and has never spoken of it since.

All her life, she'd known she was to bear the twenty-first Pendragon Queen named in Merlin's prophecy. But from her wedding day, her body had turned against her. Six years she tried to conceive; still her womb was empty as a cockleshell. Neither prayer, nor fasting, nor herbs had quickened it. Then in her seventh year of marriage, a holy pilgrim brought Mother Saint Monica's finger bone. Monica, patron saint of mothers, blessed her womb at last. The saint's small bone did great service to her and Mother continued to hold it in high esteem.

I thought long on Monica's blessing, and once asked Mother why a saint would give her a child with a devil's mark.

Mother's eyes went dark as burningstone. 'Never,' she said, 'speak that way of a saint!'

She herded me to chapel and told Father Hugh I was to kneel on the prayer stool till evensong. I had no chance to ask her if my mark were some punishment for Monica's finger bone. Did the saint wish it back? And had she given me a finger of the beast in exchange for mother's treasure?

I was not to ask. So I held the tale of Monica and my birth in my mind from that day on – a cold tale, for I was a winter's child.

On the twelfth night of the new year 1131, a blizzard swept over Wilde Island, and outside the castle walls, Queen Gweneth heard a death wraith keening. The queen thought the howl-song was for her when the labour pains came on strong enough to make her bite the cloth.

'All will be well,' said Midwife Glossen, rubbing the queen's round belly with minted goose fat. 'I've sent the king to unseal every jar and loosen every knot to ease the birth. You'll have your babe as soon as soon.'

All night Mother gripped the bedposts, screaming when the pains were on her.

An hour before dawn, she pushed one last time and I came into the world.

'A girl,' said the midwife.

Mother wept with joy. 'Praise God. Merlin's prophecy is fulfilled.' But she saw the midwife's eyes grow wide with terror.

'What's wrong?' she asked. 'Let me see her now.'

'I must . . . wrap her first.' With trembling hands Glossen bound me in swaddling cloth. She passed me to my mother and backed towards the door.

Mother touched my little face so new, then kissed my

lips, which she said were pink as a rosebud. 'Rosalind,' she whispered. 'Rosalind. Beautiful rose.'

She reached to pull the swaddling cloth away.

'Nay!' screamed the midwife. Before Mother could stop her, she fled the room, ran down the steps and out into the blinding snow.

Mother told me that her heart raced then, wondering what had frightened the woman so. In the empty room she tugged the corner of the cloth away and saw the devil's claw on my left hand.

She did not scream. She was a queen even in that hour.

'Maid,' she called to the woman waiting in the hall. 'Lock the door.'

Alone with me, and silently, she wept.

On the morrow a castle groom found the midwife's body crumpled in the snow near the castle wall. Her mouth was agape as if in prayer, or song or strangled scream. A spot of blood frozen red as a rosebud lay on her tongue.

I knew Mother was grateful to the storm for killing the midwife.

A dead woman cannot speak.

3

The Stolen Child

I WAS TAKEN BY SURPRISE ON SAINT LUKE'S FEAST
day when the warning bells rang out. High in my
solar, my nursemaid, Marn, and I peered out the
window bars. Marn was as old as the world itself, having
been the nursemaid to my mother before she was mine,
and she was near blind so I doubted she could see much
at all looking out my window. I squinted. No enemy
ships approached that I could see, no marauders attacking Dentsmore village far below. I wondered where the
trouble lay.

Marn held my arm. A chill grip and hard, but her voice
came in a whisper, 'Red clouds without the aid of sun.
Traveller beware. The dragon comes.' No sooner had she
spoken than the clouds turned red as the royal carpet
rolled out for Mother and Father on high feast days.

Over the sea he flew, his blue-green scales bright as
rippling water, his broad wings pumping. My legs went all

15

to gruel. I pressed my knees against the wall and gripped the window bars.

Marn had told me dragon tales all my life. Some said the witch Nell fed children to the beast, and I'd heard accounts of dragon attacks on the north side of our island where the villagers are wealthy in wheat and over-plump. But I'd never seen the beast close up before. The full of him. The stark of him. Like a winged demon sweeping over the world.

Outside the castle people ran for the drawbridge. Dragonslayers rushed to the stables, pulled out their gear, shouted orders, mounted horses.

Closer, closer, came the pounding of the wings. My claw throbbed in rhythm with the sound and I gripped the bars tighter to press against the pain.

'Look!' cried Marn. Even she couldn't miss the creature circling Dentsmore below. 'No!' she moaned. 'Not our little village! Can you,' she pleaded. 'Can you see the black-smith's?' Her grown son, the village blacksmith, lived with his family by the smithy.

'He's flying farther west.' Village folk dived into their shops and cottages as the dragon soared overhead, the size of the beast like hell's galleon on a fiery sea. And I saw how small the dwellings looked below his outspread wings.

Our dragonslayers thundered over the drawbridge, some still donning helmets or adjusting their scabbards as they galloped full speed down Kingsway Road toward Dentsmore. Not far below my window, more knights lined up behind the battlement walls, readying their bows.

'Did Sir Magnus put out angelica this morning?' I whispered.

'Aye, across every doorway. I heard him whispering his charm, "Step not across, thou evil beast", to ward the dragon off.'

'But if he should fly over and get to us that way?'

'Step or fly, it's all the same.' Marn said this frowning, not herself believing in Sir Magnus's charm, for now we'd seen the beast with our own eyes. What was a charm or prayer to him?

I tried to swallow, but could not, for out in the barley field south of Dentsmore, the dragon had suddenly dived and captured a peasant. Man or woman, I could not tell from so far away. I thought by the speed a man, for he'd run halfway across the field before the beast cornered him. His death was swift, first the fire, then the devouring. But the dragon's belly was not full yet.

Circling the field, he turned and flew at us. The pain in my claw increased as he came on. I wondered at it, squeezing my finger tight and tighter to make it stop, but it seemed to press the sharp pain deeper into the bone.

Down on the road the slayers wheeled about as the beast winged past. Arrows flew skyward. Thirty or more, and three at least made the mark. They struck his broad golden chest like pins tossed to a high gold-plated ceiling, then fell to the earth again.

Knights scattered under the raining arrows. They regrouped and shot more skyward. But the dragon flew out of range, heading towards Morgesh Mountain.

I ran to my east window. He was gone beyond the trees. Then out he came again, soaring over Kaydon River, the water catching his reflection as he flew towards our orchards. It was then I saw Magda, the brewer's child, coming through the apple trees, swinging her fruit basket. Magda was like a little sister to me, often running down the halls to greet me with a leaf she'd found, or a toad she'd caught by the pond. And singing, she was always singing.

Magda! She must have heard the warning bells. Didn't she know what they meant?

I raced through the door and down the hall. At the top of the stairwell, Sir Kent caught my arm.

'Let go! He's after Magda!'

'I have my orders, Princess.' He pushed me back inside my solar, shut and locked the door.

'Let me out!' I kicked the door. Pounded it.

Marn put her hand on my shoulder. 'Now, Rosie, the slayers will save our Magda. Don't you be afeared.'

I pushed her away and ran back to the window. Only an hour before I'd had Cook send Magda to the orchard.

'Apples,' I'd said. 'I will have them baked and sprinkled with sweet crumbles and no other way.' So Cook had sent the child out with her basket.

The dragon wheeled above the trees.

'Magda!' I screamed through the bars, but she could not hear me on the hill. With the dragon closing in, she hadn't time to run out to the road, nor were there any stones great enough to hide behind.

Magda dropped her basket, and clung to the apple tree, her red dress fluttering in the dragon's hot wind, and her hair, white as thistle down, streaming out behind.

The slayers raced up the hill, swords drawn, their helmets

red as coals in the waning light. But before they reached the orchard, the beast swooped down, caught Magda in his claws, and winged skyward again.

The ease of it! He'd plucked her up as gently as she'd picked the pippins from the tree and held the red-dressed girl in his claws like a bit of stolen fruit!

I clung to Marn as the dragon passed by. Circling once as if to show us his prize, he bore my Magda out to sea.

4

Dragonstone

THREE DAYS AND NIGHTS I STAYED IN MY SOLAR wretched and sleepless. Father Hugh climbed the stair to pray with me for Magda's soul. Our castle astrologer, Sir Magnus, stuffed sticklewort under my pillow to help me sleep. I didn't.

Each time I closed my eyes I saw the dragon's form, and the sounds of his attack echoed in my head. Not the memory of the warning bells, nor Magda's screams nor mine, but the throbbing of my beast mark and the dragon's wings pounding in one time together. The strange of it. The cruel wonder of it. That my cursed part should drum with *him,* even as he flew away with Magda. It was this night on night that stole my sleep. And this secret I could tell no one if I did not wish to burn.

At last on Saint Crispin's day, I left my room to ride with Father. The king was often too busy training up his knights to spend time with his daughter, so when he called me to the stables, I went. Our forest roads were dangerous. Gangs of outlaws hid in the byways waiting to rob unwary travellers, but with my father I was safe.

The day was clear when we took to the woods and the leaves hung like gold coins in the alder trees. We rode our mounts alongside Kaydon River avoiding the apple orchard where Magda's tree still stood, burned black as a crow's wing from the dragon's fire. At midday, we halted on the high hill across from Pendragon Castle. A slender sun-lit ray falling through the branches haloed Father's red hair, and fell on his blue cloak as sunlight on water.

The tall grass parted in the graveyard below where the stonemason climbed the hill. Chisel in hand, he passed the Pendragon tomb and stopped to gaze up at the Dragon-stone. The monolith was carved top to bottom with the names of the dragon's prey. My father cleared his throat as if to call out to the man, but no words followed the low rumbling. He patted his horse's neck instead.

I leaned into Galahad's mane and smelled the sweat along his neck. I wished for all the world that I could snuff out the vision of Magda's death as one snuffs out a candle.

'Come, Rosalind,' said Father turning his dark horse down the path. I steered Galahad towards a sunny spot to soak up the autumn light as I rode.

Rooks took flight as we passed the graveyard, the clang of the mason's chisel riveting my bones. The dark of my father's eyes was like the sea on winter nights when it seems nothing living swims beneath. How many slayers he had trained up to kill the dragon. Still the beast haunted our waking and our sleeping like a demon cut to the shape of our fear.

'It's not your fault,' I said.

'Nor yours, Rosie.'

'I sent the child out for apples!'

Father flinched then regained the steady look he often gave when I shouted. 'You wanted apples for Saint Luke's feast, and there was no harm in sending her. The dragon came on us swiftly, and without warning.'

We skirted the high castle wall, riding past the draw-bridge where the guards hailed us. Galloping up Twisters Hill, Father raised his hand and halted. On the sea cliff ahead of us, my mother stood with her back to us gazing out to sea. She often looked south-east in the direction of our ancestral home, though England had banished our branch of the Pendragon family six hundred years ago, and sent us here to rot.

Civil war waged across the water as Empress Matilda challenged King Stephen's right to the English throne. It was beyond my mind that I should have the power as the twenty-first queen to redeem our family name and end war besides, as was foretold in Merlin's prophecy. But Mother had high plans.

Father gazed up the hill at his queen, and I saw the sad-ness slowly lifting from his face. Putting a finger to his lips, he leaped down from his horse, crept through the grass, took Mother by the waist, and spun her round.

'Gavin!' cried Mother. 'You frightened me!'

Father drew her close and kissed her. Mother pulled away. 'Our daughter watches.'

'Let Rosie see,' said Father. 'She's fourteen and she'll be married soon enough.'

I turned Galahad about. Father had never seen the devil's mark that hid beneath my glove, so he couldn't know how his talk of marriage put a hollow ache inside my breast. Before I left the hill Mother called, 'Ride homeward now. A healer comes tonight.'

'She's well enough,' said Father. Mother made her reply as I rode off. I knew she'd say my liver vexed me or tell some other lie to justify the healer. I urged Galahad to a canter, raced past the drawbridge and up to the wooded hills. Avoiding orchard and graveyard, I headed once more for Kaydon River.

God's bones! How I hated healers! Young and sprightly or old and toothless, it did not matter. A visit meant submitting to their bloodletting or their stinking toadflax leaves. None but Mother, the long-dead midwife and myself had ever seen my naked hand. So the healers, guessing bone ache, applied poultices and charms. Others burned wormwood and sorrel to banish evil spirits, or bid me drink St John's-wort to balance my humours.

The last healer, a man with a braided beard who stank of garlic, guessed I had cramps from my monthly courses, and wrapped an eelskin around my knee!

My knee! As if that would heal my hand!

Still worse than any of these was our own Sir Magnus, who'd arrived eight years ago selling himself as a wondrous physician. Failing to cure my affliction, he'd stayed on as court astrologer and settled in the high crow's nest with his books, bones and potions. The venomous mage beguiled Mother with his starry predictions and sweetened her humours with honeyed poppy.

'I'll turn the next one away,' I told Galahad. But I knew even as I said it I would not.

What if this healer had my cure?

Across the valley, a low mist had blown in from the sea, ghosting Dentsmore below. And soft, I saw it rising towards the castle gate.

Mist was common on Wilde Island, yet as I saw the village slowly disappear the sight unsettled me and my flesh began to prick.

At twilight I was called to Mother's solar to await the healer's visit. The mist had lifted and as I watched the evening drifting slowly to dark, two swallows darted past the window.

'Look,' I said.

Mother left her loom. We watched the swallows fly round and round each other as if binding a bow.

'A sign of love to come,' said Mother happily.

'Will love come to me?' Most of the maids about Wilde Island were married by my age.

'It will, Rosie. And as soon as you are healed, we'll take you to Empress Matilda's son, Prince Henry.' She smiled at the thought.

'But if I cannot be cured –'

'You will be,' said Mother, and I saw how tight she gripped her faith, like a falcon holds its rail. She'd set her hopes on Henry. No matter that his mother, Empress Matilda, was deposed and King Stephen was in power. No matter that we Pendragons were exiles. No matter that I bore a devil's mark.

Mother led me to her wardrobe, opened the door and stood behind me, facing us towards the long mirror, my gown pale violet, hers of gold.

'Queen Rosalind Pendragon,' she said. 'Know who you are.'

I said naught. Firelight caught in the glass, burning around her gown and mine as if we were both aflame. She shut the door. We settled by the hearth to await the healer, the silence growing cold and colder between us as Mother worked her loom. She was weaving a large panel, which she hoped to finish by my fifteenth birthday. The tapestry was a portrait of me dressed in a rose-coloured gown, seated on a throne with Queen Evaine's golden sceptre in my hand. Possession of the Pendragon sceptre was Mother's dream, for the dragon stole it from Queen Evaine and hid it well on Dragon's Keep. In the last six hundred years, many a knight had sailed to the isle of Dragon's Keep to slay the beast, and regain the stolen sceptre which proved our Pendragon heritage. None succeeded.

On the tapestry, angels blessed me in the starry sky above, and below my feet mother had stitched Merlin's prophecy in silver and green. I blushed looking at the cloth so rich in colour and dream.

'Where will you hang it?' I asked, hoping the answer would be her solar or mine.

'I've not decided yet.'

Veritas Dei, God's truth, I didn't want the tapestry on display in the Great Hall for every island clodpoll to drool over. I ran my wrist along the cloth to feel the tickling threads above Merlin's words.

Three things the stars say of this queen.
She shall redeem the name Pendragon.
End war with the wave of her hand.
And restore the glory of Wilde Island.

When I was younger my mother's faith could buoy me. All seemed right in her eyes. My healing sure. My fate secured by starry prediction.

Not so now. When had I lost confidence in her dream?

Another hour passed. Still the healer was delayed. I begged Mother for a story. She quit her tapestry, her hands now astir as she told of the night long ago when she rescued her lady's maid and dearest friend, Aliss, from the frozen marsh. The incident happened while she was being tutored at Saint Brigid's Abbey. Mother missed her family dearly and one wintry night she persuaded Aliss to run away home with her. They'd only just escaped the abbey grounds and started for Pendragon Castle when they were besieged by a blizzard. I knew the tale and liked it well.

'Your lady's maid would have drowned if you hadn't pulled her from the icy water,' I said.

'No doubt.' Mother gave a half smile.

'If only I had a friend my age.' I sighed. 'One like Aliss.'

'You have friends enough.'

'Who? Bram the pigboy? I have no friends at all now that Magda –'

'Don't, Rosie.'

I turned my eyes to the dressing table, where mother's

jewelled combs and perfumes were prettily displayed. We'd had this argument before. Mother would not allow me a friend my own age. 'Because you are the princess,' she said, but I knew the real reason. Good friends kept confidences – shared secrets. I had one that could never be shared.

A bedraggled messenger arrived with news from the Sheriff William.

'Your Highness, the healer you sent for was attacked on the road.'

'By the dragon?' I cried.

'No, Princess, only thieving footpads,' said the man, fingering his filthy hat. 'They stole her horse and cloak and slit her throat besides. Only her servant boy lived to tell of it.'

I fell back in my chair, sickness rising up my throat.

Mother began to dismiss the messenger. But he stayed yet a little while to say, 'Your Highness, the sheriff bade me give you this healing pouch, which the thieves had no use for.' He handed Mother a mud-encrusted bag.

She waved him from the room and locked her chamber door.

'The healer would have lived if she'd not ridden forth to heal me.' Her death weighed heavy on me.

'You're the princess. It was her duty.'

'To die?'

Mother ignored my question and searched the muddy pouch. Frowning, she pulled out dried thyme, a wad of cinquefoil leaves and a vial. 'Your nursemaid could have gathered these selfsame herbs in the nearby woods.' She removed the cork from the vial. The smell of honeyed poppy filled the air. This being a favourite of hers, she corked it again and slipped it in her velvet bag.

'This healer would have failed us just like all the rest.' She hurled the herbs and filthy pouch into the fire.

5

Dragonslayers

AFTER MORNINGSONG THE CASTLE MADE READY TO bless the knights before they sailed north to the isle of Dragon's Keep. No man lived on the foul island though many knights quested there year-on-year to challenge the beast. This day, one-and-twenty slayers were going forth to kill our mortal enemy. At the ceremony Mother expected me to sit nobly in my gilded chair and inspire the knights with my beauty.

I had other plans.

Marn slid her cold hand along my neck as she braided my hair. 'You'll charm the knights. See if you don't.' Marn tugged my scalp harder and I winced. 'Keep still,' she warned. I steadied myself on my stool before the vanity mirror as old Marn babbled on.

'How your mother would have liked to have her hair this length when she was crowned. She wept that morning when I brushed it out, poor poppet, all shorn from her years of training at the abbey, but I was used to her tears by then.'

'Mother does not weep.' I'd seen her tears but once in my life, and that was on the night I'd tried to cut off my claw.

'Aye, well, she's a queen now. But Gwen wept her share as a lass and she was all over tears the day her mother and father sent her away to the abbey.'

I watched my nursemaid's reflection stooping in the glass to choose the blue ribbon from my drawer. She was the only one who called my mother Gwen, having suckled her as a babe, but she never called her that to her face. 'Why did they send her away?'

Marn twisted the ribbon about my plait. 'Who can say? But her brother, Bion, was the one thought to become king and they doted on him. So little Gwen was in the way, you might say.'

'In the way?'

'She was stubborn, like you, and not an easy girl to manage.'

'I'm not stubborn.'

Marn gave a dry laugh. It was nearly time to gather in the foreyard to send off Sir John Broderick and his dragonslayers.

'Have you called for the turnkey?'

'Aye, though why you'd want to see *him* I don't know. There's no time to –'

'It won't take long.'

'Ah, my little poppet,' signed Marn. 'You're all grown now and don't need your old nursemaid at all.'

I reached up to touch Marn's wrinkled cheek. She'd mothered me my whole life, and I thought to say I'd always love her. But she blushed at my touch.

'Hold still now, Rosie,' she said. 'I've got a flea.'

Marn plucked my scalp and crushed the flea with her gnarled fingers. 'A plump one,' she said. Straightening my ribbon, she stepped back. 'Ah, my pretty girl. You're ready for the knight's blessing. I'll just go and tell the queen.'

'First the turnkey,' I reminded her. She gave me an unsettled look before she shut the door.

Sir John Broderick was the best of Father's knights and I had a mind to save him from the dragon. A plan had come to me by way of Mouser. The lackwit could never catch all the castle mice, though he made great noisy scenes, rushing up and down the halls with his soiled pouch shouting, 'There's one!' And, 'stand away!' as he rammed into our astonished guests. Sick of this display, Sir Magnus mixed poison for Mouser to use against the vermin. The mice ate it well enough. But so did my cat. Poor Tilly had a fit and died.

I didn't blame Mouser for Tilly's death. Everyone knew the boy had curds for brains. The hated Sir Magnus never should have given him the poison.

Remembering Tilly, I'd devised a plan. Seeing how our good knight's arrows, those that struck the beast at all, had clattered against the dragon's scales like pebbles to a stone wall, I thought to poison him. A plump murderer in the dungeon would do nicely. We'd feed him greasy bacon, stitch poison into the pockets of his cloak, then free the murderer in an open place and let the dragon sup.

Our isle was teaming with footpads, having once been an English prison colony and a place where folk still came on occasion to serve out their time as bond slaves. Even Marn's husband had come here years ago to pay out his debt.

Many outlaws escaped custody once they reached Wilde Island, which enraged my father and mother and kept our sheriffs busy. I was sure to find a murderer in our dungeon.

Marn entered with the turnkey and I waved her from the room. The turnkey bowed and I saw traces of goose droppings on his pate – Sir Magnus's cure for baldness. The ointment wasn't working.

'List who we house in the dungeon just now,' I said. 'And tell me of their crimes.'

The turnkey pursed his lips and gazed up at the ceiling as if the answer hung there. 'Well there's Rob Thornby. He's in for stealing Madreck's sheep.'

This was not crime enough for my plan. 'Go on,' I said.

'Then there's Madreck. Held for brawling at the tavern and knocking out young Gifford for stealing his sheep.'

'I thought Rob Thornby stole the sheep.'

'Well, Madreck didn't know that!'

'Ah,' I said, confused. 'Well, who else is there?'

The turnkey crossed his arms and rocked back on his heels. 'There's Old Plimpton. He's been imprisoned years and years.'

'For what crime?' I asked, hoping it was murder.

'Well, that I don't know, Princess.'

'How is it you don't know?'

His eyes widened. He licked his thick lips. 'Plimpton's been there since I was a boy, before I ever was turnkey, Princess.'

I dropped the inquiry. No doubt the man was thin and frail, and would not tempt the dragon. I needed someone plump.

'Who else?' I said.

The man screwed up his brows. 'Pardon?'

'Who *else* is in the dungeon?'

'That's all, Princess.'

'All?'

'There'll be more after today's blessing,' he assured me hastily. 'Whenever the villagers carouse with the king's good ale, Sheriff William brings the brawlers in.'

I came to a stand. 'What about the thieves who haunt the roads at night? What about the murderers who slit my healer's throat?'

He shrugged. 'Well, they're hard to catch, aren't they?' he mused.

Was there no one wicked enough to clothe in poison? I dismissed the man, then took the stairs by threes. I was breathing hard when I reached the crow's nest.

Sir Magnus was hunched over a book of incantations. His hands rested on the table where herbs were separated into piles.

'Princess,' he said coolly and without looking up.

'I have a job for you.'

'Not now. I prepare for the knight's blessing.'

'It's for that I've come. You do not have to go through with the blessing if you take my advice.'

'And what is that?' He gazed up at last, the tufts sprouting from his brows like black wings.

'Remember how you poisoned my cat?'

'Princess, are you feeling well?'

'You can do the same to the dragon.' I told him my cunning plan. When I was done, he said, 'The beast would smell the poison.'

'Not if we disguise it in bacon fat.'

'Do you know how much poison it would take to kill a dragon?' His fingers were outspread on the table and he leaned against his fingertips.

'I . . . I couldn't say.'

'Too much.' He stepped into the adjoining alcove. As I waited, I inspected the astrolabe, his favoured instrument for reading the stars, not that he read them well. At last Magnus returned, muttering to himself and gripping stems of flowering vervain. 'Are you still here?'

'So you refuse me?'

'I have a ceremony to perform. Tell the queen to send me a sound boy to help with the herbs, and not the lackwit Mouser.'

I swept my hand across his precious piles. Brown leaves and green drifted to the floor as I left the crow's nest.

In the castle foreyard, I sat atop the platform with Mother and Father and surveyed the roving crowd. The dragon's attack must have brought them to the knights' blessing. I'd not seen so many village folk gathered there since the night

Nell was burned.

Sir John Broderick was down upon one knee.

'Why must he be sent?' I said to Mother. We were on the dais, so none could hear my quiet plea. 'He's our best knight.'

'He is,' whispered Mother. 'Strong enough and wise enough to lead the others.'

I viewed twenty men behind Sir John. They knelt in two lines spanning outward in a V like geese in flight. Some slayers were pimple-faced and slender, no more than boys in battle garb.

Sir Magnus stepped up to Sir John with our page, Anthony, at his side holding the silver tray. Waving a herb above Sir John's head, he announced to all, 'Wormwood!' then circled his hand about three times like a wheeling vulture. 'With power to protect against the serpent's bite.' He placed the wormwood in a leather bag. Leaning forward I could just make out the letters J B embroidered on the pouch.

Sir Magnus reached for the herb tray again. 'Vervain!' he said, holding up the flowering spears. 'Wear this and you will find the place where the Pendragon sceptre is hid. None, not even a dragon, can keep a stolen thing away from this truth-telling herb!'

He cupped the flowers tenderly and pressed them in Sir John's pouch.

More herbs were given. Sir Magnus reminded the slayers not to confront the dragon where thistles grow, 'for the thistle plant enrages dragons,' he warned.

Prayers were said and Father Hugh anointed each slayer with holy oil.

'Now,' announced Sir Magnus, lifting his broad hand. 'You are ready to kill the beast. Go with God, Sir John, slay the dragon, and with these men return to us with Queen Evaine's sceptre!'

The people cheered. The dragonslayers crossed themselves. Lady Broderick swooned and was caught by her son, Niles. We stood and sang a holy hymn, then marched in chorus across the drawbridge.

Sir John Broderick and the slayers rode from the castle gates, their red and blue banners fluttering in the breeze.

'All hail Sir John!' shouted the village folk. 'All hail the dragonslayers!' I felt a chill as villagers tossed lavender and wild roses before Sir John's horse.

Slow he passed before us, his armour glistening like a well-rubbed goblet. With his visor up, he gazed at Lady Broderick standing just beside me. What passed between the lady and her man was such a rush of feeling that I trembled with it. Here was the deep of love, and seeing this one glance, I knew the shallow waters I'd drunk from all my life.

The Pendragon flag with its golden lion and blue dragon bound in a ring of fire, fluttered in a windy battle as they paraded down the lane. Trumpets blared. The people cheered, tossing their hats into the air with the merry glee of the Midsummer fair. The simple folk had such faith in the slayers' strength.

It's true they were the best of men, but my heart did not rise up. Wormwood, vervain, bows, spears, and sharpened swords. In years past, I'd believed in such herb spells and weapons. But now I'd seen the beast close up. He was as a dark god to us, and our knights had little chance against him.

Dust stirred behind the horses' hoofs. A fine brown cloud rose behind Sir John Broderick, and in the wake of it, crushed flowers. Lilac mingling with dust was the smell of Sir John's passing. And beyond the trumpets and the shouts, which echoed hollow in my ears, I heard the black-birds singing.

6

Pilgrimage

THE SLAYERS DID NOT RETURN FROM DRAGON'S
Keep that autumn and the loss of Magda and our
royal slayers sickened me. Eating little and saying
less, I grew thin as a shadow wraith. Cook tried to tempt
me with puddings which I could not down. Sir Magnus
blamed my morbidity on the stars.

Father strove to raise even stronger slayers. Shouts and
loud clatterings came daily from the foreyard where Father
trained new knights on the giant straw dragon Sir Magnus
had fashioned. The great beast's wooden ribcage, con-
structed like a ship's frame, was filled with straw, covered
in green sailcloth, and bound in many ropes under
Magnus's supervision. Soundly built for persecution, the
beast was hung from a high windlass, his sailcloth wings
outstretched as if in flight.

Leaning against the mews, I watched the dragonslayers
battle the straw beast till they were hoarse from shouting

and their hair was wet with sweat. At last Magnus would call, 'Halt!' The injured dragon was lowered to the ground while weary slayers joined Father to guzzle beer and stuff themselves with sausages.

I waited in the shadows savouring this moment, for Sir Magnus would fairly weep as he inspected his dear dragon. Then he'd begin shouting at the builders, 'Fix him and be quick about it!'

Sir Magnus worried over his straw beast, but the real dragon haunted my head and heart. I'd swallowed the secret of my pounding claw. It acted like a poison in me. More than once in those dark days I flew into a rage. One week I broke Mother's vase, the next Cook's platter (this after she'd sent a slice of stuffed eel to cure my morbid liver).

Marn came to bind the spirits. In my solar she waved her wrinkled hands round and round, wrapping me in invisible cords and whispering, 'Three times winding, Four times binding. I bind all evil spirits now and cast them from this room.'

Giving me the kiss of peace, she said, 'Ah, aren't you better now, poppet?'

I wasn't.

Picking up the broken platter and eel innards, she left. At last even Marn stopped trying to cure my tempers and spent her time with Sir Allweyn in the mews.

Wandering the castle halls at night with a candle my shadow roved black across the walls. By day I rode Galahad or walked the grassy hills. One chill afternoon I fell into a fitful sleep in the orchard, leaning against Magda's burnt tree.

I dreamed.

I was a bird, or some kind of flying beast. Blue-winged and golden-breasted. I soared over Wilde Island to a shining lake. Wheeling down, all my talons went chill as I skimmed along the deep blue surface of the water. In the midst of the lake I saw a girl rising up and shining, as a flame rises from a candle.

Magda. The child fell back into the water, and I dived in after her. Down and down, then pulled her to the surface again. I stepped from the lake, thinking I still held her, but she was gone. Turning I called, 'Come out of the water!' and she to me, laughing, called, 'I can't come out. I'm dead.' I shivered and saw I was no longer a bird, but myself again.

Naked on the shore, I lifted my arms to the wind, for though I was cold, I wanted the breeze across my skin. I spread my fingers wide. And oh! My hands were bare as well and my left hand as beautiful and whole as my right. I screamed with joy and woke myself.

That night I called Father Hugh to my solar. I told the man my dream, though I did not speak of Magda, nor that my claw was healed, only that I'd felt some healing from the water.

'Healing waters,' he said with a nod. 'It's said Saint Columba once dwelt in a cave near a lake on the far side of Morgesh Mountain before he returned to Scotland. In those days pilgrims came to the hermit's lake for healing. Columba's Tear, the lake was called. And many found remedy there when the water was astir.'

'Do the sick still venture to the lake?'

'I've heard of no healing there since the days of Saint Columba . . . five hundred years ago? Or is it six?' He scratched his bald head.

I would not be turned away by a thing so small as time. 'Once a place is sacred,' I said, 'is it not always so? Would God remove his grace once given?'

'Oh, Princess,' he said, his brows tilting. 'Not likely.' He frowned then, thinking. 'But if there were once roads to that rough place across the mountain, there are none now. And no holy hermit there to greet a traveller once he comes. It would be a two-week journey at least, and that on a healthy horse and in the milder months of summer.'

Later when Mother came, I told her of the lake. 'A pilgrimage?' she crossed her arms.

'This lake, Columba's Tear, is just over the mountain. It's a place of holy healing. My dream told me so.'

'Would we follow a dream?' mused Mother.

I grew hot. 'Your healers never cured me, I've chewed my fill of horehound and pressed one too many dead men's teeth against my skull! So if a dream showed me –'

'A journey up mountain.' Mother nodded and gave a sad smile. 'It is time.'

My heart leaped, but Mother seemed troubled. She touched her saint's pouch. 'We should present you to Prince Henry before high summer. And I have it on my heart that you will go ungloved.'

'Ungloved,' I breathed. 'I'll cross the sea and feel the wind blow through my fingers.'

Mother smiled at that.

Mother told the king we were going to Saint Brigid's Abbey for a time of prayer and fasting. The nuns there were cloistered from the world. And so no one, not even Father, knew where we were going. Another lie to protect my claw, but I counted it a small sin. Thus late in the afternoon on Saint Bertilla's feast day, I slipped Father Hugh's map into Galahad's saddlebag, and Mother mounted Aster. To begin our pilgrimage aright, I scattered dried lavender as we rode across the drawbridge. Galahad's and Aster's hooves crushed the purple blooms, and a sweet, stark smell rose up, blessing our journey.

We chose the woodland path through the valley, which lay below Morgesh Mountain like a great green skirt. Father Hugh's map had unicorns galloping along its edge and the giant's head peeping over Morgesh Mountain. This gave me pause, but I hoped the lake at journey's end would show itself to be real.

That Mother had changed her mind, and so quickly, puzzled me. She was not one for mountain rides. And never rode without full escort. Was it the strength of my dream that swayed her? Another thing. What had she meant by 'It is time.' Her voice, usually clear, was husky when she said that. And I heard old tears unwept behind her words.

These darker thoughts soon vanished. Such beauty all around! Twilight stars pricked the sky and the moon bloomed white as meadowsweet. Wings flitted overhead. A chorus of toads croaked in the streambed. I took these sights and sounds in as Mother turned onto a path that chased up the mountain.

Hours passed and night came on. Pine boughs stirred as if to sweep the stars from the sky. As the trail grew steeper, I gripped the saddle with my knees. How brave Galahad was, and true: and how he loved long journeys.

It was late when we came upon a dim-lit cave and tethered our mounts in the sapling grove. Galahad hoofed the ground anxious to be away again.

'Soon,' I promised in a low whisper. He shook his mane, then nibbled the dry grass with Aster.

The cave was welcome enough, for I was tired and chill. There was no door, only a boulder betwixt cave and path, and I could see the crackling fire painting the entry walls pale gold. Mother slipped inside. I marvelled at her daring, then entered myself.

I should have known by the sudden smell of rotting meat, there were no kind folk here. An old woman wrapped in a muddy shawl was crouched over a table, her back to the door. She turned as I came in and placed her hand near the pile of leaves and scattered bones.

'Come closer,' she said, pointing to the fire.

I gripped my cloak. 'Why stop here?'

'Hush,' said Mother. 'Meet Demetra.'

I stayed my place near the entrance.

'So this is she,' said Demetra standing up and stepping closer. She leaned down peering at me with her moonstruck eye. The milky whiteness of it sent a chill to the back of my neck.

'She's a tidy beauty,' said Demetra. 'If a little frail.'

I felt as if she were eyeing me for the cook pot. 'I'm fourteen,' I said. 'And strong.'

'I know your years.' Demetra gave a gap-toothed smile. 'For don't I know her starting spark to the day?'

'What does she mean by that, Mother?'

The queen adjusted her skirts as if seeking an answer in the folds. 'Rosalind,' she said hoarsely. 'I would not have come here if there were any other way –'

'Aye,' clucked Demetra. 'You've taken your time about it.'

'Let's go,' I said tugging Mother's arm. She seemed fixed to the floor. 'We should ride farther tonight,' I pleaded. Still no movement from Mother. 'We have a long way to go.'

'I'd say you have arrived,' laughed Demetra. She waved her hand at two birch stools near the fire.

Mother sat.

'You've hexed her, you witch!'

'Rosalind,' commanded Mother. 'She's done nothing to me. I came here on my own power. Sit down now, daughter.'

'I don't understand.'

Demetra clapped her hands and a serving woman appeared from one of the tunnels at the back of the cave. Her clothes were ragged, her golden hair pulled back into a braid. Mother started when she saw her, but the woman did not notice, for she kept her eyes on the floor.

'Fetch tea, Ali.'

The servant fled down the tunnel and returned with a tray of steaming mugs. I watched her pass Mother a cup. Her hands were red and the tips of her slender fingers

cracked. Beautiful hands once, I could see, but they had
been hard worked. She gazed up at Mother, her brown eyes
pleading, Mother's going soft, then hard in turns. It was
clear from that one look they knew each other, though I'd
never seen this woman or the hag.

All seemed inside-out. The black night a place of safety,
this warm cave full of danger.

'Serve the princess,' ordered Demetra. Ali handed me a
tea that was sweet to sip but bitter going down. I drank it
only out of thirst. Ali refilled Demetra's cup, then flitted
back down another tunnel.

'You took long enough to bring her,' said Demetra.

'We left only today,' I said.

Demetra snorted.

'I had some hope the village healers . . .' Mother took a
sip of tea. 'I knew she must be ready to take your cure. I'm
sure she's strong enough to face it now and live.'

Strong enough for what? This woman was no healer.
'Mother,' I said through gritted teeth. 'We have our pilgrimage to make.'

Demetra peered at me like one about to gut a fish. She
poked the fire, sending sparks from the burningstone.
'Who says there's a cure for her?'

'There must be,' said Mother.

My gloved hands felt cold around the steaming mug.
And the tea quaked below the rim.

'Some things are sealed in their making,' said Demetra.

Mother stood up to her full height. 'Not this,' said
Mother, her voice low and ominous. 'The girl is innocent.
Did you think I would have drunk the slime from that

giant egg if I'd known what lay within?'

Giant egg? I'd never heard of this. The cave walls began to swim. 'Saint Monica healed Mother's womb,' I said through chattering teeth.

Demetra laughed. 'So that's what you told the girl, eh? Well, saints or slimy potions, you said you'd do anything to conceive.'

'But the egg –'

'You sought a child and won one.'

Mother grabbed my upper arm and pulled me closer to the hag. My tea spilled on the stony floor. 'Look at her, Demetra,' said Mother, her words coming out in gulps like one drowning in a sucking sea. 'She's lovely, pure and sweet. A beauty. Well-schooled, with a sound mind. She'll be the twenty-first queen.' Mother tightened her grip. 'She's *the one!*' Her last words came out more like a cry than a vow. And I saw by the lift of Demetra's brow that she heard Mother's uncertainty.

I struggled to pull away, but Mother had both arms about my waist and held me before her as if I were her puppet. Demetra reached out and ran her gnarled fingers through my hair. 'I know Merlin's prophecy,' she said. 'But the time may not be ripe with England in civil war –'

'Merlin saw her ending war.'

I strained against Mother's grip, the three of us so close I could smell Demetra's leathery breath. At last I pulled free and the two faced one another.

Demetra licked her lips. 'Wizard words,' she snapped. 'I don't see his vision playing out with the girl's witch mark.'

Witch mark? She knew? I had to leave now! But I

couldn't move.

Mother swayed. 'How do you know what ails the child?'

'I knew there would be some mark on her from the cure you took. Could it be . . . hiding on her hand?' She tipped her head and smiled.

Slowly, I backed towards the entrance, but before I could escape, Demetra's moon-struck eye caught me in a milky stare. I would run when she looked down.

'Mayhap,' mused the hag, 'you should try for another girl. A perfect one without a mark to threaten her power.'

I stepped back once and twice, as if walking through thick snow.

'No,' shouted Mother. 'Rosalind's *the one*. The only hope we have. There's but one thing in the way, and we've come to be rid of it by God's power, or by potion!'

'Well, not by God's power *here*,' laughed Demetra. 'But a potion sure. That or a good sharp knife.' Saying this, she unsheathed her blade.

I screamed and raced outside.

A rush of hot wind hit my face as I flung myself forward. Heart beating, blood rushing, feet pounding, I ran into the night not caring where.

'Stop, Rosalind!' called Mother.

I scrambled like a hunted thing, with Mother and Demetra in pursuit. Feet flying over root and stone, I rushed down the winding path.

'Come back!' called Mother. 'You'll catch your death!' But I thought to myself that death was not chasing me as hotly as those two.

I took a sharp turn, nearly falling as I ran. Fearing that

they'd catch me on the path, I dived behind a blackberry bush and watched them hasten by. Mother's cloak shining in the moon and Demetra's grey hair flying out behind her like moss caught in a river. I bit my lip as Mother called, 'Rosalind!' across the craggy mountain.

Twigs scratched my cheeks and arms as I crawled deeper in the underbrush. The smell of sage filled my nose, mingled with the dust my hands and knees stirred up.

'Find her,' called Demetra from further down the path. 'She's a tender girl and there's a hot north wind a-blow tonight from Dragon's Keep.'

I nestled under a sapling tree. Hot north wind, a dragon sign. I'd felt it as I ran myself, and there was a strange smell on it, like a putrid wave bringing dead sea creatures to the shore. I was afraid then. Still I did not call out to Mother, for in her wake ran Demetra, and in her hand I'd seen the knife.

7

The Kiss

DEEP IN THE NIGHT, A NOISE AWAKENED ME. 'Mother?' I whispered, though I knew she was back in Demetra's cave by now. A beating sound came from the starry sky. I sat up, gripped the stunted tree and listened. There it was, a strong dull sound like that of Marn thumping a rug with a stick. Then darkness sped betwixt the moon and me.

'Just an owl,' I said for comfort. But the smell in the air told me otherwise. Burning leather, putrid flesh, rusting metal: a smell somehow familiar.

The dragon.

Overhead I saw him. Power. Muscle. Red-tipped wings wide as the church wall. His underside was gold. His back and wings blue-green. I was afraid, but could not turn away.

Beat. Beat. The wings shook out their shadows like dust from old carpets.

In the foothills below, sheep gathered on the grass like small clouds clustering in a darkened sky. The beast circled over them. Where was the shepherd now?

Oh run. Run. Don't let the dragon catch you! My claw throbbed in time with the flapping wings as it had the day the dragon killed our Magda. I clenched my teeth, willing it to pound to another time, but it fell into the rhythm of the giant wings like a soldier to a marching drum.

Run, sheep!

They scattered beneath him. Then I saw the shepherd rushing down the hill. Two beats more and the dragon swooped down, caught the shepherd in his claws and flew skyward again.

I could hear the poor man screaming as the dragon flew closer to the cliff where I hid, and landed on a broad flat stone not more than sixty paces from me. The beast was the length of our drawbridge and his scales shone eerie white with the moonlight as if he were cloaked in teeth.

The captive man screamed and flailed, his cloak and breeches bloody in the encircling talons.

My legs twitched. I should run now! But the beast blocked the way before me, and the cliff edge was just behind. I shivered in my hiding place, praying the dragon would not notice me.

The beast held the man on the tips of his talons and opened his powerful jaws. *Stop*, I screamed with mind and heart, but not with my mouth. There was no saving him. Eyes closed, I pressed my hands to my ears, still I could not shut out the sounds of the dragon's teeth crunching the shepherd's bones.

Finished with his feast, the dragon looked about and sniffed. I hunched up close to my small beech tree.

'Rosalind!' My mother's voice called from somewhere up mountain. The dragon turned, and pricked his ears.

'Rosalind! Come back!'

He lifted his head higher.

'Rosie! Oh, Rosie! Answer me!'

Slowly the dragon's wings unfurled. He would follow her call and do to her what he'd done to the shepherd!

I leaped up from my hiding place. 'Dragon.'

He turned. I could see his nostrils flaring, green about and red within.

Blood pounded in my ears.

I searched the moonlit ground for a weapon: bushes, slender grass, pebbles. Nothing.

The dragon's tongue lashed out like a devil's whip. He lowered his head, saying, 'Sweet morsel.' Dragons know many human languages, being sharp-witted and slit-tongued, so the words did not surprise me. But the voice did – a voice like stones thrown into a river, deep and clear and sharp all at the same time. I could tell by the tone the dragon was female.

She inched closer, belly to the ground like a stalking cat. The gold of her underside was the colour of my gloves. Her eyes were large as lanterns slit with yellow fire. These were the soft spots – all else was scaly armour.

'I am not afraid,' I said, my heart thrusting in my ribs. The dragon stopped and peered at me. This was not what she was used to hearing, nor what I'd meant to say.

The dragon blinked and crooked a sharp-toothed smile.

'You're nothing but a winged lizard,' I shouted. 'And it's sure you sleep on a flat rock in the sun and your brains are all in your gut!'

Moonlight spilled across the dragon's head, glinting green as tarnished metal. She opened her mouth; her dagger teeth still red with the shepherd's blood. 'The morsel has no fat,' she said, her voice loud and creaking as the drawbridge. 'But I see she has a fire in her belly.' Then lifting her head, the dragon breathed silk-blue fire into the sky. I felt the heat across my face and chest. The firelight shining like a thousand bluebells in a starry field. I swallowed hard, my tongue swelling in my mouth.

She bent closer, smoke swirling about her head. Then lifting her forearm, her five-taloned claw gleaming black and washed in moonlight, she paused, and lowered it again. Her eyes had fallen on my gloves.

'Gold,' she breathed.

Quickly I tore them off and tossed them at her feet. The glittering threads of my gloves distracting her, I seized the moment, thrust out my hand and scratched her right eye with my talon.

She roared, rearing back, and the ground shook beneath her.

I leaped to the right. She caught me in her claws, like a wee mouse to a cat. I worked to breathe in her grip, and with every gasp, my chest was shot with pain.

Now we were face to face. Drops of blood pearled along the gash beneath her eye. The smell of blood and burnt flesh filled my nose and I felt as if I were in the grip of a mountain. I thrust my arm out again, to make a second wound but I was too far back.

Some trance shrouded the dragon as she stared at my naked hand: my scaly blue-green claw, the sharp black talon still wet with her blood. A shiver raced across her back and made the dry sound of rustling leaves.

I kept my hand stretched out where the smoke curled between us. A strange wizardry was here, though I knew not what. I was afraid to move.

The dragon's slit pupils opened slowly like curtains parting to a fiery chamber. She was so still that a yarrow moth lit upon her head and stayed there opening and closing its wings in the moonlight.

I felt a calming come over me then, a peace down to my core. And though she had me in her grasp, and I could not kneel or cross myself as I'd been taught, I loosed my soul to meet my end. In a twinkling, with a shift of soul, I was prepared to wheel upwards into heaven. Ah, but I wasn't ready for what happened then.

The dragon's warm wet tongue thrust out and wrapped about my arm. It twisted like a serpent, the slit ending at my fingertips. She held her tongue there licking my talon as my blood chased through my veins. My claw had never been so gently touched.

I heard a rushing in my ears as if the sky had sent a river down.

At last the bright red tongue unfurled and slipped into her mouth. Letting go her hold, she set me down, uprooted my small tree, and flew over the cliff's edge. I watched her drop the sapling to the valley floor below as she sped across the sky. The clouds blushed in her approach, and darkened again as she passed, like tapestry near a wavering candle.

I was left standing, my arm still outstretched against an invisible foe. A cool breeze played about my flesh, my claw still damp from the dragon's kiss.

8

Angel's Betrayal

AN ANGEL LEANED OVER ME AS MY EYES OPENED TO the light, her golden hair blowing loose in the wind. 'So I am come to the afterworld,' I mumbled, still half asleep. The angel's small brows tilted. I noticed then she had no wings.

Rain began to fall, and with the rain, awakening.

Alive.

A girl of an age to me. No angel. Who was she then? The ground about us darkened with the drops. She helped me to a stand in the prattling water. A cool north wind blew droplets towards the overhanging cliff.

'Are you the shepherd's daughter?' I asked. She began to walk. I followed her up the muddy path, my thoughts scattering like thistledown. The dragon. A female. She saw my claw and kissed it.

After an hour's walk, my bones ached from my night outside and my belly growled with hunger. We drank at a mountain brook. By the time we crossed it, I'd formed a plan.

Father Hugh's map and food were in my saddlebag. I'd find the trail I'd run down last night, slip into the copse where Galahad was tied and ride him north to Columba's Tear. The waters there would heal my hand. I would be free. But how was I to find the trail when I'd only seen it in the dark?

The sharp wind caught my cloak as I followed the girl along the path, thinking.

A voice cried, 'Ah, you've put yourself to some use, Kit-cat!'

The girl had led me to the wolves!

Mother rushed from the cave, her face mottled, her eyes red and swollen with tears. 'Ah, God, Rosie! I thought the dragon –'

I did not stay to hear the rest, but flew away from her.

'Rosie! Don't run off again!'

I stumbled back down the muddy path, running fast and hard. But they caught my sodden cloak, and dragged me screaming back into the viper's den.

'Well, you're back home now,' said Demetra, tying a leather strap about my waist and securing it to a metal ring on the wall. Home? This wasn't home. With Ali's help she'd pulled me down a maze of darkened tunnels to this small cell in her lair, where I was forced onto a narrow cot.

'Leave us, Ali,' said Demetra.

Damp with sweat and breathing hard, I tried to regain strength for battle as Demetra sped about with wooden bowls and stinking herbs. Mother entered my cell.

A grey cat leaped onto the table. The carving knife rattled as she trotted over to sniff a wedge of cheese. Demetra shooed away the cat and turned to Mother. 'The cost before the cure.'

Mother put her silver on the table by the bread loaf. The hag snatched the coins and dropped them in her waist pouch.

Peeling off her golden gloves, the queen sat beside me while Demetra crushed dried mustard seeds with a stone pestle. The room filled with a pungent smell as she worked.

All was silence but for the rhythm of mortar and pestle. Then wiping her hands on her wool shift, Demetra left the cell.

'Untie me quick, Mother. Take me home.'

She patted my arm. 'No, Rosie. This woman will heal your mark. She has great powers.'

'Dark powers!' I spat.

Mother flinched. 'It's time to take this cure. No one else has healed you. If there were another way . . . You must be brave, Rosie.'

There were tears in Mother's eyes as she said this, but I felt no pity for her. She could free me if she chose.

I tugged on the leather cord about my waist, working the knot whilst Mother turned to dab her eyes. The knot befuddled my gloved hands so I slipped the right glove off to undo the knot. Nothing. I'd only managed to tighten it. In the copper firelight the knife blade shone beside its bread loaf. I was reaching for the blade when Demetra swept in and caught me by the wrist.

'You must be hungry, child, to reach so far for bread,' she said with a wry smile. I was indeed famished, but she knew what I'd been after. Demetra let go her hold, then clapped her hands once and twice. Ali appeared, received her orders and returned with the honey and a horn of goat's milk. The hag tied my wrists firmly to the cot on either side of me as Ali sliced the loaf and dripped honey on the bread. Mother fed me until my aching belly calmed.

My betrayer came to take my horn and I saw a ring of dirt beneath the girl's fingernails, still her hands were slim and beautiful, and I felt a pang. If I had God's power to order, 'Let her hands be mine,' I'd do so. What would it matter to this girl who betrayed me to the hag? Who would care if *she* had a claw?

'Who is the girl?' I asked when she'd left the cave.

'Ah,' laughed Demetra. 'She might have walked in your shoes.'

'Quiet,' ordered Mother.

Demetra left the cell, her grey hair lifting like cobwebs in the breeze. It was the first time Mother had crossed the hag since I'd been recaptured. But it was in defence of another.

'What does she mean to you?' I asked, the words echoing from the hollow ache in my chest.

'Nothing at all,' said Mother. 'She's Ali's bastard, Katinka.'

So Katinka went from angel to bastard in a single day. How strange the world was. Then I remembered the look Ali had given Mother when first she'd seen her. 'You knew Ali before she was a servant here,' I guessed.

Mother started. She would have denied it if she could, and worn a fixed look of indifference, but I'd read the truth in her face already. 'She was once my lady's maid,' Mother admitted.

Marn had told me about the lady's maid expelled from mother's service for bedding a wandering minstrel. 'And wasn't she rounding with child already before she left?' said Marn. 'Ah, she was spoilt. And here she was as pretty as an angel.'

Demetra still hadn't returned, and Mother was softening to me it seemed.

'Free me.' A command, not a plea this time.

Mother sat and kissed my damp hair. 'You will be healed, Rosie. And later when you're married to Prince Henry, you will thank me.'

'Take me to the lake. I'll find my healing there.'

'The lake?' asked Demetra as she darted back in.

'Columba's Tear,' said Mother patting my arm.

Demetra laughed. 'It's nothing but a marsh now.'

'I don't believe you!'

'Well, now, do you think I'd live here if a lake could do my healing? I'd stir the waters myself and charge good coin for folk to come and take a dip.'

The hag slit a prune and removed the pip. Then humming to herself, she took a jar down from the shelf, pulled the cloth from the lid and drew out an enormous spider.

Its legs flailed in the air.

'Mother,' I said, hoarsely. 'Order her to take the thing away!'

She knew my fear of spiders. I'd always run at the sight of them. A year before this, when a fat spider crawled into my solar, I'd screamed and leaped up on my bed. Mother had bolted the door and made me stand beside the spider. 'A princess doesn't show her dread,' she'd said. And so the spider crawled up the wall while I held my breath. Thus she'd taught me to swallow my fear, to let my blood scream in my ears and not give voice to it.

Blood was screaming in my ears now as Demetra held the spider by its leg.

'Mother! Tell her to get rid of it! I don't mind my curse at all. I'll wear my gloves till death.'

'Till death you say?' laughed Demetra. 'That may be.' Demetra dangled the spider above the fruit then stuffed it in the shrivelled plum.

I tried to sit up, the leather cinching my gut so tight I fell back on the cot.

'Keep her still,' ordered Demetra.

'Marn!' I screamed as Mother held me down. My nursemaid was far away down the mountain, but she would have stood between Demetra and me, old bones to old bones, and kept the horrid spider away.

I clamped my jaw against the fruit. If that spider crossed my lips, I was sure to enter a strange world knit by the devil's needles; a world where a loving mother would pay out silver to have her girl tortured.

Demetra bent over my cot, her breath smelling of

turnips. 'This is for the swelling.' She thrust out the puckered plum, the spider's leg wiggling out one side.

'Take it Rose. It's for your good,' said Mother.

I bit my lips, but Demetra pulled my jaw open, dropped the spider-fruit in, and clamped it shut.

Oh, Saint Alodia, protector of children, come wrap Demetra with your cord and drag her into hell, I prayed. But there was no saint. No cord. And the only thing wrapped was my tongue around the wretched prune. I pressed it to the side of my cheek while Mother stroked my brow saying, 'Soon all will be well, Rosie.'

Demetra moved my jaw up and down to make me chew the spider-plum. I never will forget the crunching sound the spider made between my teeth.

9

Flying as in a Dream

MOTHER HAD NEVER LET ME SHOW MY HAND TO anyone in the world but her, but all vows were broken in Demetra's stinking cave. She dismissed Ali and her child, then carefully removed my glove before the hag. Demetra's glance was hungry, as if she hoped to toss my severed claw into a soup and sup upon its power.

'Woman!' said Mother impatiently, 'Will you but stare and stare?'

The hag applied a hot poultice of mustard and stinging nettles. Anon I learned the reason I'd taken spider-fruit for swelling. She wrapped the mustard cloth and nettles tight around my scaly claw. Stinging heat seared my flesh, flamed into my hand and burned up my arm. Soon my hand began to swell like a ripened peach.

'Stop,' I cried. 'Make her take it off.'

Mother kissed my forehead. 'Hush now,' she said.

'The nettles sting.'

'They fight your cursed flesh,' said Mother.

A small shadow hovered in the hall, an edge of skirt appeared. Mother adjusted the poultice, so no part of my claw could be seen. 'Enter now, Katinka.'

She came in with a tray of mint leaves.

'Mint,' I called.

Katinka held out her tray. Mint would cool my burning claw. I could stand the pain a moment more, knowing it was near. Mother laid the wet mint leaves on the backside of my hand just above the burning poultice.

'Be gone.' Demetra pushed the girl from the room. Katinka tumbled to the floor in the shadowy hall, but she did not cry out.

I waited for the cooling mint to work, holding my breath and thinking of a rhyme Father used to say when I was small. 'Hug her and kiss her and take her on your knee, and whisper very close, darling girl, do you love me?'

'Darling girl, darling girl . . .' I whispered over and over, but my hand grew redder and rounder till it seemed like a wormy apple torn from the branch to rot.

The fire in the pit crackled as Demetra unwrapped the poultice. I felt a moment of relief, then she added more hot mustard smear and nettle leaf.

'My claw. It's stinging like a thousand bees.'

'Enough,' ordered Mother turning to Demetra. 'Stop her pain.'

'Sleep potion has a cost,' said Demetra above my screaming. Mother tossed more silver on her table. Demetra pocketed the coins and took a sea sponge from her little shelf.

'When Rosalind's a good girl, she'll have her cakes and custard,' said Demetra holding out the sponge. 'But when she pouts and cries, she'll have nothing but hot mustard.' Demetra laughed at this, her gap-toothed mouth showing her grey tongue. Leaning over me, she pressed the sponge to my mouth. I thrashed and screamed into the strange smelling sponge.

'What's in it?' asked Mother.

'A good sleep potion. Poppy tincture and hemlock —'

I drifted away from the hag, my mother's worried gaze, the cell with its crackling fire. In my fevered dreams, I faced a legion of angry sprites who cut off my arms with their grass-blade swords. No matter how many arms the fairies cut, I grew more back, till I had eight arms in all.

Rousing from a strange dream, I found Demetra sitting at my side. Her rough voice still echoed in my head as if she'd spoken through my sleep.

'Ah,' said the hag. 'Your eyes are open now.'

'Where is Mother?'

'Oh where, oh where has your Mother gone?' taunted Demetra. Her cheek twitched as she peeled the poultice from my hand. I tilted my heavy head and looked down. On my puffed-up hand my blue claw seeped green ooze.

Mother slipped into the cell, shadow quiet. Demetra touched my swollen claw with her long fingernail.

''Tis softened now,' she said.

Mother was all concern. 'Can she feel you?'

'She feels it but far away. The poppy and the hemlock have her still,' said Demetra. 'I'll peel the putrid flesh down to the girlish skin.'

'Do what you must,' said Mother, tightening her jaw. The cave swam as Demetra lifted my hand, grasped the flesh at the base of my claw, and pulled. I screamed. Demetra ripped a layer of blue scales down to the nail then dropped it to the floor.

Blood poured from the wound. The hag raced for a leather thong, tied it tightly round my wrist, pinched the flesh again, and tore.

My screams increased.

'You said she could not feel!' cried Mother.

'She'll not remember this,' said Demetra.

Another dream but this one familiar to me. I was a flying thing, an angel or a bird with a mighty wingspan that cast a great shadow on the earth below. I was full of power as I sped across the sky. Never in all my life was I as happy as this. I swooped down, but not into a lake as before. Instead my body pulsed to the sound of hoofs as first a flock of sheep, then, in the deeper woods, a herd of deer, raced under my broad shadow. Wind singing in my ears, a fearsome roar filled the wood and swift, I downed a deer. Fire. Torn flesh. Smoke. Blood. And a raw taste on my tongue.

A searing pain awakened me. My hand was bandaged to the wrist. Mother sat close by stroking my head.

'How long was I dreaming?'

'You've slept three days, dear, and called out in your dreams.'

I looked into her eyes then, wondering if she'd heard the same beast cry I'd heard inside my dream, but her eyes were cool and unafraid. 'It's over now if all is well,' she said, twisting my hair about her finger. 'So pretty,' she whispered. 'We'll pray there are no scars to mar your beauty.'

Mother leaned close to my cheek. 'If Demetra's doctoring is true, the claw will be gone.'

Hope rose in me. 'And the golden gloves?'

'We'll burn them! Yours and mine together.'

'I'll light the fire and toss them in.'

'Aye,' said Mother with a little laugh, 'but hush, Demetra comes.'

It was time for my uncovering. Time to see the girlish flesh hidden fourteen years beneath a devil's curse. My heart was hopping like a hurried rabbit.

Slowly Demetra unwrapped the cloth. The sour smell of dying flesh went all about the room, and I felt the shame of it.

''Tis no bother,' soothed Mother, but her nose wrinkled just the same. With pounding pulse, I watched the slow unfurling of the bandage, but when the last bit of cloth dropped to the floor, Mother jumped back with a scream.

The finger was still blue-green and spined like a lizard's, but now it was larger and was crisscrossed with purple, as if my flesh had creeping roots.

'The curse is worse than before,' shouted Mother.

'I take pride in my craft,' said Demetra. 'And if the poultice and the tearing did not cure, my good knife will.' She pulled her knife from her belt. My heart leaped against my ribs as the blade glinted in the fire.

'Wait,' screamed Mother.

'The claw must come off,' Demetra said, stepping forward.

Forgetting my tether, I tried to intervene, was caught about the middle and pulled back against my cot.

'Maim her?' cried Mother. 'No prince would have her, maimed!' She grabbed Demetra's arm and they struggled near my cot, banging into the table, knocking over wooden bowls and scattering damp herbs across the floor. Mother wrestled the knife from Demetra's hand, and with a sudden force, she pressed the hag against the wall.

Demetra's eyes bulged; she breathed roughly as Mother held her by her hair, pressing the knife to her throat. Even in the dim light, I could see the veins on Demetra's neck protruding against the blade. Much as I hated the hag, I did not want to witness murder.

'Don't, Mother,' I pleaded.

'Quiet, child!'

'Know this,' gurgled Demetra, fixing her moon-struck eye on Mother. 'I've sent a sealed scroll to a friend. To be opened if I should meet untimely death. On the scroll Rosalind's secret curse is writ in full.'

'Who has this scroll?' demanded Mother.

'The scroll, the scroll. Who has the scroll,' taunted Demetra.

Mother screamed, cut a hunk of Demetra's grey hair down to her scalp and threw it in the fire. Then she pitched the knife against the stony wall with a clatter. Demetra hunched over laughing as my mother covered her face.

I curled my knees to my chest. My claw throbbing, my breath coming in gulps, I closed my eyes to shut out the world. The odour of my mangled claw mixed with the stink of Demetra's burning hair.

That very night my mother wrapped me in her cloak and led me from Demetra's cave. Wending below maple trees and pine, we urged our horses down the twisting path. A rustling sound and Ali burst out from the bushes with Katinka. Mother halted suddenly.

'Take my girl,' pleaded Ali.

'I cannot.'

'I've done all you asked. Don't deny me this.'

'She stays here.'

'She's not a burden. She makes no sound.'

I looked at Ali's daughter, shivering in her threadbare gown. Her pale face and hair drank in the moonlight.

Katinka drew farther back into the shadows.

'No,' said Mother.

'She's fourteen,' said Ali. 'She'll work sun to moon as I did for you. And she'll eat but little from the table.' She lifted her hands. 'I've accepted all. Done all, but my girl's life is in danger.' Ali tugged the corner of Mother's cloak. 'Demetra beats her,' she whispered fiercely then stepping

68

back, she pulled up her daughter's ragged gown.

Indeed, dim as the light was, I could see the blue-green bruises from her ankle to her thigh.

'I want her,' I said suddenly. 'Give the girl to me. I can use a lady's maid.' After her betrayal of me in the hag's cave Mother owed me this. Even in the starlit dark, Mother's face looked royal-blooded as she tilted her head.

'She'll never be a grief to you,' said Ali, pressing her daughter closer to Mother's mare.

A linnet trilled in the woods. Silence from Mother, but I saw she was considering. 'Marn could use help carrying the chamber pots out to the privy,' mused Mother.

'Give her to me,' I said again. And this time Ali lifted her struggling daughter up. I felt a rush of joy as Katinka took the saddle in front of me. She reached for her mother. I held her tight. Booting Galahad, we started back down the path, Ali ran after saying, 'Goodbye, my precious girl. It's for love we say goodbye. Remember, Kit. Remember that, so some day you'll understand!' Behind us she crumpled on the path, weeping.

With my arms wrapped about her, I felt Katinka's heart flutter like a small bird caught. She squirmed and tugged my elbow. 'The girl wants to jump.'

'Hold her fast, Rose. Katinka is yours to lose or keep.'

Only hours before this, I'd struggled against my own bonds, so I whispered, 'I'll not harm you, Kit.' I meant my promise. She'd betrayed me to Demetra, but I'd seen how the hag treated her. A slave will do her master's bidding while in bondage, and she'd been kind enough to bring the mint. 'You're free from Demetra,' I added. 'She'll not beat you again.' No thank-you from the girl, but then, she could not speak.

None could replace Magda. This girl would not follow me about skipping and singing the way she had, but her hair was the self same colour as the stolen child's, and she was fourteen like myself. I'd found a friend to keep me company when the heavy winter snow bound me to the castle.

Just before dawn we crossed the drawbridge and left our horses in the stableyard.

'Where will Kit sleep?' I asked.

'With Cook's new girl.'

'No, with Marn. If she's to be my lady's maid.'

And so Katinka was moved into the chamber adjoining mine. And there she stayed, herself like a treasure box and I was the one with the key.

10

Friend and Fowl

'COUNT THE SEEDS,' I SAID, HEART POUNDING. THE orchard had been harvested but there were still a few apples on the ground. I'd slit one in two and given it to Kit. We were trying the newest love spell I'd garnered from Sir Magnus's book. Kit was quiet on her feet and she knew well how to slip silently into the crow's nest and smuggle out a text.

The castle escorts stood along the edge of the orchard, guarding us from the common footpads hidden in the woods. They were posted far enough away for me to say the charm out of their hearing.

I'd sliced the apple with my knife, and said the spell over it chanting the name, Henry, three times as the book instructed. We'd even gathered the grave soil to bury the seeds should the charm prove unfruitful.

Cut in two and count the seeds. Even and your marriage day comes soon. Odd and you're sure to be a spinster.

Kit's brows were tipped as she nimbly wrestled out the apple seeds. They must be counted right.

She looked up. No smile on her face, but then she hadn't smiled once in her month here at the castle though I'd done my best to ease her. Kit missed her mother, I knew. Still she slept in a soft bed, rode my best roan, Marigold, and came on outings with me when I could leave my lessons. The girl might have lost her smile long ago in Demetra's cave, but I was determined to find it.

'Even?' I asked hopefully. I read Kit's eyes.

Odd.

Spinsterhood.

'The grave soil,' I whispered. Kit crouched under the tree, and dug a little hole. This she did for me since I couldn't soil my gloves. We tossed in the seven seeds and poured the pouch of grave soil over all to bury the charm.

Kit found another bruised apple on the ground. Should we try again?

I sheathed the knife and shook my head. I was done with the apple charm. Clouds coiled overhead as if to ensnare the tree tops. A storm would ride up soon from the sea. Kit stood and dusted off her blue gown. I saw she took some care with that. The day after she arrived I'd gone to Mother's solar.

'I'll give Kit my old gowns,' I'd said.

Mother had bristled, but I stood strong by the loom. 'They're too small for me. Should I give them to the pimply scullery maid instead?' I cupped one hand in another, my claw still aching from Demetra's 'cure'.

Mother frowned as she worked the threads. 'I'll leave

you to your folly, Rosalind. But don't let the lady's maid come close to your heart. Remember she's a bastard.'

We left the orchard on horseback, the escorts riding not far behind. Bitter over the apple's fortune I kicked Galahad to a canter. We managed to get ahead of the escort, galloping above Dentsmore and past Witch's Hollow. Kit's cloak blew out behind her and her cheeks were pink.

In just a month she'd learned to ride apace with me. And she'd go anywhere on Marigold except to the hunt. She was too fond of animals for that.

Her love for wild creatures was greater than I'd guessed until the day the robin came. Sister Anne, Kit and I were in the study where I sat misreading Latin. I'd just stumbled through another passage when a robin flew straight into the window. The crash of beak to glass made me jump and the stunned bird fell like a stone.

Kit leaped up and ran from the room.

What was this? Kit was fast on her feet. I called after her and chased her down the stairs with Sister Anne in tow. We raced through the kitchen, out the postern gate, and to the shallow place in the moat where the maids do the washing.

With a loud splash, Kit leaped into the muddy water to save the bird.

'Kit! Come back before you drown!'

Sister Anne and I waded in up to our knees. Cold water stung my shins. I reached above the swirling water, trying to grab Kit, but she pushed further out. 'Turn round and come to me,' I ordered.

The mute girl seemed deaf as well. She plunged in after

the bird. Behind me, Cook was on the shore, shouting 'Princess! Come out of the moat!'

I lunged for Kit just as the water swallowed her. 'My friend!' I screamed, 'Someone save her!' Sister Anne and I were held to shore as in an iron brace, for neither of us could swim. Water rushed against my thighs. I made to leap, but Sister Anne pulled me back.

Across the moat, Kit came up sputtering. Holding the robin above her head, she gasped for breath and paddled toward us.

'I've never seen the like,' said Cook. 'What witch-spell aids her in the water?'

My heart raced as Kit came to a stand in the shallows. Her hair was laced in green milfoil, like a dead spirit rising from the water.

'God's heaven!' I pulled her to the bank choking back my tears. 'I thought you dead! What devil possessed you?'

Kit didn't even look at me, her heart was all for the bird. Kneeling on the muddy ground, she stroked the sodden red feathers on the robin's breast.

I heaved a breath. 'The bird broke her neck when she crashed into the window. You've nearly killed us all to rescue a dead thing!'

The incident at the moat was all but forgotten by winter when the rains came in thick grey curtains across the sea. In my solar, Marn was stitching me a pretty cloak out of soft rose-coloured wool.

'I hate the rain.'

'Aye, well. You should be glad for it.'

'Why is that?'

Her needle stopped mid-air as she squinted up from the cloak. 'Dragons never attack on stormy days. Rain soaks their wings and downs them.'

'That's just an old story.'

'Is it now? Tell me when you've heard of any attack in foul weather like this?'

I tapped the window, thinking.

'There, you see?' Marn was satisfied and went back to her stitching.

Bad weather might have kept the dragons away but it didn't hold the healers back. In the week the first winter snow blanketed the castle, Mother brought a healer from Burnham. Indeed my claw had troubled me since Demetra's painful cure, but this healer could only guess at my trouble. Assessing me, he went to work, shearing off a third of my hair, burning it to ash, mixing it with goose fat and rue and smearing it on my face. I broke out in pimples. Mother sent him to the dungeon until my face cleared and my hair grew back again.

Three months he was imprisoned there, and I was glad of it. All that time I took my meals in my solar. Kit stayed hidden with me until my hair grew back, and my skin renewed. In those three months we read the lives of the saints, played countless games of chess and though I'm a clodpoll at tapestry, Kit showed me some tricks so that even Mother began to complement my work.

As the snow deepened Kit stood at the window, hand at

her throat, looking up at Morgesh Mountain. She was pale as a swan shadow in a pool.

'Your mother's safe,' I told her.

No movement from the window. Kit felt betrayed but I knew Ali had sent her away to save her.

'Come.' I set up the chess pieces. 'I'll win this time, see if I don't.'

She sat again. Her eyes gleamed. Like Mother, she would not weep in front of me. Kit pursed her lips with concentration, forgetting her sorrow for the moment as we challenged each other with our knights.

Kit would not smile nor speak; still I counted her a friend after those pimply, hairless months in my solar. In early spring when the snow in forest and valley melted, Marn took us herbing. I wore my new cloak, the best Marn had ever made. I was glad now she'd taken the time to embroider roses on pockets and hood. The day was chill and bright, and we tired Marn out as we raced through the hills.

At the top of a steep grade, Marn leaned over. 'Thimbles, how my back aches.'

Kit patted her shoulder.

'Ah, well, I'm old,' said Marn.

In the greenwood, Marn showed Kit where to find wolf's-bane, how to pluck holy thistle, and schooled her on the uses of sticklewort. 'Now this herb protects against evil spirits and poison, but mind it's not taken by mouth.' She pulled it up by the root. 'Sprinkle these leaves on the windowsill and you'll keep shadow wraiths at bay, place them under the pillow and you'll aid a poor sleepless soul.'

Kit had need of sticklewort that very week. Aside from my welcome flying dreams a new dream haunted me. In this one I saw again the dragon devouring the shepherd on Morgesh Mountain and woke myself up screaming. Marn and Kit came bustling in.

'There, there,' said Marn. She lit seven candles to chase away evil. 'Now tell us what frightened you so.'

'I dreamed of the dragon.' I could say no more than that. Neither knew about the poor shepherd, how the dragon had held me in her claw, or, stranger still, her parting kiss.

Kit spread sticklewort along the window and put more leaves under my pillow while Marn said her charm to bind the spirits and ward off bad dreams. 'Three times winding. Four times binding. I bind all evil spirits now and cast them from this room.'

Marn moved her hands over me as if tying invisible knots, then crossed herself for good measure. 'Now,' she said with a half-smile. 'That's better, isn't it, poppet?'

She rubbed oil on my temples as she began a tale of long-ago days when Wilde Island was a magic place full of tree spirits, and fairies. ''Tis said Merlin himself spent a year on the Isle of God's Eye in the midst of Lake Ailleann. And didn't he learn his magic there?'

'What sort of magic?' I asked, yawning.

'Well, the sort that mages know. How to read the stars and such.' She puffed up then. 'And isn't that a good thing, for he read the stars for you, Princess. And told the world about you six hundred years ago.'

'Oh, don't talk of that,' I said.

Marn frowned under her nightcap. 'Thimbles!' she fretted.

Kit smiled, a first for me.

I giggled.

'Ah, so the cure's working now,' said Marn proudly.

I nodded covering my smirk with a coverlet. Kit's smile widened.

Marn turned to my tapestry. Mother had finished it just before my fifteenth birthday and we'd hung it in my solar. There I sat enthroned, Pendragon sceptre in my hand. Below me were the words of Merlin's prophecy. And under that was the body of the dragon shot full with countless arrows like a great green pincushion.

'The sceptre,' mused Marn, still looking at the tapestry. 'Proof of your bloodline. I'll tell how the evil dragon stole it from Queen Evaine right in the middle of the Saint Crispin's Day celebration.' Her face beamed in the flickering candlelight, for she loved that story the best of all.

I fell asleep, thinking not on the stolen sceptre, but on the small found treasure of Kit's smile.

II
Diviner Eggs

SNOW AND RAIN GAVE WAY TO SUN, AND NINE MORE
names were added to the Dragonstone. Still, Sheriff
William reported more deaths from footpads than
from the dragon that spring. Bands of murderers and
thieves were attacking travellers, and looting and burning
villages all over Wilde Island. Father allocated funds to the
sheriffs in every shire to pay extra men to hunt the outlaws
down.

Spring filled the air with sweet scents. Bram the pigboy
celebrated the season by stealing honey from our hives.
Bram's enterprise sorely disturbed our bees who chased
him round the garden and stung him twenty-seven times. I
know the number of the stings, for Kit and Marn were
mending my gowns the day Bram went for the hives, and I
was the one who tended him.

Bram swelled up like a prickly pear. I treated him with
pork fat and thrashed yarrow and swaddled him in bandages

saying the charm I'd found in Sir Magnus's book. 'Sting, sting of the bee. Remove thy sword and set me free.'

That same afternoon, Bram, on some fool's errand, staggered into Dentsmore, still swathed like a dead man. This caused Jossie to swoon into a well. Bram pulled her out, though he told me later how she screamed as he did so, thinking he'd come to fetch her to her grave.

Spring warmed to summer. On the day we held our yearly Midsummer's fair in Miller's Meadow but three miles south of Dentsmore, I went with Kit full of hope, planning to glimpse my future and test Merlin's prophesy in a diviner's egg.

What a day Kit and I had together under the near-blind eyes of Marn. We downed steaming roundcakes and drank mugs of cider as we wandered past the stalls. For a penny you could buy a lace or gobble down a sweet. We watched jugglers and tumblers, avoiding the far end of the field where the barber was pulling teeth for a penny. (Screams and pleading cries to Saint Apollonia, patron saint of toothaches, came pouring from his booth.)

We cheered along with Father when Niles Broderick – now Sir Niles – won the jousting match. After mourning his father's heroic death he'd thrown himself into his training and won himself a knighthood. It was well deserved.

Kit and I sat under the maple tree with our apple tarts. A large grey cat crept up the lane towards the fair. Darting in and out of the stalls, it soon stirred up the dogs.

'Be gone, hex cat!' screamed the miller's wife, jumping up from her bench to slap the cat across its rear. The cat howled and raced past the acrobats who tumbled from their human tower. Sheb Kottle's filthy cur chased the cat about, barking and snarling, and children ran to their mothers screaming. The curs in chase knocked over three beer barrels. A barrel burst and, quick to the spigot, dogs and revellers went belly down lapping up the brew.

'Get ye out of there!' Bram's mother dragged him from the frothy puddle. Beside me, Kit's eyes were sparkling. When the barrels were righted, music resumed, and as the pipers played 'Come Ye to the Greenwood' the villagers went back to their stalls.

Niles Broderick, who'd been eyeing Kit from afar, came up to us and took off his hat. 'Will you let your lady's maid come dance?' Kit blushed, but I made her go. How well they looked together and how gracefully she moved her feet in time to his. I watched him swing her round as the sun sank behind the hills.

When the tables were laid along the edge of Miller's Meadow for the Midsummer's Feast Mother left the festival. She hated eggs above all other food and diviner eggs, served raw as they were, vexed her innards. Father bid me sit at the high table near the Earl of Warwick and his lady, but I wedged myself between Kit and Marn. Lord W. and his wife turned up their noses. Let them sneer. I would choose my own best company.

My gut still full from the doings of the day, I awaited Father Hugh's blessing, then picked at the food. First came trenchers of venison in cream sauce, then stuffed peacock, fruits, cheeses, and sculptured jellies washed down with apple beer and elderberry wine. Last came the destiny cakes and diviner eggs.

Candles flickered in the summer wind as the chandler's wife, Tess, took the goose eggs from her basket. Tess was a true diviner. Dressed in a blue gown with a crown of lavender on her head, she looked every bit the queen of fairies.

'We'd better go now,' said Marn.

'I'll stay for the divining.'

Marn frowned. 'I shouldn't keep you out so late on the night of the fairies' high feast.'

'There's no reason to fear the fairy feast,' laughed Tess, sweeping back her auburn hair. 'Fairies have not been seen around here for more than six hundred years.'

I felt sad hearing this. I'd wanted to believe the fairies still dwelled in our deeper forest lands where folk rarely wandered.

'Kit's egg. Will you divine it, Tess?'

'Oh, aye.'

Marn strode down to the far end of the table, the more to gossip with her son's wife, Fiona, as Kit broke her egg and dropped it in her bowl. Tess jiggled Kit's dish, her luminous eyes widening. 'Why poppet, you shall break a heart. What do you say to that, my girl?'

'She does not speak,' I said.

'Now that's a pity with such a pretty face.' Tess moved on to me. Crack! I broke my raw egg and dropped it in my dish. The diviner wrapped her fingers round my little bowl, and bent low enough for me to smell her lavender crown.

'Ah, true love,' she said, gazing at my egg. 'For the sweet and thorny rose bush is bound to call the bee.'

'What bee?' I asked thinking of the prophecy. 'Is it Prince Henry you see?'

She swished my bowl about then drew back, her dark brows tilting.

Looking down, I spied a drop of blood next to the yolk. 'What does it mean?' I asked, a coldness leaping to my skin.

Tess turned her back, her hair shining russet in the candle glow. I grasped her elbow and pulled her close. 'You'll tell me what this means,' I whispered.

Tess looked about. 'Not here. Anon at Miller's Pond.'

I dumped my bloody egg on the ground. Let the dogs lick it up.

The villagers held a Midsummer's game floating little candle boats across Miller's Pond. Niles fashioned boats for us, but I left Kit and searched for Tess. On the far side of Miller's Pond, I spotted her at last in the barley field. She was walking and speedily. I bounded after. 'Tess! Tell me what you saw in my egg!'

'I cannot speak now. I have someone to meet.'

'Someone more important than your own princess?'

Tess began to run.

'You'll tell me what you saw,' I shouted, but she disappeared into the barley, the lavender crown falling from her hair. The edge of the night sky was scarlet. The barley whispered, *red clouds without the aid of sun. Traveller beware. The dragon comes.* It's nothing but the last stain of the day, I thought as I quit the field.

On the beach, the castle musicians played 'Threading the Needle' as the villagers danced in and out like needles through cloth. I would leave the fair and rush to the chandler's cottage, where no doubt the woman hid. There I'd shake Tess hard and force her to spit the omen out. I was turning my foot toward Dentsmore, when Father caught me up.

'Dance with me,' he said, twirling me around. We danced. Eased our parched throats with mead and danced more. I could not escape. From that hour on, Father never let me from his sight.

When we arrived home late that night, everything was a-stir inside the castle. Servants ran up and down the stairs, Sir Magnus shouted; steam filled the kitchen, Cook wept. Mother had fallen from her horse riding home from the fair. She'd lain alone for hours, bleeding and unable to move. At last she'd gathered strength enough to ride back to the castle and now lay recovering in her chamber.

Hearing the news, Father flung his cloak aside. 'Why did no one come for me!' he shouted. Sir Magnus bowed. 'The Queen only just arrived herself. We'd thought her all this time to be with you at the fair.'

Father rushed to her solar. I paced the floor with Kit and Marn and waited as Sir Magnus went in and out with herbs and bandages. At last, Mother called me to her bed. I greatly feared the sight of her, hearing from Cook that she was gashed and bloody.

'A rotting branch broke and fell right acrost her path,' said Cook, her fat cheeks trembling. 'It was a fairy spelled the branch, for didn't it startle her horse so bad he reared and threw the queen to the ground? She tumbled through a thorn bush, struck her head on a stone, and all was black. There she lay torn and bleeding for hours, poor thing. And here we were having our supper the whole time not thinking a thing was wrong. Ah,' she cried. 'She should never have ridden home alone on Midsummer's Eve, for that's the night of the fairies' high feast, mind. You'd never catch me out of doors on Midsummer's Eve. Fair or no.'

When Father bid me go, Kit kissed my cheek for courage. I tried to put on a smile before stepping into Mother's chamber. I'd hoped to make her laugh with stories of the fair. But I lost my purpose as I slipped through the door. Propped in her bed with scratched cheeks, a swollen eye, and head and arm all bandaged, Mother looked for all the world like Sir John Broderick on the day he'd skirmished with a boar. Her torn gown and bloodstained gloves lay on the corner chair. Sir Magnus's herbs soured the room.

'Come by me,' she whispered. I sat on her bed, clinging to the wooden post and looking at the fire to keep my eyes from her swollen face.

The logs popped and I could see a roll of charred vellum burning in the fire. The edges of the vellum had already turned to ash.

'There's nothing to fear now, Rosie,' said Mother. She told me of her fall. I learned the horse awakened her with a nudge, and finding herself scratched and bruised, she climbed back in the saddle.

'Why did no one come for you?' My throat was thick. Even this was hard to say. Mother touched my trembling chin. 'No one knew I'd fallen, Rosie. Your father thought me safe at the castle. The servants here thought me at the fair.' She tipped her head. 'I was foolish to ride alone, but the evening was so fair and I long to be alone at times.'

'Not with so many footpads about. You've told me yourself never to go without an escort!'

'Rosalind, don't talk to me as if I am your child. I knew what I was doing.'

Her eyes were hard as wet stones. I remembered what Cook said and told her, hoping to soften her eyes again. 'Cook said a fairy spell spilled you from your horse.'

Mother tried to smile, her swollen cheek puffing out with effort. 'Well, that's Cook,' she said, her voice a little lighter than before. 'It wasn't a fairy. A raven startled my mare.'

I frowned. 'Cook said you told her a branch fell across your path.'

'A what?' Mother looked startled. 'Oh, don't believe Cook,' snapped Mother. 'She wasn't there. I was!'

Again the hard tone. 'What's wrong?' I asked, confused.

'I'm tired and sore. That's all.' Her voice was low again, but heavy. She leaned forward and touched my hair. 'You look so fair tonight, my little rose.'

Tears rolled down my cheeks.

'Don't weep now. All will be well with your Prince Henry across the sea.'

'I cry for you. Why do you always have to bring up Henry?'

'Because he's our hope, Rosalind! Do you think I want my girl to rule an island plagued by dragons and footpads?'

Why shout at me? I toyed with her coverlet thinking I would be glad to rule here. Wilde Island was my home. But mother was hot and cold by turns. Whatever happened when she fell had changed her. I hoped the change would pass away when her wounds were healed.

'It's late,' said Mother. 'You should be abed. But call Lady Beech before you go, and tell her to burn the bloody gloves and gown. They're torn beyond repair.'

I called the queen's lady-in-waiting and left Mother's solar, the smells of serpent's tongue and blood mingling in my nostrils.

12
Witch's Hollow

B Y THE NEXT DAY WE'D LEARNED MORE OF THE
strange events following the Midsummer's Fair.
Sheriff William came early to tell us Kent the coppersmith was attacked and eaten by the dragon on his way
home from the fair. And more than this, the woman Tess
was missing. The sheriff suspected witchcraft here, though
he would not say in front of me the reasons he suspected
this. Father closed the door. Pressing my ear to the crack, I
tried to listen in, but their voices were too low.

After the sheriff left, my head was in turmoil over Tess.
I visited the mews, but Sir Allweyn was rude, the hawks
agitated. Later I could not attend to my lessons. Sister
Anne was schooling me on the dragon wars, the battles
and broken treaties when I asked, 'Is it true dragons cannot cry?'

'What year was the treaty with France signed,
Rosalind?' she asked.

'Tell me, is it true?'

Sister Anne sighed. 'I am told this is so.' She put down her book. 'Tears put out their inner fire. Once this fire goes out, a dragon dies.'

'So they cannot repent,' I said.

'You should ask Father Hugh that.'

'I'm asking you.'

Sister Anne crossed herself. 'It's better not to ask such things, Princess.'

'Why not? A dragon ate the coppersmith, and mayhap Tess as well. Even now they look for her. A murderer can repent before he's hanged, but can a dragon?'

'You cannot hang a dragon!' said Sister Anne with alarm. 'I think,' she said, 'you've had enough study for one day.' And she left with the haste of one who has need of the privy.

With the dragon on the hunt, I was forbidden to leave the castle without Mother's or Father's consent but, late in the day, I tugged Kit down the stairs. Sneaking out the servants' door we crept over the drawbridge. On the grassy hill we climbed the maple tree for a better view of Dentsmore village and woods beyond.

Up the lane in the graveyard, I heard the clanging of the stonemason's chisel, carving Kent's name in the Dragonstone. My spine shuddered with each pound of the hammer.

High in the boughs, Kit and I watched the sun running

off with the last of the day.

'Look,' I said pointing to a woodland meadow on the outskirts of Dentsmore. 'See the horsemen riding round in Witch's Hollow?'

Kit peered through the branches to spy the sheriff's men, her blonde hair spilling from her cap. I shivered looking on. Was the sheriff searching for Tess in that cursed place?

'There sits a princess on her perch!' shouted Bram the pigboy, giving us a whistle as he came up the hill.

'Hush, clodpoll.'

'Call me clodpoll and I'll keep my news to myself.'

I snorted. What sort of news could a pigboy have? 'Have you stolen more honey? Where are your stings?'

'No honey, princess,' he said rocking back on his heels.

'Go away.'

Kit covered her nose. Bram's stink reached us both even in the branches.

'Aye, you won't hear of the murder then.' He swung his arms as he started down the hill.

'Wait!' We scrambled down the tree. 'Tell me who was killed,' I said, my mouth going dry as salt beef.

The pigboy crossed his arms. 'Tell your maid to kiss me and I'll say.'

'Say now by order of the queen!'

'I see no queen here,' said Bram, looking round the stand of maples.

'You see the future queen. Now speak!'

Bram leaned against the tree. 'Six bread rolls from Cook's larder and half a pound of cheese,' he bargained. The boy was always hungry.

'Three rolls and a quarter-pound.'

Bram gave a nod and pointed to his right at the forest beyond Dentsmore. 'They found Tess the chandler's wife there in Witch's Hollow.'

My skin pricked. I'd last seen Tess running through the blowing barley, saying she had someone to meet.

'Was it the dragon that killed her?' I asked.

'There were dragon signs there. Aye, the beast had come to Witch's Hollow, but this killing was not his. He ate Coppersmith instead or haven't you heard?'

'I knew it,' I said.

Bram picked up a stone and flung it toward the castle.

'How do I know you speak the truth about Tess?'

'Ah,' he nodded. 'I saw the corpse myself about an hour ago as I was coming through the woods. Sheriff William's men tugged me away, but not before I saw the pool of blood on the grass. Stabbed three times, she was. The last time in the heart,' he said licking his lips. 'Aye, and it was gruesome sure. More blood than I ever saw at a pig killing. Much more.'

Bram rubbed his hands together. 'She must have put up a fight. I was close enough to see the scratches on her face and arms, and there was dried blood under her fingernails. Ah, but the witch knife did the trick, and she was left to bleed to death whilst Demetra flew back to her cottage.'

Flew? My flesh crawled. 'How do you know of Demetra?'

'The mountain hag? She used to hobble through Dentsmore with her herbs till the villagers chased her away.'

I pressed him for more. 'But how do you know it was Demetra killed Tess?'

Bram clicked his tongue. 'Ah, well,' he said, the brownness of his teeth showing too much as he smiled.

'Tell me!'

'Didn't you see the grey cat at the fair?'

'Aye, Kit and I both saw it.'

'Twas Demetra's kith-beast, creeping hither and thither,' he said wiggling his filthy fingers, 'frightening the wee ones, and spelling the dogs till they frothed at the mouth.'

Kit grabbed my arm and I felt her cold hand through my sleeve.

I'd seen a grey cat in Demetra's cave, but cats were common enough. 'The dogs weren't hexed.' I laughed, showing my ease to dispel Kit's fears. 'The hounds frothed at the mouth from lapping up spilled beer.'

'Spilled beer, was it?' Bram gave a guilty look for he'd lapped it up himself. 'Never you think so.'

'A stray cat proves nothing of Demetra's part in this murder.'

'No? All signs point to Demetra. Didn't she fly back to Tess's cottage?'

Bram's logic had begun to vex me. 'How do you know this? Did you see her?'

'Myself?' said Bram, offended. 'I do my best to stay clear of witches. I have pigs to look after,' he said with pride. 'But I'm told she left the mark of the witch along the chandler's walls. Scrolled in blood it was.'

Kit and I crossed ourselves three times.

'Too, she stole some coins, and magic stones, and a scroll.'

'Scroll?' I said through a strangled throat.

'Aye, some scroll she'd given Tess to guard. Her husband knew where Tess hid it and he told the sheriff it was missing.'

'How do you know this, pigboy?'

'Didn't I follow Sheriff William back to the chandler's cottage so I could hear him break the bad news to the chandler? Oh and I could hear both men well enough through the shutters.'

The sky was growing a deeper purple, and there was the smell of roses and lavender in the air. But my skin was cold. I wrapped my arms about my chest and leaned against the tree. Coins, magic stones, a scroll.

Could this be Demetra's scroll on which my secret curse was writ? If this were true, why would Demetra kill her and steal it back? There was a roll of vellum burning in Mother's hearth. Fear rose up my throat, but I swallowed it back down. It couldn't have been the scroll. Mother fell from her horse on her way home. She had the bruises and scratches to prove it.

Bram flopped down, plucked a blade of grass, and chewed. 'Look,' he said, pointing to Witch's Hollow. 'The sheriff's men are searching all around the woods for more murder clues.'

Torchlight flickered from the village below as one by one the people gathered on the road. They moved of one accord along the winding street and stopped outside the chandler's hut, torches wavering against the darkening sky.

'The villagers will be after Demetra now,' said Bram chewing on his grass. 'Death by hanging,' he mused. 'Or by cleansing fire if they've a mind to.'

Kit stood flushed and trembling beside me.

'No,' I said to calm Kit. 'They'll let the sheriff chain Demetra up and bring her to Dentsmore for her trial.'

The pigboy rolled back his head and laughed. 'Oh aye, they'll stand aside like docile lambs whilst the sheriff sees justice is done.'

'Get away from me, pig brat!'

He left, but not in the direction of the castle. Bram was running fast to meet the villagers.

I stepped away from the tree and took Kit's hand. The torches in the village below circled like starlit water in a swirling moat. Then the crowd took off, marching up the road leading to the mountain path.

Kit's hold about my hand tightened and her eyes sparked like burningstone. Her mother, Ali, was in Demetra's cave, and who was to say she wouldn't be seen as just another witch to hang or burn as the people liked?

Down the hill we flew, through the foreyard to the castle stable. I tossed a coin to silence the stable boy, and we led the horses across the drawbridge. We took the road that crossed Morgesh Valley and galloped to the base of the mountain.

'Don't worry, Kit!' I called. 'We'll save your mother sure!' But my voice did not sound as confident as I wished, and I hoped Kit could not hear the fear behind it.

We galloped in the wind, riding up the steep path, leaping over fallen branches. I was thankful then that I'd taught

Kit to straddle her horse snugly as a man does, to duck her head, and to centre her weight on the saddle just before a jump.

Part way up the trail, I pulled Galahad to a halt and looked over my shoulder. Not far below us the villagers' torches flickered like star spit. Our mounts were speedy but those on foot were already swarming up the trail.

'Faster,' I called. 'They're heading for Demetra's cave.'

I urged Galahad to a gallop, praying all the while to Saint Hippolytus for protection from a sudden fall. We happened on the cave. I say this because I was lost by the time we reached it. Dismounting stealthily, we hid our horses in the copse to the right of the trail, and sneaked inside.

The fire burned low. Newly gathered herbs mingled their goodsome smells with rotting lamb bones scattered on the table. We crept through the stony maze in search of Ali. I prayed Demetra was deep in a cavern bent over an absorbing spell, or better still, gone altogether. This close to the hag, I could taste the fear in my mouth. I set my jaw and prayed I would not meet her moon-struck eye.

13
The Hag

STUMBLING INTO A SMALL ROOM, I BUMPED AGAINST a broken eggshell the size of Cook's great cauldron, spilling bones and dried herbs on the floor. It could not be an egg by all rights. No bird was that big, but I had no time to wonder at it with the villagers on their way. Racing down the hall, I found Kit leaning over her sleeping mother. She wept soundlessly as she kissed her cheeks.

'Child,' said Ali.

'Hush,' I whispered. 'You must come with us now!' I pulled her up. Ali, obedient to my harsh whisper, grabbed her cloak and shadowed us out of the cave. Hearing the crowd close by, I took her hand and tugged her into the shelter of the copse where our horses were hidden.

We crouched behind some thick gooseberry bushes, and waited. I rubbed my sore knee and eyed my gloves. Both were filthy and the right one was torn. Mother would be angry.

'Who comes?' whispered Ali.

'Villagers. Their blood burns for Demetra.'

The crowd wended up the trail and surrounded Demetra's cave, their torches and rushlights crowning the stone entrance in pale gold.

'Out, witch!' called Brock the tanner.

In the gap between Brock and Kate the miller's wife, I saw the entrance of the cave and the low fire within. No sign of Demetra. The villagers shuffled their feet, their shadows dancing on the stony walls.

'Out, I say!' Brock shouted.

Four men strode into the cave. A soft wind blew up-mountain as all outside waited. Then there was a clattering noise and a scream, and out they came with Demetra. With her hands bound behind her back, and her grey hair blowing loose as a spider's web, she looked every bit a witch.

'You have spelled your last spell,' shouted Brock.

'Why have you bound me?' cried Demetra. 'I've done nothing untoward. I've been away at herbing these three days.'

'Gathering hex potions!' shouted Kate. 'Wilde Island will not abide a witch!'

'Where have you hidden the knife you used to murder Tess?'

Demetra narrowed her moon-struck eye. 'Tess murdered? This is the first I've heard of it. I say I've been up mountain.'

'It's true,' whispered Ali. 'She's been gone three days.'

'Aye, gone,' I said, 'but who is to say where?'

'Unbind me!' snarled Demetra. Just then I saw her grey

cat in the cave behind her. It jumped from the table where it had been nibbling on sheep bones. Skirting the fire, it scurried outside.

'See her kith-beast!' called Jossie. 'Same as the one we saw trancing the dogs at the fair!'

'Kill it!' shouted Keith.

Kit fairly leaped out to aid the cat, but I grabbed her by the cloak and held her back. Arrows flew as the cat darted into the woods on the other side of the path and disappeared.

'Never you mind,' said Keith. 'The kith-beast will die when the witch does.'

'I have to help Demetra,' whispered Ali.

'Stay,' I hissed, tugging her behind the bushes. 'They'll call you a witch as well, and your neck will be in the noose!'

Kit pulled her mother closer.

I wished to be away but could not move. Any sound we made above a whisper would give our hiding place away. Tim the chandler ran into the cave, returning with a handful of stones, and Demetra's knife.

'I could not find the scroll. My wife never let me see, but I thought to myself that there might be witchcraft written on it. Ah, I warned Tess about that, but she wouldn't listen. She . . .' Tim's face contorted in the torchlight. 'But here are coins I found in the cave, and five magic stones like my own dear wife's!' he cried. 'And I found the knife she used to do her butchery!'

The crowd roared at the sight of the knife.

'The coins and stones are mine,' called Demetra. 'And the knife is for cutting meat like any on your tables! You'll not find a scroll here. I didn't do the deed. Your princess is cursed!' she cried. 'Ask the queen who killed Tess!' My body burned and shook – fire and ice in the witch's words, but Demetra's cries were covered by the crowd shouting, 'Burn her! Burn the witch!'

Fast the rope went round Demetra. She screamed louder still as the men drove her into her cave. They tied her to the table where her herbs and bones were strewn, and the people tossed their torches in.

'Oh, come,' I moaned. 'I cannot bear to stay.'

The villagers howled as flames engulfed the inner cave. Smoke filled the air about us. With all the shouting and Demetra's screaming, none heard us mount our horses. Ali rode ahead with Kit on Marigold. We headed down a secluded trail, putting bushes, boulders, rowan trees and oak between us and the burning.

The horses followed Kaydon River down the mountain. Leaning close to Galahad's mane, I tried to shut out Demetra's screams, and clear the smell of death smoke from my nose.

I slept.

Later in the night, a strangled sound awoke me. I tensed, sat up and looked about. The growling increased, a sound wild and menacing. What beast hunted us here so close to home?

The growl changed to a moan, more human now than animal, and it came from just ahead. Ali turned to me, cheeks pale, eyes wide. 'Something is wrong with Katinka!'

A strangled sound poured from Kit's mouth. We dismounted in the high orchard. At the base of an apple tree,

Ali held Kit on her lap as she convulsed. My friend's face was pale as candle wax, her lips were deep purple.

'What is wrong with her?' I gasped.

Ali rocked her. Soon the noise increased. With a garbled cry, a shadow emerged, birthing black from Kit's mouth. My skin burned even as it went cold. I wanted to run, but love for Kit held me there.

'God!' called Ali. 'Help us.'

I put my arm about Kit's neck as we watched in muted terror, the birthing of the shadow wraith.

How slow and with what pain this shadow wraith escaped my poor friend's mouth. An hour passed, yet there seemed no end to this writhing form that came feet first from her lips. I would have pulled it from her throat, but there was no touching it. The thing wasn't made of flesh.

With strange howls, the shadow wraith emerged, until at last it ripped itself from Kit's mouth. With a final scream, it spilled onto the earth and sank.

A black hole formed where the wraith was sucked into the orchard floor, and a stench of burning bone rose from it. We left the pit.

'Oh my Katinka!' cried Ali. Kit looked so small on her mother's lap. I closed her mouth, and wiped the drop of blood from her lip.

'I did not know,' wept Ali. 'Demetra must have hexed her.'

She gripped my cloak. 'Katinka had a voice when she was small. She cooed, and wailed as any babe. Demetra couldn't abide the babe's cry. There came a night when her wee mouth opened and no sound came from my daughter's throat.' She stroked Katinka's hair. 'But I swear I didn't know Demetra hexed her.'

In case the wraith should think to come again, I said Marn's binding charm over Kit. 'Three times winding. Four times binding. I bind all evil spirits now and cast them from this girl.'

Tying the invisible knots, I kissed my friend's damp forehead, whispering, 'There now,' and 'You'll feel better soon,' with the kindness of a mother, the way Marn always had with me.

In that dark hour as we held Kit, still as death and grey, though breathing softly, I thought of Demetra, a woman cruel enough to stuff a shadow wraith into an infant's throat. The hag was dead now, a witch's burial set for her bones. She would be thrice scattered and thrice buried so the villagers could be assured the witch would never rise. I was glad of it. Let them dig and scatter the hag's bones. Ah, let them cast her into unending darkness.

The chill air wrapped about us, and we thought to move. It would be hard to get back inside the castle unseen at this late hour. Yet before we left the orchard, I learned how close joy can follow on the heels of sorrow, for in the moonlight, Kit stirred in her mother's lap.

'Muth . . .' she said hoarsely. Then frowned, forming her lips again to strain out the word, 'Mutheer.'

'Aye, Katinka.' She bent and kissed her brow.

Kit took my arm. 'Roosie,' she whispered, her lips forming like a rose as she said my name.

My heart swelled. 'Aye, Kit,' I said embracing her. 'I am your Rosie. I will always be your Rosie.' A quiet jubilation filled me as I held her close. My dearest friend and companion was released.

I could still feel the stiffness of my claw beneath my glove. I was not healed with Demetra's death. But Kit's releasing gave me hope that some day I might be unbound and touch the world like other women.

An owl hooted from above. I wondered as I stood to untie Galahad, what other curses died this eve. How many hellish spells had gone down with Demetra?

Ali looked at me. 'You must return home. The queen will worry.'

'We left in view of no one.'

'Getting back inside the castle might be a different matter.'

'You're coming with us,' I said hopefully.

'I cannot. The villagers know I served Demetra. They'll burn me for a witch.'

I would have argued, but it was true.

'Mother?' Kit gazed up at her. She'd only just got her back after their year apart.

'Where will you go?' I asked.

'To Saint Brigid's Abbey. I lived there for a time as a girl. The nuns will shelter me.' She looked to the south and worked to hold her face steady, the night wind blowing back her hair.

My heart pounded. 'You're . . . Aliss,' I whispered.

She gave a sad smile. 'My full name is Alissandra. No one has called me Aliss for a long time.'

'You were my mother's lady's maid and her dearest friend.' My eyes were brimming. Aliss and Mother, Kit and myself, I should have seen it long ago.

Kit took her mother's hand. I had the power to order her to return to the castle with me, she was my lady's maid, but there was cruelty in that. Kit had missed her mother this past year. I was fifteen now, and strong. I should bless my friend and let her go. Yet I gripped Galahad's mane, and leaned my head against his side, working hard to tame my breath.

None spoke. I stared at the castle on the far hill; beyond it stars salted the sea with specks of light.

'We are free now,' said Aliss. 'The shadow of Demetra fades.'

'Aye.' Kit pulled off her hood to let the breeze play in her hair.

I could not tell Kit to go. Could not demand she stay. Torn between kith and kin, Kit fingered Marigold's mane and faced the road stretching down the hill.

Aliss touched Kit's cheek where a smear of dirt rested from her ordeal. 'You know my love for you?'

'Aye,' said Kit.

'And you know of Rosalind's love?'

Kit nodded.

'We both long to have you with us, but . . . your place is with Rosalind now.' Alissandra embraced her girl.

'I can't,' said Kit, her eyes wet with tears.

'The princess needs you, and I'll be safe enough.' Aliss brought her forehead close to Kit's. 'I was born near Brigidshire, and the nuns will be kind to me.' She wiped the damp hair away from Kit's brow.

'Take Marigold,' I said, suddenly generous. 'Kit will ride with me.'

We mounted our horses. In the orchard where we passed, a flock of startled birds flew helter-skelter into the dawning sky.

'Wait,' called Aliss. Turning Marigold about, she took a silver brooch from her cloak, and gave it to Kit.

'It says *omnia vincit amor*,' said Aliss. '"Love conquers all".'

She turned and rode southward.

14
Punishment

O N OUR RIDE DOWN THE PATH, I WARNED KIT NOT to speak to any in the castle. We might tell of her cure in time, but I sensed Mother would find Kit's voice good reason to dismiss her. The queen liked it well that my lady's maid was mute.

In the graveyard we dismounted. 'We'll take the secret way inside.' I felt along the wall for the tinderbox the sexton kept hidden there. Candlelit, we entered the Pendragon tomb and passed Queen Evaine's carved effigy atop her stone casket. In a deeper chamber down more stairs I found the jagged crack and gave it a push. A squealing sound of stone on stone and the wall moved back.

'This is our way of escape if the castle is ever under siege,' I whispered. 'Father showed it to me last year, but you must never say you've seen it.'

'Aye,' whispered Kit hoarsely. And whom would she tell being mute to all but me?

We looked down the dark passage. The tunnel seemed a living thing, a long serpent wending beneath the earth. The dank air wafting from the opening smelled like rotting meat. I stepped inside but Kit held the small doorway. 'I feel a chill, Rosie.'

'A wet passage,' I said, shouldering my misgivings. Together we closed the door, and walked the muddy floor in the flickering candlelight.

Down the dark tunnel, I heard a soft scuttling noise across the walls. Rats. I wanted to run, but this was our only way in. Side by side, we stepped along, following the passage that ended in the wine cellar, and as we pushed against the door, I spied the casks all lined against the wall.

The door creaked when we pressed it shut and we held our breaths, but no one came to check the noise.

We might have made it to our beds. And sometime before dawn, I might have mended the tear in my glove to leave off all suspicion. But Marn was far too motherly. Awakened by the cold, she discovered Kit and I were missing. Marn caught us creeping down the hall, drew us both into her chamber and shut the door.

'Now, where have ye been!' she scolded. 'I'm of a mind to thrash you both!' She squinted at our soiled gowns. The bit of blood still stained Kit's mouth, though I thought I'd wiped it clean.

'Who's harmed you?' she cried.

'She took a fall from her horse,' I said thinking of no better lie.

'A fall? Ah, my precious girl! Are ye hurt?' She held Kit close and wept into her hair. 'Wicked girls,' she scolded through her tears. 'How could you think to go riding at night without so much as a sprig of wolf's-bane to protect ye? Ah, I'm such a fool to let you slip out so!' She wept as she undressed Kit and searched her for blood wounds.

'God be praised,' she said, dabbing her eyes with her shawl. 'The fall did you little harm, poppet.' She clothed Kit in her nightdress, tucked her in her bed, and turned to me. 'Come, Rosie,' she said. 'I'll be putting you to bed now. Wild girls, the both of you! On the morrow you'll have your punishment for this!'

I followed Marn down the hall like a dog its master. Any punishment awaiting us could not touch my joy now that Kit could speak. Marn shut the window tight. Then pulling me to my bed, she set me down and lit the rushlight.

'Ah, dearest,' she said, helping me into my sleeping gown. 'I love ye like a daughter. To think you rode out without a guard and Kit fell off her horse, and I wasn't in the knowing of it. A better nurse would have felt the trouble in her bones, but I've grown old and useless.' She sniffed and brushed away a tear.

'No,' I said, 'you're the dearest old Marn and I . . .'

'There's no telling what the queen will do when she hears of this!' said Marn tossing back the covers. 'There's punishment on the morrow for us all, mark me!'

I slipped into the bed. 'Ah, Rosie,' said Marn, stroking my hair. 'Never steal away again. Promise your old Marn. There's a deal of evil in the world you have no knowing of, and I would not have you touched by it.'

Marn kissed my cheek and looking down, she saw my soiled gloves and the tear. 'Filthy!' she said. 'And torn. The queen will fly into a rage!' She hovered over, wringing her hands.

'I fear her anger more than dragon fire,' she whispered. And I saw in her wrinkled face that it was so.

'Wash them,' she said to herself with a nod, and quick she tore the gloves off. Her swift action startled me and I had not time to hide my hands.

Seeing my claw, her jaw dropped and her hand flew to her mouth. 'Le . . . leprosy,' she stuttered. 'Ah, God!' Her face went tallow-coloured. My gloves fell to the floor. 'So that's what drove you out. You went to see the lepers encamped up in the hills! And now you've caught their blight!'

'No,' I argued. 'I did not go to them! This thing. This curse . . .' But already Marn was rushing to my door wailing, 'Leprosy!' And from the hall, I heard her moan, 'We're all undone!'

Still sickened by her cry of leper, I buried my face in my naked hands, Marn's scream at the sight of my claw making the whole of me feel unclean. Kit had been healed, but I was still a leper in Marn's eyes.

I heard Marn knocking on a chamber door as I picked up my discarded gloves and slid them back on. *Leper. Leper. Leper.* Marn's judgement echoed in my mind with every knock, her scorn piling dirt over my body like a burial spade. Down the hall, the door opened, then shut again, cutting out all sound. She'd gone in to Mother! She'd tell Mother! I couldn't move under the piled-up earth. Now there was only my scattered breathing caught inside my quilt, and the rattle of the night wind at my window.

In my dreams, there seemed no peace that night, but a swirling and a twirling, all the world going widdershins from God. Still I would never have wished awakening had I known what dawn would bring.

Hadn't Marn said we would all have our punishment on the morrow? Aye, the wild girls got their punishment with the breaking of the dawn, just as Marn had warned, and it was worse than any whip.

'Rosie!' Kit was on her knees by my, her hair askew, her face puffy.

'What is it? Did the dragon attack?'

She shook her head, no.

'Was Aliss accosted by footpads on her way to the abbey?'

'Marn!' she choked, 'It's Marn.'

'Is she ill?'

Kit could not answer. I leaped from my bed, threw on my cloak heading for her chamber, but Kit pointed down the hall.

'Where is she?'

I raced behind Kit, my head more full of pleading prayer than any beggar's chapel. We reached the edge of the moat where a crowd of servants gathered. Bumping into Cook, I pressed through the crowd, and I found my Marn.

'God, no!' In the moat Marn floated, her shawl still wrapped about her shoulder. A dead rat and three bright plum leaves tangled in her hair. Water swirled around her.

And the morning rain pattering on the moat made ring on ring that broke against Marn's body.

The servants hovered behind me, weeping. And Cook lifted her hands to heaven calling, 'She's killed herself! What sorrow brought the woman here?'

'Hush, wench!' shouted Sir Allweyn as he poked Marn's hand with his pole.

'Don't,' I pleaded. I could not bear him poking at her so. There was the hand that had held me when I was small, picked my berries, mended my gowns, and just last eve had stroked my head. With steady motion, Sir Allweyn drew Marn from the moat. The chapel bells rang, and all of us were weeping.

Cook was wrong. I knew Marn had not leaped to her death. She was a sturdy soul. She'd wept when sorrow took her. Rocked herself and said binding charms when she was sore afraid. But never would Marn drown herself. I knew this to the bone. Someone had pushed her. Some devil killed my Marn. And were a knife within my hand, I'd kill the one who'd done it sure as the morning. I'd slit his throat and watch his blood spill on the ground.

Sir Allweyn laid Marn's body on the shore. I wept over her swollen face, kissed her cheek and pulled a bit of moss from the corner of her mouth.

Cook leaned over Marn and screamed. The other servants joined in till all about the water's edge there was a sound like the death wraiths keening.

Sir Allweyn waved his pole and tried to hush us, but on we went. We wailed all together, Kit holding me as I lifted the wraith song up to the sky.

15

Her Spirit Unbound

ALL OF MARN'S DEATH DAY, KIT AND I HUDDLED BY my chamber fire, our eyes swollen with tears. The day passed outside my window, but I didn't care to see the sun. On we sat, heavy with grief. When the sky grew purple Kit leaned in close to me and said, 'Do you mind the day Marn told us about Sir Magnus?'

I nodded. Just three days before, we were all in the walled garden. Marn had talked of Magnus as she tidied the herb bed. My nursemaid had come to Wilde Island as a young wife after her husband was banished from England for poaching on Lord Headington's land. 'Though he was innocent as a lamb,' she'd said. Then she'd told about our castle astrologer.

'Thinks he's God's gift to the world, he does,' said Marn. 'But Magnus is a twisted man, I say, and I know well, for he came aboard the same ship I did to serve out his years of punishment here on Wilde Island.'

Marn weeded round the rosemary. 'And what was he banished for, my dears?' She'd tightened her lips, looked about, and lowered her voice. 'Murder, I say.'

'Murder?' I'd felt the thrill of the word churn through me as if I were milk on my way to butter. I sensed the man was evil, but never guessed he'd killed anyone.

'Aye,' said Marn, 'And I'm glad I've told ye now, for some day you'll be queen, and you'll need to know not to trust the man.'

'I never have,' I said truthfully. 'Whom did he kill?'

'His sweet young wife. Poisoned her for her money.'

'We would have hanged him for that here on Wilde Island,' I said proudly.

'Aye, and they would have in dear England too, but some say he coin-pursed the judge, and so came here instead.'

I grabbed Marn's arm. 'Does Mother know?' I asked, but my question was drowned out by the sound of footsteps on the far side of the garden wall.

'Who's there?' asked Marn startled. Kit and I climbed the apple tree. No one was below on the other side. Kit looked wide-eyed at me then, mouthing the word *Magnus*. Below us in the garden, Marn had crossed herself.

In my solar Kit's cheeks were flushed as we each recounted the tale. 'Magnus must have listened beyond the wall that day and overheard her telling us,' whispered Kit. I stood agitated, then sat again.

'Then yestereve,' Kit went on, 'when Marn was alone, Magnus took his chance to . . .'

'Hush,' I warned. 'Someone's coming down the hall.'

The door opened. In stepped Mother.

'Leave us,' she ordered. Kit left the room, her soft grey gown rustling as she went. Mother locked the door. 'Put these on.' She tossed a pair of her golden gloves on my lap. I tore off my filthy ones and Mother threw them in the fire. A putrid smell rose with the smoke as they burned. I choked, slipping the new ones on. They were too large, but I said nothing.

'It is a sorry day.' Mother's face was still scratched and swollen from her fall. I looked away, silent.

The fire popped. A small bright piece of wood fell near my gown. Mother leaped up and struck the cinder back with the poker. Her sleeve fell back showing the scratches along her arm.

'It doesn't matter if you speak,' she said. 'I know you sorrow for your nurse, as we all do. But you left the castle unguarded with Kit yestereve.'

'We rode to save Ali from burning.'

'You took this on yourself?'

'We saw the villagers coming up the hill with torches and so we went.'

'Did you not think to come to me?'

I watched the shadows on the wall, silent, black, roving.

'Such risks you take with your life, Rosalind. You know you're not allowed to ride without an escort.'

'You did.'

Mother's neck stiffened. 'I'm not a child.'

'Nor am I. I couldn't let the villagers burn Kit's mother!'

'So you ran off with your lady's maid, who should have kept you here!' Her eyes narrowed. 'Listen to me, Rose.

This lady's maid has led you into trouble and so –'

'You wouldn't have wanted Aliss to die, would you?'

Mother's look wavered and for a moment she couldn't speak. 'How did you know it was she?'

'I guessed. She didn't speak of it.'

The fire cast a trembling light across Mother and it seemed she eased in the glow, bathing in the memory of a happier time. I'd missed that look.

'Of course,' she whispered. 'I'm glad that she . . . that Aliss lives.'

'Why did you send her away?'

'She was with child, Rose, and out of wedlock.'

I thought there must be more to it than that. 'But why to Demetra?'

Mother reached into her waist pouch, pulled out the silver vial and sipped her poppy potion. This she did to harden herself again, I think. But I didn't want her hardened. I wanted to weep with her for Marn, who'd been her nursemaid and mine, to feel her holding me the way Alissandra held Kit when the fit was on her.

'You rescued Aliss from the frozen water when you were a girl. Why shouldn't Kit and I save her from burning now?'

Mother coughed and screwed on the lid. 'That's different.'

'It isn't.'

'You risked the future of our island, Rose.'

'As you did when you saved Aliss.'

'No. I was nothing then. No one knew my brother would die of the pox and that I'd be the queen.'

I heard the word *nothing* like a sting. I wanted to correct her, say that she was never nothing, that she mattered even when her brother was alive, even though her parents sent her away to the abbey. But Mother went on and the sting grew worse.

'Marn came to me crying that you'd gone to see the lepers,' said Mother. 'She saw your scornful part.'

'She shouldn't have . . . she knew never to take off my gloves.'

'She saw the tear and thought to mend them!' Mother's look was cold. She had a way of stripping me with her eyes. 'Well?' she said. 'What have you to say to this?' She folded her arms across her chest, the gold threads in her gloves sparkling with the firelight.

I kept silent.

The flames sent a copper glow all round Mother's head like the golden halo that crowned the stained glass angel in Saint John's chapel. No shadow marred the queen's fixed expression as she thought out her next words.

'Poor Marn,' she sighed. 'It shocked her so when she saw your wretched claw. It was the horror of your deformity made her jump.'

'Never! Marn would love me if I were covered with sores from head to heel! She would love me without hand or arm or if my face were ruined with the pox! It was not my claw that made her jump!'

'What then?' asked Mother, her lip a-twitch. 'What else would drive the woman to it?'

'Marn was pushed!'

Mother started. 'Pushed? Who told you this?'

'No one.'

'Then keep away from lies!' The vein pounded on the side of her neck as she tugged open her saint's pouch. 'Here,' she said. 'Swear on Saint Monica's sacred bone.'

'Never. She was pushed!'

'By whom?' asked Mother still dangling the open pouch so close I could see the saintly finger bone.

'Sir Magnus. Marn told Kit and me how he came to Wilde Island on the ship with her so many years ago. He served out his sentence in Hessings Kottle, did you know? Sold as a bond slave for the crime of murder.'

'Gossip,' snapped Mother.

'It never was!' I bit my lip to keep the tremble still.

'Sir Magnus has been with us nine years, Rosalind. Why would he wait so long to kill Marn if she knew his crime?'

'He might have overheard Marn talking of it in the garden. Never had she risked telling me until –'

'A story.' Mother huffed. 'When you're queen you'll have to know the difference between truth and tattle.'

The room was astir with far too many shadows. I felt the heat of the fire across my chest, the skin on my face pinching in the yellow light. There was another hand that could have pushed Marn in the moat. If I could form the words that gripped me hard about the throat. If I could but look into my mother's eyes and ask her.

Mother closed the saintly pouch and drank more poppy potion. She shut her eyes and breathed in deep awaiting the dream. How lovely was her face then and how calm.

I looked down at my shrouded hands. Was it so? Was

Marn so overcome by the sight of my claw that she threw herself into the moat?

We buried Marn on the feast day of Saint Peter. Mother and Father did not come because they said she'd shamed Pendragon Castle by taking her own life. I still thought this a lie and I fought with both of them to let me go. Nothing would have kept me from this last hour with my Marn. And so, clad in grey, a nosegay in hand, I walked with Kit and Sister Anne up the lane to the graveyard.

The castle servants travelled in our wake, and behind them came a crowd of villagers.

The bearers placed the coffin by the grave. Across from us Marn's grandchildren huddled by their mother. All in black they were like a nest of fledgling rooks. Marn's son, the blacksmith Gerbert, hovered over his brood as the service began, his face hard as an anvil.

A robin called from the maple branch above as Father Hugh led us in 'Come the Way Over', a song that tells of heaven where the blessed souls all go. Then down they lowered the coffin on its ropes, and my heart lowered with it.

Kit flung her lilies in the grave to protect Marn from evil. And on Marn's coffin, I tossed my marigolds, remembering how she'd said they made a sleeper's dreams come true. I prayed as the blossoms fell that Marn now dreamed of heaven.

Father Hugh crossed himself above the grave and we sang another hymn, but he would not say the final prayer of releasing, because he said Marn might have killed herself.

'I'll say it then!' cried her son, his neck going red as coals. 'We here all know my dear mother was half blind,' he said. 'It's sure she stumbled to her death not knowing the moat was so close by!'

Father Hugh bowed his head. He was a good man for it. The Father could not say the prayer himself, for none of us there knew if Marn were pushed, jumped in herself, or only stumbled in the dark. So her son said the releasing prayer hard and solemn, and Marn's spirit was unbound.

Each year we celebrated Saint Peter's feast by offering bread to the poor, killing an innocent lamb, and serving a great banquet at our table. Cook was already roasting the lamb.

Mother came in with a golden coronet for me to wear to the feast.

'I'll not go tonight,' I said.

'You will, Rose. And you will wear your coronet with pride.'

I had stood to argue my case then slumped back into my chair. Marn's death had robbed my strength.

Mother motioned to Kit. 'Come with me.'

They left me alone by the fire.

In the early eve before the guests arrived, Kit and I watched Tim the chandler light the candelabrum in the Great Hall. It held one hundred candles, a great expenditure of tallow. As Tim lit the last wick the room was draped in honey-coloured light. The glow spread along the rush-strewn floor and up the walls, gilding the tapestry where a line of huntsmen chased a red fox through the woods.

I stood close to the burning, wishing all the brightness would enter me and chase the sorrow of Marn's death away. There was a warmth there, but it seemed to circle round me, and not settle closer in.

The guests arrived then to the sound of trumpets, Father and Mother entered the hall. Father Hugh gave a solemn blessing and the guests began their meal. I had no taste for food, so the dogs were pleased to rove beside my chair. They bashed my legs with happy tails as I dropped chunks of lamb to the floor.

Kit sat beside me. From across the table, Niles tried to cheer us up with stories of a knight's valour, but we neither one could smile. I was worn from my sorrow over Marn, bristled from the work of holding up my chin to keep my coronet from slipping, and angry at the guests for being so merry on the day my nursemaid was buried.

'I'm tired,' I said. Niles glanced at Kit as we left the table and I wondered if Henry would ever give me that same look when we met over the sea.

I told Kit, 'I saw a loving look just now.' We rounded the corner and our shadows met upon the wall. With none around to hear, Kit whispered, 'Where?'

'From Niles Broderick.' I thought how sad the boy had been after his father's death and how hard he'd trained for his own knighthood. So it warmed my heart to see Niles's love for my lady's maid. Love lost. Love found. I thought to say it thus to Kit but she closed my chamber door saying, 'Sit here while I build up the fire.'

I did as she commanded me. As Kit tossed a shank of yew into the hearth and set to with the poker, she told me why Mother had called her to her chamber.

She might as well have jabbed my heart with the poker.

'The nunnery? Never! I won't let Mother send you!'

'You cannot stop it.' Kit brushed the bark dust from her hands.

'I will! When the feast is over I'll march to Mother's room and tell her you will stay!'

Kit sat down beside me, the flames washing gold across her cheeks.

'It's done, Rosie. Your mother blames me for putting you in danger.'

'But we had to go and warn your mother.'

'She won't have me here with you any more. She says I am not honourable.'

'Not honourable?'

'Sit still,' said Kit, 'and speak softer, someone may come down the hall.'

Our words were circling round and round the truth. This wasn't about rescuing Alissandra, but about our friendship. Mother thought we were too close, that I might share my secret with her. And she couldn't risk that.

'It's my fault,' I said suddenly.

'It's not.'

'But –'

Kit silenced me with three cool fingers on my lips. 'It's

done, Rosie. The queen won't change her mind.' She leaned closer to my ear. 'Your mother must never know what happened to me in the orchard. Promise me this, Rosie.'

I didn't move.

'You know it's not safe for me here now that I can speak. How long before the queen discovers it?'

'We'll keep it secret.'

She tipped her head. 'Think, Rosie.'

I couldn't look at her face, her eyes.

Kit unclasped the silver pin her mother had just given her and held it out to me.

'I can't take this,' I choked.

Kit shook her head and pressed it into my glove.

The next morning I watched Kit ride away with Sister Anne. Clouds shadowed the moat dark as stained wool as their horses crossed the drawbridge. In ten days' time Kit and Sister Anne would reach Saint Brigid's Abbey, where Kit's mother awaited. I clutched her pin to my breast, my mother watching Kit's departure beside me at my window.

My breath came wild and gulping as my bright swan shadow rode down Kingsway. And in Kit's hand I spied a slender apple bough. She held it out, the small green leaves dipping in the wind, and I knew the message there. 'Never betray our secret,' it said. 'Never tell how I came out of my spell in the apple orchard.'

PART TWO

Wolf's-bane

16

The Listing Ship

THROUGH AUTUMN I WAS WRAPPED IN SORROW, thick as a sea mist. And when the winter snow fell, I stayed by my hearth. But no matter how close to the fire I sat, I never could get warm. Mother brought more healers to Pendragon Castle. I submitted to their salves and I drank their potions, sour to sour.

Winter's chill grip loosened, yet no news of dragon attack came that early spring. We were soon to find out why.

One March morning, I left the castle at long last to ride again with Father. A mile south of Dentsmore we galloped past Miller's Meadow and rode through fields of buttercups and wild iris till we reached Lake Ailleann.

Father slowed to a trot. 'I've seen you sorrowful all season, Rosie.'

'Aye.' We let the hoofbeats measure out the silence between us.

'More than foul weather brought you down,' Father said at last. 'Still you mourn your nursemaid.'

I nodded.

'And you miss the little lady's maid? You have a good heart,' said Father. 'I'm glad for the prince that will marry you.'

I held my reins, gave Galahad a pat, and watched the first beams of sunlight winking on the lake.

'You're of an age to marry now,' continued Father as we rode on. 'I wed your mother at sixteen. But we're still waiting on Empress Matilda. Merlin's prophecy rests heavy on us.'

'It may be the saving of Wilde Island has nothing to do with marriage.'

Father pulled Crispin to a halt. 'What? You think never to marry, a beautiful maid like you? It would be a sin.'

His words were fresh as bellows to dormant coals. And a little hope-fire kindled in my chest.

'You'll have Prince Henry. Only the best will wed my Rosie.' Then turning Crispin, he raced along the shore, the reeds swaying as he passed like slender pilgrims bowing to their lord.

The breeze picked up as we skirted Lake Ailleann where the water shone blue as a giant's tear, with a dark speck in the middle. God's Eye seemed a sombre place to me, it being the last vestige of what Wilde Island had once been six hundred years ago when Merlin took a year of silence there.

I'd wondered when I was small if my destiny to restore Wilde Island's place under the sun, as Merlin predicted, meant to return it to its magic days, and I'd asked Marn about it. 'Ah, poppet, you're a dreamer,' she had said to me. 'It's sure the isle is swathed with a great many healing herbs from its magic days. But now it's trodden down with all manner of men. The wild beasts will not speak to us as they did in Saint Columba's time. Nor will the water sprites or fairies come out. They've all run skitter-tail from us. And it's not likely they'll return.'

I slowed Galahad to a trot. Above us the sky was pearled with small white clouds. The freshly risen sun beamed over the earth, and as I looked to the water, it seemed the magic was not gone, but dozing like a sleepy child that would one day leap up, as a bairn does from her slumber, and greet the world again. I dreamed of this as I rode behind Father, the larks high in the alders calling down to us as we rounded the lake.

Lake Ailleann lapped lazy as a dog's tongue on the shore as we wandered to the place where the yarrow moths were waking. We watched them one by one break apart their waxen tombs and struggle out. All the while Father stroked his beard and said, 'Look ye, Rosie. Out of death to life.' And I crossed myself as I watched a yarrow moth creep from her shroud, unfurl her yellow wings and flit skyward.

Father traipsed through the rushes and picked up a stone. 'Come closer by the water,' he called, 'and make a wish, my girl.'

I followed to the water's edge, chose a round rock as small as a sparrow's lay, and looked out to Lake Ailleann where the ripples whispered one to another. I knew if I could have my wish I'd bring Marn back from her drowning death, rescue Kit from the nunnery, and go herbing in the woods with them forever. Marn would stoop in the cool shade calling, 'Ah, here's a rue plant, dears. Sniff the leaves, and your head will clear in love matters.'

I turned the stone over in my glove.

'You think too long,' said Father. 'Make a wish,' he said, closing his eyes. 'Toss the rock.' He tossed his. 'And be done.'

I closed my eyes, tossed the stone, and saw neither Marn nor Kit behind my eyelids, but the image of a lover with his arms about me. In that vision my hand was fully healed, my finger shone pink as a rose petal. And I saw my gloves fall away like the torn cocoons the yarrow moths had left behind.

Marn once said, 'It's the roundness of a stone that brings about a wish. That and the rings that go acrost the water.' But I think Marn wasn't right in this. I think the answered wish comes from the hand that tosses in the stone.

We left Lake Ailleann behind, skirted the woods, and rode up Twisters Hill. There on the windy cliffs, Father pulled Crispin to a halt and strained forward.

'A ship,' he called through the swirling wind. And as soon as he said the words, the chapel bells rang out six times across the valley.

'Something is wrong,' said Father. 'See how the ship is listing to the left?'

I held my gloved hand to my eyes to shield out the sun and saw the ship tilting to the side, its sails fluttering small as moth wings.

'She may sink!' said Father. We raced toward Dentsmore. Father galloped past the cottages, calling all the boatmen out. None had been to fish that day, it being Sunday and what some womenfolk called 'My good man's day-o-slumber'.

I waited on shore with the other women whilst Father and the fishermen leaped to their boats. Many were still clad in their nightshirts, Father having called them from their beds.

As the boats pulled away, the women crowded on the docks to call, 'Not too far out! It be a Sunday!' And, 'Heed the warning waves, my dear!'

Sheb Kottle stumbled out of the Pig and Thistle, late to the news of the listing ship, but early with dire warnings. Padding to the dock he called, 'She'll sink before you reach her!' And though the men on the Dentsmore boats were too far out by then to hear him, he went on. 'She's sure to be a serpent's supper! Daft fools! I say turn back, afore ye all go down together!'

Kitty Wells, whose man was on a ship, took up a shank of driftwood and whacked Sheb Kottle on the head. He left off his predictions but set to moaning like a wraith, which spread the fear all round.

Standing apart from the others, I looked straight on to the wind, myself unsettled as my father's boat reached the larger vessel. By now the broad white sails tipped sharply as a knife to bread. I felt sure the ship would tumble over and go down a moment after. The craft did not topple as I feared, but escorted by the Dentsmore boats, slowly headed for the harbour. I could not see what set the boat a-kilter till they came closer in.

A carriage arrived. Hearing the chapel bells, Mother had come to greet the ship surrounded by her castle escort. She called me from the shore, but I stayed on the creaking dock. I meant to stand there until Father's boat was safely on the dock again, for the tilting ship, growing ever larger as it neared the shore, gave me a sense of foreboding.

'Ah! They've caught a whale,' called Kitty waving the driftwood above her head.

'Nay! Not a whale,' called Mavis. 'But a serpent sure!'

I shielded my eyes and looked out. There, lashed to the side of the vessel, cresting and bobbing in the sea, was the thing that had nearly sunk the ship. First I saw its giant head, hanging limp, snout down in the sea. Then I saw the blue-green scales across its back glinting in the water. Blood washed from the deep gash in its side.

'Dragon!' shouted Sir Allweyn running down the dock.

'It's dead and conquered!'

'We are free!' shouted the people on shore.

Suddenly, everyone was dancing: Jane with Kitty, Sal with Jossie, Sheb Kottle with himself. Then Jossie Brummer threw her arms around me shouting and jumping as if a mouse were in her kirtle. She spun me round and round in a jig, till the sea and sky were all one colour. All the while I reeled, joy and loathing mixed strangely in my heart.

Mother flurried onto the dock arm-in-arm with Sir Richmond and Sir Kimball.

'This will be a day of celebration for all Wilde Islanders!' she cried, and she herself twirled round on the dock with Sir Richmond.

By the time the ships reached us, we were all a-scuttle to the tune of 'Hey Diddle Da', pipes tooting, drums pounding and children singing all out of tune. By now I was swept into the joy of the dragon's death and had put away the strange sorrow I first felt when I saw the beast.

Father hopped onto the docks and wrestled Mother away from Sir Richmond. Fairly pushing the knight into the water, he kissed Mother there and then in front of all the world.

The villagers shouted and clapped as the sailors hopped down to tie the galleon to the docks. Then, herding all but the royal family back to the shore, the fishermen set to work cutting the ropes away from the dragon.

I could see only the snout, the beast being on the far side of the ship. I stood close to Father as the captain, dressed grandly in a torn cape and bloody clothes, stepped down to greet the king and queen. He doffed his hat to the cheering crowd on the beach, and bowed to Mother and Father. 'I am Lord Godrick,' he said. 'I've come with greetings from the Empress Matilda.' And Mother swooned.

It was too much for Mother to see in the same day the downing of her mortal foe, and greetings from Empress Matilda. Here was the captain of Matilda's ship, come to Wilde Island to pay homage to its king and queen, to invite the princess to Matilda's court, and strapped to his vessel, our mortal enemy, slain.

When Mother came out of her swoon, she ordered a banquet brought from the castle to the very beach where we stood. There with billowing flags and bonfires we would celebrate our victory over the dragon.

The boatmen tugged the dragon to shore. The music ceased. The only drumming now was the surf itself, pulling and pushing against the dead beast, washing over white then swirling pink with dragon's blood.

A youth with eighteen years or so on him came down the plank and stood beside me on the dock. He was of high rank, dressed as richly as Lord Godrick. His hair was black and his skin a rich brown, yet his eyes were blue. I'd never seen dark and light so finely combined in one person.

By now the fishermen had pulled the dragon ashore, and laid the creature on the sand. Waves swept up to meet the beast, which lay head-to-tail the length of the ship that brought her in.

'It's a female!' shouted Sam Denkle, wringing out his wet nightshirt.

'Ah, it couldn't be!' called Sir Richmond, then coming round front of her, he laughed, 'Why so it is!' All seemed aghast at this, but I knew this news already, having faced the dragon once on Morgesh Mountain.

My tongue went of a sudden dry as I looked on our mortal enemy. Ropes still wrapped about her, she lay tousled as a gown thrown on the floor. Her golden throat and underbelly gashed; her eye half open to the sun to show the black slit pupil and the yellow iris blooming out from it. The dragon's neck was strangely twisted like a tumble of seaweed on the sand. And I thought as I looked at her how someone should take the time to right her head.

'Come, Rosalind!' I heard the fear in Mother's voice, but I held my place.

Village folk were gathering a distance from the corpse. Even in her death the dragon had a power that struck coldness to the bone. Salt wind stung my cheeks. I could not take my eyes from her to come away as Mother wished. Here was the monster who had year on year consumed our noblest knights. Here was the dragon who'd streaked our sky blood red. Burned our cottages. Feasted on my people. Stolen Magda. Captured me, and kissed my claw.

'Sad,' said the youth beside me.

I drew back. 'Sad? Her death is Wilde Island's greatest victory!'

He crossed his arms and turned to face me, his dark hair blowing across his eyes. 'It's good we killed the monster then,' he said, frowning.

Lord Godrick marched down the pier and slapped him on the back. 'It's our best victory, Kye,' he said. Then turning to me he doffed his hat. 'Princess Rosalind, meet my son, the dragonslayer.'

Kye bowed and his father smiled. I cast my eyes downward then and saw a thing that sickened me. Hanging from Lord Godrick's side was a fearsome weapon. Not a dagger as any man would have, nor a sword, though just as long, but a severed claw, green-scaled and curving down to a sharp black talon.

'Rosalind,' Mother called again. 'We'll return here soon enough!'

I fled the dock. I was so unbalanced over Lord

Godrick's trophy; the boards seemed to totter under my feet like a ship's deck. I'd heard of dragonslayers sporting a severed claw in the dragon wars. And I'd seen many a man waving a bloody boar's tusk above his head, or riding home with a stag's antlers strapped tightly to his stallion after a day's kill, but this prize haunted me.

Steadying myself, I walked as nobly as I could to Galahad, held his mane and laid my head against his strong neck.

'Ride with me,' said Mother opening her carriage door. 'Sir Richmond will lead your horse back home.'

I kissed Galahad's soft neck and breathed his sweet grass smell before giving him to Sir Richmond. Then into the carriage I crawled. Door shut, we left the harbour and bumped along Kingsway toward the castle.

'It's all come to pass,' said Mother merrily. 'With the dragon dead we'll soon recover Evaine's treasure. And with the Pendragon sceptre in hand, there'll be proof beyond all doubt that you're descended from the Pendragons.' She clasped her gloved hands and brought them to her chin, her eyes brimming with joyful tears. 'Oh, Rosie. I'm so happy!'

I looked out the window, my stomach wild and churning.

Back in my solar, Mother locked the door.

'It's Sunday eve,' she said pulling out her knife.

'Not now.'

But Mother removed her gloves, took my left hand and peeled my golden glove away to the horny blue-green flesh.

'Don't cut the nail too close,' I whispered.

'I'll take good care.' Always she promised this. The

knife's edge flashed in the firelight as she cut and scraped. A familiar sickening smell arose, the scrapings falling to the floor like a scattering of beetles. *Veritas Dei!* If only I'd not seen the severed claw. I wanted so much to believe I wasn't dragon's kin.

'Mother,' I said. 'That egg you drank to quicken your womb when you went to see Demetra . . .' I bit my lip remembering the giant shell I'd stumbled on when rescuing Alissandra.

'Done!' said Mother slipping on my golden glove. She shoved her knife back into her sack, tossed the leavings in the hearth and padded to my wardrobe.

'In De–Demetra's cave,' I stuttered.

'Don't talk of the hag now, Rosie. Our happiness is here.' She petted the sleeve of my blue velvet gown. 'You must shine like a jewel tonight. Lord Godrick will see your best side and he'll tell Empress Matilda what a perfect match you'll make. Ah, my heart is dancing. They say Prince Henry is quite manly,' said Mother discarding the blue velvet. 'Red-haired and strong-bodied.' Mother shook her head and tossed the yellow gown aside. 'You'll wear the green,' she said. 'It brings out your eyes.'

'How can we go to Matilda's court? I'm not yet healed.'

Mother paused, looking first on my face and then to my gloved hand. She sat beside me again and stroked my tangled hair. 'Your father took you riding too far this day, Rosie,' she said. 'I'll order beef broth to restore your strength before we go.'

'I don't need restoring!'

She touched my cheek. 'Hush. You are cold.'

'It doesn't matter what gown I wear or how beautiful I appear. We both know I cannot marry!'

Mother's eyes filled with tears. 'Don't spoil this happy day. I promise you the fates have turned.' Putting her arm about my shoulder she leaned in close. 'What say you to this, Rosie? You and I will go to a holy man in Wales before we meet Matilda.'

'Why should he be any different from the rest?'

'He healed a girl run over by an ox cart.'

I was unimpressed. Mother went on. 'She suffered a severed arm. In prayer, this holy man rested the bloody appendage against her shoulder, and the arm grew back just as before. The girl got right up and drew water from the well!'

I shook my head.

'By all the saints it's true. Sister Anne heard it from a monk who saw it with his own eyes.'

'Well this *is* news,' I huffed.

Then slow and soft she began to tell her fairy story about sweet Princess Rosalind, pretty as a windblown flower, travelling across the sea for healing. Hands freed from her gloves, in France she met her dear Prince Henry, and he loved her with the full of his heart. I'd heard the tale of my future life a hundred times, but this night it warmed me like a balm.

How happy the story was, how much we would love each other, how great was our power when the usurper Stephen was overthrown and Henry and I were crowned the rightful king and queen of England. Mother's tale ended in the old song, 'Lady come ye over. Over the sea.

And bring your heart with you. And marry me. I will be lonely and never be free. Until you come over. Over the sea.'

Meek to her love, I took on her fairy-dream and followed Mother to the feast.

17
Demon Fire

AN HOUR BEFORE SUNSET WE ARRIVED, AND WERE escorted to the beach. It was my intention to ignore the captain's trophy as best I could, but as the fates would twist it, Mother wedged me between Lord Godrick and his son at the high table facing the shore.

All the tables, abstracted from the castle for the occasion, were set in a half-circle on the beach facing the dead beast. It was the wish of King and Queen to hold a royal banquet within sight of the creature that had lorded over Wilde Island all these years. And the people loved them well for it.

Across the sea the sun dozed, unfurling crimson veils from sky to water. A pink wave washed up to touch the dragon carcass, and the damp wind blew the dragon's death-stink to my table. I felt distemper in my liver, but neither the knights and their good ladies, nor the villagers seemed to mind the fumes. All were making merry with the blackmanger, stuffed quail, suckling pigs and wine. Cook had outdone herself as if it were a saint's day feast. And every villager had his joy's portion, as the minstrels strolled about the tables strumming lutes and blowing pipes.

I watched Lady Warwick go after the quail on her tray. She cut the meat, her pale gloves moving swiftly as clouds in a high wind. Though hunger hollowed me after my long day of riding, I picked at my quail, nibbled on a wing, and ordered wine. The cupbearer filled my goblet. I downed it swift and held it out to him again. Sir Magnus nudged Mother who looked hard on me. I took no notice, the wine flowing like a warming fire through my flesh.

The bonfires grew stronger with the coming of the dark. Trouble slipped away from me with the goodsomeness of wine. Thus, I had begun to reel upon the bench when Lord Godrick stood to give his speech.

'Good fellows,' he began, the claw at his side fairly touching my cheek. 'I am a modest lord of some acquaintance with Empress Matilda.'

The crowd cheered.

'A man of ships and swords, and if it be known, a man who fought in the great Crusades.'

More cheering. I tried to lean away from Lord Godrick's middle and ended nearly cheek to cheek with his son, Kye. Father smiled. I belched and blushed.

' . . . but never was a battle sweeter than when my son slit this monster here!'

Another shout from the people.

'No sooner had the dragon swooped down than I had

my sword drawn. I scored blood, gashing her thigh, but she grabbed me in her cruel talons. Then Kye was to the demon's heart and here!' He drew his sword, thrust it in the candlelight and knocked over his goblet. 'And here!' He thrust again. 'He slashed her with his sword! You see the creature there?' He pointed to the dragon. 'She'd measure longer than my vessel if you counted in her tail. I say she had me in her death-grip. My ribs were fairly crushed. I couldn't breathe for the pain. The dragon's teeth were dagger sharp and when she opened her foul jaws, I smelled the putrid breath flowing from her mouth.'

I nearly swooned as his dragon's claw dangled near my brow, the black talon glinting in the fire.

'More wine!' I called, but the cupbearer was lost in reverie.

'That's when my good son, Kye, shouted, "Meet your death!" He slit the dragon's throat and with a mighty gash, he vanquished her!'

'Hooray!' shouted the villagers.

'My only regret,' said Lord Godrick, 'is that Kye's dear mother, whom I married while on crusade in Palestine, wasn't here to see her son become a true dragonslayer!'

'Kye! Kye!' shouted the villagers. They clapped and called his name until he stood beside me.

'Show us the sword!' shouted the miller. Kye drew his weapon and waved it above his head. Father came to his feet and raised his goblet. 'Let it be known,' he shouted above the crowd, 'that this day in March will be Kye Godrick's feast day here on Wilde Island from now until the end of time!'

'Hear, hear!' shouted all. Horns and goblets were lifted to the heroes. I held mine up, though it was empty.

Kye sat again. His troubled eyes wandered along the dragon's spine where seagulls were now landing. 'I bested it,' he said under his breath, 'and now there are no more.'

I turned and looked at him. His dark face swam before me. His head was tipped and I saw a kindness there about his eyes. I understood the words he spoke under his breath. It was good to have the fearsome dragon dead at last, but there was a sorrow in it, for there were no more dragons now, maybe no more in all the world. The dragons' creature-time was over and they'd not be seen again.

The minstrels played their lutes. Kurt the jester strode out and did a little dance. He sang a knotty-pated tune and shook his bone rattle, till all were laughing.

Sheb Kottle, brave with ale, and stumbling in his boots, wended his way down the beach. Spreading his arms out wide, he turned widdershins before the dragon. The village children joined him, arms outstretched and spinning. 'She's dead. She's dead,' they chanted, till they fell on their faces laughing.

Full of little more than wine and ready for my bed, I stood, swayed, but Mother waved her gloved hand and bid me sit.

Now the children were up again, crowding near the dragon, playing their clapping game. 'Bright fire. Dragon's fire. Broken sword. One black talon ends the war!'

'Merlin's prophecy,' said Kye beside me, but I'd known the rhyme only as a children's game.

The children tossed sand on the carcass and completed

the chant. 'Turn them into mincemeat! Bake them in the flame! Cut them up! Spit them out! Start the war again!'

'Why add those words?' Kye said with disgust.

'Hush, son,' warned his father. 'It's just a game.'

Sheb pushed the waifs aside, climbed upon a broad stone near the dragon's mouth, and launched into a speech. 'Sal Conroy!' he shouted. 'Went down the dragon's throat when I was just a lad. And my dear mother with her.'

He wept and Keith the miller came to take him from the stone.

'No! Let me speak!' Sheb cried, pushing Keith away. 'And in the next year, Cal the goatboy,' he called wiping his nose on his sleeve.

I crossed my legs, uncrossed them, crossed them again, my belly churning.

'And Sir Harmond,' cried Sheb, 'who rode out with his dragonslayers. Then Meg Dillon was et, and after that . . .'

One by one Sheb listed those who died in the dragon's mouth. I'd seen those names on the Dragonstone. Sheb was nigh on sixty years old, and he had a fair memory for a drunkard.

As Sheb went on with his blood-list, Brock the tanner ran up to the dragon, and kicked her in the teeth.

'This is for Coppersmith, et on Midsummer's eve!' he cried. 'And this,' he kicked again, 'is for Sir John and his slayers!'

The villagers howled, but I bit my lip, never had I seen such doings with a carcass, and the chill running down my back told me it was wrong.

'Stop!' Kye shouted. 'Move away from the beast!'

I stood beside him swaying, but Brock went on.

'Ah, see whose teeth are spoilt now?' cried Brock, leaning over the great head. 'You're nothing but a fat old turd, are ye,' he screamed tugging on the skin ruffles that sprouted like two fans behind the dragon's ears. 'A crawly thing with curling claws,' he shouted. 'And you stink like a privy!' Then Brock dropped his breeches and wagged his bottom at the beast.

'Maynard the baker,' called Sheb. Just then the bare-bottomed Brock turned and pissed upon the carcass.

'Enough!' screamed Kye, rushing from the table. He dived at Brock, knocking him on his back. Quickly he pulled the simpkin's breeches up, saying loudly, 'Think, man, there are ladies here!'

Brock jumped up howling like a cur and boxed Kye's ear. Now they rolled in the sand, the villagers laying money on the winner.

'Stop this, Father!' I called.

Lord Godrick laughed. 'Never you mind. My boy will beat the poor man flat!'

Kate, the miller's wife, skirted Kye and Brock's battle. Toddling down the beach, she danced about, pouring beer over the dragon's snout, and spat in its open eye. I cringed. Then she ran round and round the dragon, tossing seaweed over the beast's head. 'Ah,' she cried. 'Such an ugly face needs a veil!' She cleared a table with the help of other villagers, and pulled the cloth from it. The children twirled about singing, 'Dragon's dead! Dragon's dead!' as Kate flung the tablecloth over the beast's head.

This was beyond my heart. I fled from the feast and ran

for the dragon. 'Rosalind!' called Mother as I lunged for the cloth. 'Come back!' shouted Father.

I had the corner of the cloth in my hand and was about to pull it off the she-dragon's head when Sir Magnus marched down the beach and gripped my arm. 'Back to your table!' he shouted.

I fought the mage but the cloth slipped from my grip and he forced me up the beach.

The villagers broke out in a merry brawl then, screaming and tossing bones at each other across the tables. But if a war was to be fought, it was not ours to wage.

Red clouds unfurled. Another dragon came.

Thundering like the riders of the apocalypse, the dragon tore from the sky, roaring fire. He lit the village and trees behind us, encircling us with towering flames.

People fled screaming. Tables overturned. Platters and goblets came crashing down. Some villagers raced for the wall of fire, others to the sea, but all were pressed back by the water or the flames.

Sir Magnus left me on the beach where I stood rooted to the ground as a sapling until Kye took my arm, dragged me to an overturned table, and pressed me down behind. There we hid, the air above us churning with the mighty dragon's wings and the flames behind burning maple trees and cottages.

'Stay down,' said Kye. He put a protective arm around me.

I drew close to him and felt his strength. 'Tell your father to hide the claw,' I whispered. 'If the dragon should smell it on him . . .' Kye called to Lord Godrick who pitched his claw behind us. It landed in the wall of fire.

The great golden-breasted dragon swooped low. Catching the tablecloth in his sharp talons, he pulled it from the she-dragon's head and tossed it to the sand. Then landing beside the body, the dragon brushed the seaweed from her face, and with his bright red tongue, kissed her.

'Her mate!' whispered Kye in awe. 'And here I thought there were no more dragons in the world.'

The beast lifted his great head, and let out a cry to deafen heaven. 'Charsha!' he roared. I covered my ears, but the roar rattled my skull and shook me to my bones. Blue fire spilled from his jaws and rose up in great silken sheets to the stars. Villagers joined him in his screaming, the fear of their own impending death sharpening their voices to a painful pitch.

I felt the fire at my back and saw the yellow of it reflected in the sea. All was fire and fury, till the dragon ceased his cry. Then raising his great foreclaw, he gashed his lady's belly open.

My breath caught in my throat as I saw five eggs tumble to the sand. Each egg was large enough for a child to curl up in. And all were blue-speckled as a robin's lay. Mother screamed, and my flesh flamed as the she-dragon's blood spilled round the eggs.

It was half dark when I'd collided with the shell in Demetra's cave, but I knew by the size that the eggs on the sand were the very image of the egg Mother sucked to spark her barren womb. Behind the table where we hid, our eyes met. I saw the truth of what she'd done in her stricken glance. How the world tumbled over inside me then.

The dragon was occupied with his eggs. Some villagers dared stand and look about for an opening in the wall of fire. But the beast roared, 'Be still!', his voice loud and grinding as a millstone, and they leaped behind the tables again.

Children about me whimpered, and the women moaned as the dragon gathered his eggs and laid them on the tablecloth. Then with clumsy claws, he knotted the cloth about the eggs. I saw how tenderly he covered them, like a father to his babe's bunting.

Grasping the knot, the dragon lifted his brood, flew them to Sam Denkle's fishing boat, and laid them in the rocking vessel. Waves pounded on the shore, fire blazed behind, but all else went still as the dragon pulled the boat away from the docks and dropped the anchor in the sea.

Back he flew to lift the she-dragon, and as he did so, Kye tightened his hold on me. 'He came for her,' he whispered, 'As a man would for his lady.'

One foreclaw round her throat and the other on her forearm, the dragon pumped his wings to lift his lady's corpse. But his mate was the size of him, and the work of his wings could not lift her.

As the dragon struggled to take her, a passel of villagers raced for the harbour boats to make a swift escape. The beast turned from his labours and shot out flames, setting the docks afire. The villagers screamed as the flames spread to the fishing boats and to the larger vessels. Folk scattered this way and that, while on the sea the flames hissed, sending up great clouds of steam as they touched the water.

Grunting with effort, the dragon tried again to lift his

lady. He beat his wings, straining against her weight. Then dropping her, he raised his head and roared.

He set his lover's form on fire. Her flames rose up yellow as the daffodils, dancing in the wind. Beside me, Kye's face glowed with the shining from the fire as his eyes took in the sight.

Long did she burn, and long did her mate watch as the wind swirled around, lifting the flames higher. Smoke tumbled in waves above the dragon's head blanketing the stars. The sharp smell filled my nostrils. He stood completely still till her very bones tumbled in upon themselves. Then, slow, he turned to us.

In his splendour he was as large as Lord Godrick's vessel fore to aft, which was now ablaze in the harbour. Standing on legs the breadth of oak trees, he stepped toward us. I sickened and my body reeled. Caught between the fire and the shore, we were sure to be the dragon's meat.

The great beast thrust out his foreclaw and, one by one, knocked those still standing by the tables face-down on the sand. They fell like threshed wheat to the sickle.

He towered over us snout twitching and nostrils smoking; his blue-green scales glinted in the light of the bonfire. Some villagers in complete despair leaped up, raced down to the water, and plunged in.

The dragon let them go, knowing they would drown. Leaning over, he swished his tail and growled, 'Wretched crawling things! Snoutless brood of beasts! Flat-toothed, and without talons, you sharpen steel to do your killing! No fire in your bellies, you stoop to use a tinderbox!' He breathed flames over our backs, till I thought my very gown would catch fire. 'Who saved your wretched race?' he roared. 'And what have you given us but war?'

He flashed out a claw and drew Brock high above our heads. Tearing off his shirt, as Cook would pluck a bird, he ate him.

Brock's wife howled, and I bit my wrist to keep from screaming. The dragon licked his jowls, pacing back and forth as we lay like scattered leaves to his feet.

Four knights rushed out and were crushed beneath the dragon's feet. We were prostrate sinners to our confessor, but there was no benediction here. The dragon's heart was like molten metal, poured to shape a killer's blade. Across the water a fierce wind blew, stripping the cloth from the dragon eggs. Waves pounded the shore. One washed over Sam Denkle's boat and swept an egg to sea.

'The eggs!' I screamed.

Spewing fire, the dragon flew to the little fishing vessel. He plunged his legs in the black water and skimmed along the surface, all the while screaming to the pitch of the storm. Then flying up, he checked his dripping claws. Empty.

With a final roar, he flew towards us again and set the last of our harbour ships alight. Kye gripped me harder as we watched his father's vessel burning bright as a tallow candle shedding gold on the spoiling water.

Soaring over us one last time, the dragon's great wings pumped a fierce hot wind across our backs. Then he sped out to sea, and pulled up the boat's anchor. Lashing the rope about his leg, he flew above the black water, towing his eggs homeward to Dragon's Keep.

18
The Shell

HALF OF DENTSMORE WAS DESTROYED AND MOST of the boats in her harbour, including Lord Godrick's ship. Four castle knights were dead, as was the tanner, Brock. Seven more were drowned from seeking safety in the sea, so twelve were dead in all. More would have died if the dragon hadn't left to save his eggs from the storm.

Others were injured, villagers with fire burns and broken bones. They buried the dead, then after a goodly time of mourning, began to rebuild the burnt cottages and fishing boats.

None blamed Kye or his father for the attack. For years we'd thought there was only one dragon flying hither and thither over Wilde Island, coming down to snatch sheep or sup on villagers. It may be the knights who sailed to Dragon's Keep saw the both of them, but they died before they could tell us there were two.

After the killing of the female and her burning to a bony ash, there was but one dragon now to be sure, but he tended four speckled eggs.

Cook said, 'Ye'd best pray the boat was tipped over and all four eggs spilt in the sea.' She worried her apron with her hands. 'It's our only hope for a bit of peace in future,' she said.

I tried to pray for such a wind as would tip Sam Denkle's boat, but could not make myself. Stranger still, alone in my chamber, I dreamed of the dragon's eggs. Four of them, blue as a robin's lay. They were all of a size to me, and when I drew my knees against my chest, I thought of blue-green dragons curled up sleeping in their shells.

In the days that followed, Lord Godrick rode to the castle when he could spare an hour. Busy rebuilding his ship, he'd come after sunset to confer with Mother and Father. It had been the man's intention to stay but a little while on Wilde Island, to apprise me of my Princess worth, and to garner knights to return with him to France. Empress Matilda was mounting another campaign to over-throw King Stephen, and she had hopes of recruiting all our knights.

Mother and Father were pleased to have the empress's interest at last. Father whistled as he walked about the cas-tle and was measured for a new suit of armour. And Mother set the maids to work sewing me new gowns. So everyone was a-scuttle. The villagers building new cottages, Lord Godrick and his men restoring their ship, and father's journeymen fitting his vessel for war. Soon after the men's departure, I was to sail on Mother's ship to France. Her vessel was receiving much attention, for Mother liked to sail in luxury.

When I could get free from tending those broken and bruised by the dragon, I galloped to the cliffs where I could see the workmen repair the ships in the harbour below. I could tell Lord Godrick and Kye from the others as they milled about on shore. Each wore the red of lordly men whilst the sailors and journeymen worked in plainer cloth. There on my cliff edge I watched Kye, axe in hand, chipping bark.

As night came on, I stood at my window and looked through the bars at God's starry script. Merlin saw my life written in the heavens six hundred years ago. He'd seen a redeemer who would end bloodshed and restore Wilde Island. But I wondered as I looked up at the stars if Merlin saw a woman who would know a man's love?

Early one morning, a fortnight after the dragon's fire had scorched our shore, I was kneeling in the garden gathering wintergreen and wolf's-bane when Kye stepped up beside me. I knew him by his stance, though I did not look up.

'Why wear gold gloves to pluck the greens?' asked Kye, leaning over me.

'A princess never bares her hand to any but –' The words *her husband* caught in my mouth.

'To any but . . . whom would you show your pretty hands to?'

'Not you,' I said.

'Don't you like the feel of daffodils?'

I squinted up at him. His velvet hat was askew, his eyes playful.

I uprooted some wolf's-bane. The small blue flowers bobbed in the breeze.

'Flowers for the table?'

'Wolf's-bane for the villagers' ills.'

He tipped his head. 'I thought it was poison.'

'I make a salve for joint pain. Many suffered injuries at the feast and not all were from the dragon.'

'Who taught you the healing arts?'

My heart dropped. 'My nursemaid,' I said crossing myself.

'Why cross yourself?' said Kye. 'Is she a holy person?'

'Dead. Drowned. And she was a saint or close to it,' I admitted. Kye may have seen the fervour on my face when I said this. He stepped back a little. A soft wind blew his tunic. I bit my lip and went on plucking.

'My mother was skilled with herbs,' said Kye. 'A Muslim by birth, she secretly read from the Koran and kept her faith until she died. I learned much from her. I wish now she'd taught me more about herbs.'

We shared the silence in my garden. Mine for old Marn and Kye for his mother.

'If one of my father's men should suddenly take sick?' asked Kye.

'Mother would send a healer, but if he could not come, I would. I know many cures.' I did not mention how many 'cures' I'd suffered.

'And who needs oil of wolf's-bane?'

'Sheb Kottle for one.'

Kye put his hands on his hips. 'The man who cursed the dragon.'

'He was drunk.'

Kye laughed, his shadow overpowering the patch of winterberry where I knelt.

'You're in my sun.'

'I thought I might give you shade,' he said, 'but I see you want exposure.' He left the garden for the castle.

'Wait,' I whispered, and the look of his blue eyes lingered in the air as if he were haunting me behind the bluebells. In the wind his voice was asking, 'Not touch the pretty daffodils?'

I was alone, well hid behind my walls. Keeping my eye to the door, I stripped off my right glove, ran my fingers along the bobbing lilies, tickled my palm with the daffodils, and felt the sweetness of the roses in first bloom. Kye's gaze and his laugh must have stirred a madness in me, or I would not have been so bold. But with my right hand free, I flew about the yard, arms outstretched and fluttering like the sparrows.

Before sunrise the next morning I rode up to Twisters Hill. At the top I halted Galahad and gazed out to sea. A stone flew past me and arced over the cliff. I gripped my reins and looked behind. 'What fool tosses a stone so near his princess!'

'The simpkin, Kye.'

Kye rode out from the shadowy willow whose greenery was still dark to the day. 'Come,' he called, 'there's something you must see.'

'Is one of your sailors ill? Shall I bring herbs?' Kye did not reply but kicked his horse and galloped down the hill.

'I take it you have good purpose for this ride?' I shouted as I rode in his wake.

Kye took a narrow path at the edge of the woods that ran alongside Kingsway, but passed the turnoff for the harbour, and for Dentsmore.

'Tell me where you're taking me.'

'I take you nowhere, Princess,' he called back. 'It's you that follows me.'

All honour and dignity schooled me to leave the ride then, but I warred against my better mind and followed him. We came to Witch's Hollow. From my saddle I could see foxgloves and daisies all dew-covered in the green grass. But the ground of Witch's Hollow had been watered with blood and the seeming innocence of the grass made the place twice deadly.

I was grateful when Kye turned his back on the meadow and rode toward Lake Ailleann. Cautious, I urged Galahad on. Near the shore, Kye stopped and gazed out over the lake to the isle of God's Eye where it is said Merlin once took his year of silence.

'It's there I'll go,' he said more to himself than to me.

'God's Eye is forbidden.'

'Why?'

'My father, the king, protects it.' Then thinking what Cook once said, I added, 'Some say Merlin's ghost walks there.'

'All the more reason to go.' Kye gave his horse a kick and galloped off through the long grass.

I followed more confused than ever. In half an hour's time, we turned down the path leading to the sea. On the beach, Kye dismounted and tied his sorrel mare to a bleached log.

The rising sun spilled a golden road across the ocean. I leaned forward in my saddle. 'Why have you brought me here?'

'You know we sail in four days' time?'

'Aye, and my father makes ready to follow you to war.'

Kye gripped his hilt. 'War calls.'

'Does it call to you?'

'To my father.'

'And to mine,' I said, alighting from Galahad.

We stood beside a pile of driftwood logs, the salt wind having blown the trees bone-white. Kye kicked a stone. 'Before I go to war . . .' He looked at me, his eyes moist with sea wind then turned away. I thought in my deeper self, that Kye was caught in love's sorrow, and my heart beat in answer to it. If this dark sea-bound boy should love me. Wouldn't I give my kingdom for that?

'There's something you must see,' Kye said at last.

'What have you?'

Kye would not say.

'If you brought me here to tease –'

'Come. This is for your eyes alone.'

'Why? Are my eyes better than another's?'

Kye's jaw tightened. 'I saw the way you looked at the dead she-dragon.'

'As I did you.'

This seemed to startle him. He stepped back, crossed

his arms and glared at Morgesh Mountain, the peak washed pink in morning light.

I could not seem to speak with him. Every word was an offence, every silence, a harm.

I touched Kit's silver pin. 'Show me what you brought me here to see.'

Kye led me up the beach to a small cave where he crouched low and entered.

'You've not found a corpse?' I asked before going in.

'No. Don't be afraid, Rose.'

I entered the damp cave. There on the tawny sand lay the thing Kye could not speak of.

A dragon's eggshell.

It was but half the shell, empty of its pip, the outside blue-speckled, and what I could see of the inside was milky white. And broken in this way, it stirred my memory to the half-shell crammed with bones I'd seen in Demetra's cave.

'I found the shell washed ashore last night and brought it here,' said Kye. Then like a father to a cradle, he knelt down beside it and ran his hand along a jagged crack. 'There's no telling what would become of this if my father should see.' He looked up. 'Do you . . . like it?' he whispered.

A thrill raced up my back. 'It is the blue of cornflowers.'

'Or robin's eggs,' he added.

Or your eyes, I nearly said, but I bit my tongue.

'Beautiful,' Kye whispered touching the smooth outer shell. He motioned to me. 'Come round here and see this.'

I crossed the sand, stepping soft as a cat, and knelt down beside Kye. There, etched on the white shell, was the pale green outline of the dragon pip. The sea had torn the pip from the shell and nothing was left now but the etching of her curled form. I saw in the outline how the tip of the pip's tail came to her mouth, as if she'd thought to suckle it. The sea had left three blue-green scales behind. Stuck to the shell, they were the size and shape of rose petals.

Kye leaned forward. 'See the wing shadows?' he whispered, tracing the wing outlines on the shell.

I felt an aching in my throat. Ah, how that shadow troubled me, the poor pip dead now in the stirring water.

'Rosalind?' Kye touched my cheek.

I tipped my head back. But his lips did not brush mine.

He stepped outside and I followed. Kye crossed his arms and leaned against the rock wall. A gull flew past, casting a shadow across his brow. 'Since coming to Wilde Island, I've heard talk of a prophecy about you.'

'Ah,' I said, disappointed. 'Merlin saw my fate writ in the stars.'

'I'd not heard of it before.'

'You wouldn't have. Our side of the family was erased from history when they were banished. But before Arthur's younger sister, Evaine, was sent here to Wilde Island, Merlin promised her there would be one born to reclaim her family name.'

'Merlin read much in the stars,' whispered Kye. His eyes met mine and for a breath I was lost in the cloudless blue sky of each.

A wave hissed up near his boots. Kye crouched and drew a spiral in the sand. 'I'm confused by this prophecy as I've been about another.'

'Another?'

Kye glanced up. 'Merlin saw it in the stars. A day when the dragon wars would end and there would be peace between men and dragons.'

'Like the childish rhyme?'

'Aye, only they butchered his words.'

'It may be Merlin misconstrued the stars this once.'

Kye stood and held my shoulders, but his touch was gentle. 'Why did you warn the dragon about his lost egg, Rose? Why should you care if all his brood were drowned at sea?'

'I . . . I warned him to save us. If I hadn't called to him about the eggs, we would all have died that night.'

Silence. Kye's warm breath washed across my forehead.

'And . . . that was all?'

'Aye. That was all.'

He dropped his hands to his sides, brushed past me and marched down the beach.

'Don't go,' I called, but Kye mounted his horse with a grunt. 'I thought you would be truthful,' he said. 'I see that I was wrong.' He turned his mount and sped off.

I stumbled back to the little cave. A surge of anger empowered me. Godlike, I used great strength to roll a large stone before the entrance until the dragon shell was well entombed.

Let it rest where no one else would see it, touch the blue of it, nor trace the pip's outline inside the shell. Burial done, I mounted Galahad and rode homeward. Salt wind slapped against my cheek in the place where Kye had touched me.

19

If Wolves Should Come

TWO DAYS BEFORE SAILING TO WAR, MY FATHER, having grown tired of Cook's eel pie, called for a hunt. Knowing Lord Godrick and his son would join the hunting party, I wrapped Marn's cloak about my shoulders and hid in the chapel. There I prayed for strength. I must look to the future of our island and set my heart on Henry.

I was deep in prayer for Kye and Father's future battle, humbly addressing Saint George, protector of soldiers, when Father came mouse-silent up the aisle.

'Galahad is saddled,' he whispered.

'I'm praying,' I said, not looking up.

'I've taught you how to hunt, and by the saints, Rose, the trumpet's about to sound.' He crossed himself for raising his voice in God's house.

'I'll not have you seem disobedient as Lord Godrick's son,' he added.

This intrigued me. 'How has he disobeyed?'

'He went to God's Eye without my permission and spent the night alone there.'

'Has he returned?'

'Aye. He's come back with his head full of visions. If he were my son, I'd show him the whip!'

He crossed himself again for shouting a second time in chapel. 'Come, Rosie,' he said more softly. 'Hunt one last time with me before I leave.'

'Don't go.'

He wrapped his arms around me. 'I go to win you a kingdom, Rosie, so you can marry Henry.'

'And if I should love another?'

Father pulled back. 'Do you love another?'

'No,' I said standing suddenly.

'Then join us. Let's show Lord Godrick how a Wilde Island princess handles a horse!'

Thus challenged, I ended my prayers, and went to the stable yard. Mother arrived soon after, crimson-cloaked and regal on her chestnut mare. Lady Broderick and her son, Niles, rode up beside her. Lord Warwick joined the castle knights, and Lord Godrick came with Kye.

Kye was brown-capped and brown-caped, like the muddy ground about us, but his eyes were like a clear sky after much rain. I made an excuse to check my saddle and turned my back to him. Still I felt the power of his glance warming my shoulder.

Trumpets sounded. The hounds were loosed, and we were off. The hunting party galloped up the grassy hill. Hoofs pounded, dirt and grass flew, people shouted. With all the noise we made, it's a wonder we didn't frighten all the animals off the island. Once surrounded by tall pine trees and yew, I rode behind Father, whose image changed from man to ghost as he raced into the clutching fog. The dogs ahead of us all howled. 'They've picked up the scent!' called Father, and he galloped through the mist.

I urged Galahad onward, but my horse slowed, the fog about us thick as porridge. Galahad was a fine horse as ever cantered up a trail, but fog had always put him off his mettle, and he would not quicken in the midst of it.

Down the trail behind me, I heard Lord Godrick boast, 'Hunting a stag be little sport when I have downed a dragon!' Not wishing to meet Kye, who was riding abreast of his father, I peered about, and seeing a small trail, turned from the broader path. I rode there until the fog breathed grey about me. Galahad and I seemed the only stirring creatures in the wood.

I'd left the sound of hunter's calls, the howling dogs, and in the cold embrace of fog, I trailed on for an hour. As I passed under the swaying trees, an eastern wind sang in my ears. Marn used to say, 'When the wind is in the east, 'tis good for neither man nor beast.' I shook the warning off and rode on. The path narrowed. So deep and grey the forest was, it seemed as if I rode my steed at the bottom of the sea. And the moaning wind all round was like the swirling of the water.

Lost, hungry, cold, and pushing against fear, I kept on going; sure my small path would meet the main trail once again. My heart lifted when at last I heard the howling of the hounds. Turning left where the path forked, I headed for the sound.

'Come, Galahad,' I said. 'We've found the hunters.' With a swift kick from me, Galahad bolted forward. We raced into the mist, the woods taking shape as we passed. Faster. Faster, then Galahad slipped. The earth fell away as we hurtled over the edge of a ravine. I was thrown from Galahad's back. My ankle broke with a loud crack as I hit the steep side of the hill. I screamed with pain as I tumbled through fallen branches and thick bracken and came to a muddy halt at the bottom of the gorge.

I cradled my ankle, which was already swelling around the break. My arms and legs were scratched and bruised, and blood filled my mouth where I'd bitten my lip, but it was nothing to the ankle pain. I looked through the mist. 'Galahad?' No sight of him. 'Come, Galahad.' I licked my bloody lip, panting against the pain and watched the forest floor tipping up to meet the sky as if all were on a tilted platter.

'Galahad?'

A crow screeched in the oak branches above and I felt for my charm pouch. Gone. I had no wolf's-bane or sorrel to protect me from the evils of the forest. The sound of crunching leaves came from behind. I turned and shouted, 'Galahad? Good boy! Good . . .' My heart clutched. There was a stirring and a panting in the bushes, but it wasn't Galahad or the hunting dogs.

Out of the fog grey on grey, they padded closer, ghostly things that made hardly a sound. Their scouting could have been a rustling in the leaves, their coats a thicker fog. But their eyes shone like flecks of moon on a dark sea and

I saw they were not ghosts, but things of flesh, fur, tongue, and teeth. And I felt the wolves' hunger.

I scarcely breathed as they circled me. Noses in the air, they sniffed and sniffed.

Clinging to the stump, I tried to rise, but like a sapling to the axe my ankle gave way. I tumbled sideways just as the great wolf leaped on me.

I screamed for help, thrashing and kicking his belly till he leaped away. Blood poured down my gown and soaked my riding cloak. The wolf crept closer, his sides heaving, the others sniffing and waiting behind. I hurled a stone at his head and missed.

Pressing hard against the stump, I tried again to stand, but the lord of the pack leaped and pulled me down, his jaws tearing a gash in my arm. I howled, punched, kicked, grovelled and bit his foreleg. Blood filled my mouth and nose, the stench of him mixing with the bile in my throat. Then suddenly the wolf yelped. He leaped back and tumbled on his side in the mud.

I turned and wretched. Sucking in my breath, I saw what seemed to be a bird hovering above the wolf. Wiping dirt and blood from my eyes, I looked again and saw it was a feathered arrow deep in the wolf's chest.

Kye came crashing down the ravine and slid to a halt above the dead wolf. He lifted his head and howled wild as an animal.

The wolves scattered, but an elder wolf with great shoulders raced up to my saviour and knocked him flat. Flipping over, Kye grunted, wrestling with the beast. The grey wolf had Kye's shoulder in his jowls. Kye grunted and drew his knife. He stabbed and stabbed as I tried with all my strength to pull myself towards the fight. The blood-soaked knife slipped from Kye's hand. Knife and arrows gone, he battled raw, blood flowing down his face.

I was downed and bleeding, pulling hard towards the knife and weeping for the wanting of it. Then with a shout, Kye pushed the wolf from him and was a-top his kill. He'd won, with no arrow and no blade. I choked for breath as if water churned about me. The knife I'd sought wedged beneath a fern, still a body's length away. Kye stood over his second kill.

Smelling their brothers' blood, the wolves fled into the forest. Twigs cracked beneath their paws, green bracken rustled in their wake as they ran, until the woods all about grew silent.

Kye rolled the grey wolf's body over with his boot. Sure the beast was dead, he turned and came to me. 'Here, dearest,' he said. 'We must stop the bleeding.' He stooped, bloody-cheeked and breathless. Taking off his shirt, he uncovered a red gash across his shoulder, the blood weeping from the wound.

'Your face,' I said. 'Your shoulder.'

'It's not deep,' he said, tearing his shirt in strips. 'Show me your arm.'

I held out my blood-soaked arm. My ankle pained me more, but my skirts hid the broken bone from him.

As Kye touched my wound, his face hovered so near to mine, I could smell his skin. My lips trembled. Even in my pain I wanted him to lift my chin and kiss me. But Kye saw my wounds more than my wish. He squinted as he ripped my sleeve. Seeing the teeth marks and deep gashes down my arm, he pulled off my left glove to further view my wounds.

The glove dropped with the soft sound of a dead leaf.

The woods went still all around us as Kye looked at my bloody hand and my naked claw.

I wanted to hide my curse behind my back, but Kye had seen it, and his face hardened with the seeing of it.

I'd have rather been the wolves' supper than have seen that sickened look upon my beloved's face. Still he clenched his jaw, bound my wounds and wrapped me with his torn shirt.

At last Kye stood and limped about, gathering his bow and arrows, and wiping wolf's blood from his knife. I could not speak. Like a harlot shamed by love and gathering her coin, I slipped the golden glove back on to hide the hideous thing, though the gold cloth shrouded nothing now. Kye had seen I was a monster.

While I covered myself, Kye crossed his arms and gazed into the mist as if to seek his lover there. Then seeing I was gloved, he stooped and took me in his arms. He gathered me like kindling, with no more love than a man would have for branches.

Through the parting mist, I spied Mother on the ridge above. And she saw it all. The dead wolves. Kye shirtless, bleeding. Myself crumpled in his arms. And her scream was like the cry of a kestrel before it swoops to kill.

20

Twine Unravelled

KYE CARRIED ME, WRAPPED IN MY CLOAK, UP THE ravine, and as we reached the trail, Father rode up on his steed. 'Rosie,' he called, and Kye lifted me to him.

'Take her to the castle,' said Mother. Father cradled me, holding tight my bleeding wounds, and as we turned toward home, the hunters searched for Galahad. Halfway down the ravine he was, lying with his foreleg broken, and as we rode away, Father ordered Galahad slain.

'No,' I screamed, but Father kept riding, saying, 'Hush, Rosie. It's for the best.'

At times there is a sorrow beyond tears. I was quiet then beyond weeping for nothing would save my Galahad.

In the coming days I lay abed in my solar, my wounds wrapped and my ankle strapped to a splint. The ankle had swollen broad as a pig's jowl and the flesh was plum-coloured where it was not green. My body ached. Each time I woke I felt as if I'd been dragged over sharp stones.

Sir Magnus called for a bloodletting. 'Less blood, less swelling,' he said. When I complained, he bid me chew elder twigs. Mother came twice a day to lay boiled serpent's tongue on my bruises, which eased the pain but little. At last Mother dripped her prized poppy tincture on my tongue. I'd seen her sip this to ease her worries and to bring on dreams, but I'd not taken it before. The potion tasted mild and sweet.

Pain abated, dreams came and I saw behind my curtained eyes the snarling wolf pack circling. Later still I dreamed the dragon tore out his talons one by one. He hurled the bloody claws at me as if they were a troubling of knives. But worse than these visions, I dreamed of Kye. In my drugged sleep I saw him kill the wolves again – saw him tear his shirt and kneel down, saying, 'Here, dearest.' But the dreams turned bitter then. My naked hand exposed, I'd watch Kye's expression sicken at the sight of my hideous claw.

Once I awoke sweat-drenched to find my mother laying serpent's tongue across my arm. Noting the kindness in her countenance just then, I asked a question. 'Kye's wounds,' I murmured. 'Do they heal?'

Mother nodded. 'Lord Godrick's son will heal. You must not think of him.'

'But the wolves . . .' I said. 'I would have died if he –'

'Hush, Rosalind, and rest.'

Leaning over my leaf-wrapped shoulder, Mother said, 'Tell me, dear. When Kye tore his shirt to wrap your wounds . . . did he strip away . . .' She took a heavy breath. 'Did he remove your glove?'

A sudden heat filled my throat as if I'd swallowed coals. 'No,' I choked.

'Good, then,' said Mother, bending to kiss my forehead. 'No one could love you as I do, Rosie.'

She brushed my hair from my damp cheek. 'Why do you weep?'

'The pain,' I said, and it was true, but it was not my wounds I spoke of. Mother dosed me a second time with honeyed poppy. I sucked the sweetness of it down, grateful for the sleep it brought.

The next day I awoke to the coolness of a man's hand against my head, and turning, murmured, 'Kye.'

I opened my eyes to find my father sitting on my bed. 'Rosie? Poppet?' he said, leaning over me. 'Are you feeling better?'

Before I could answer he held out a small bouquet of bluebells and bleeding heart. I sat up slowly and took the little posy.

'I leave for France tomorrow,' said Father. 'Let me take you to the walled garden and see you in the blossoms before I go.'

I was still weak, but tired of the stale air in my solar. 'Would you carry me down?'

Father stamped his foot, playing like a horse, 'I would, milady.'

I laughed. I'd not made the king prance about since I was six. 'I have a wish,' I said pulling back my hair.

'Granted.'

'I've not yet thanked my saviour, Kye. If you would ask him to come to the garden –'

'Ask another wish, poppet.'

'Why? Is it wrong that I should –?'

'Lord Godrick's ship has sailed. Kye is gone.'

My heart was already cracked, but this one word *gone* was the stone that broke it. I dropped the flowers on the coverlet.

'When?' I choked.

'This morning.' Father went to my window. 'I can see his vessel yet.'

'Lift me.' My head spun as I swung my legs over the bed. Father carried me to my window seat and slid a second chair closer to prop up my splinted foot. I laid my flowers on the sill.

'I cannot go as far as the garden,' I gulped.

'Shall I call Sir Magnus?'

'No!'

Father flinched.

'Just . . . leave me by the window here.'

'The sun will heal you.' Father kissed me on the head and called, 'I'll order you some broth,' as he went out the door.

The sails of Lord Godrick's ship were white as winter geese against the blue sea. It was too far out to spy any folk on deck, but at the prow I knew Kye stood, his black hair blowing back. With every gust of wind my love was sailing further from me.

Kye had turned his back on me. His eyes were forward now to France, to England, and to war. He would wash all memory of me from his mouth with brine, spit me out, and never tell another soul he'd fallen for a twisted girl.

That I'd heard him call me dearest was but a teasing light in a world meant for the dark. I'd never know the taste of his lips on mine or hold his children to my breast.

In that moment as I watched through my glassy window, it was not death I wished for, but more and greater still, that Rosalind Evaine Pendragon was but a dream that never woke to flesh; never found face or form. That I had never been born.

The next morn I was taken by carriage to the harbour. Sir Kimball carried my chair down to the dock where I awaited Father's farewell. In the sea mist, I sat splinted, my wolf-wounds swathed in bandages, the sea around all whispering. Mother came ghost-like up the dock, stood beside my chair, and bid me smile. I could not forge one. All the pageantry with which we were sending Father off to war did not mask the sorrow of his going.

The water lapping on the posts and the gulls circling over brought back the day the dragon died. I remembered how Kye had stood beside me on this dock and watched the she-dragon's body dragged to shore.

'Sad,' he'd said. Before he even knew me, he'd let me in his mind's chamber, for no other person on Wilde Island would have understood his sadness for the slain creature.

Kye and I had been bound together in the dragon's death.

When the last barrel of cider was loaded onto Father's ship, trumpets sounded and the farewells began. Father came up the dock and handed me a silver box.

'Open it,' he said.

A golden cross lay inside nearly the size of my palm. It bore five rubies, one on each point and the largest stone in the middle; each shone like a bright droplet of blood.

'Put it on, Rosie,' he said, and I hung it round my neck. Then sweetly he bowed to kiss my cheek.

'Don't go,' I said, taking his sleeve. 'I don't have to marry Henry.'

'Ha!' laughed Father. 'You think saying this will stop me from this war? Don't worry, Rosie. We'll win out for Empress Matilda. I'll see you married soon.'

'No,' I pleaded, but Father gently pulled my hand away and stepped aside to grace Mother with a gift. Another cross, though more jewelled than mine. Mother's was covered in emeralds, and boasted three sapphires the colour of her eyes. She wept silently as Father slipped it round her neck. Then the king went down on one knee and Mother scattered salt over his head.

The women on shore tossed salt on their good men as well, praying for their safe return, for many fighting men were set to sail with their king that day and join Empress Matilda in her war.

Father gave a grand speech that promised victorious return, then, under the flurrying flags, he boarded his vessel.

Trumpets playing, drums pounding, the ship set sail for France where the empress waited to gather her armies against King Stephen. More than one good woman wept as the white sails caught the wind, so my tears and Mother's were among the many.

Mother and I went to Saint John's Chapel more often in the days after Father's departure. We spoke little, preferring silence and prayer. So ardent were our pleas to heaven, nine and twenty candles in the chapel burned down to their stubs.

My knees troubled me and my ankle ached while I prayed. Mother was with me all the while and she didn't complain though I saw her strain and wobble when she stood after hours of kneeling.

We left the chapel like two feeble women, I with my crutch and she rubbing her sore back.

'Go work on your tapestry,' I said one day when her face was too grey with worry. She'd always found joy in her weaving.

Mother shook her head. She'd never in her life been weak. Iron-willed, Father said of her. Now that he was gone the iron seemed to have seeped from her core. Sir Magnus stepped in, taking advantage of her fears for Father. He drew daily charts predicting Father's fortune, and quizzed the stars to determine the best date for our own future journey. When the star casts displeased Mother, he treated her with an excess of honeyed poppy, and soused her forehead with rue and vinegar to cure her headaches. She grew thinner and more brittle.

Weeks passed. More days than not, Mother's eyes shone and her motions quickened as if she suffered fever. Long into the night, I heard her pacing in her chamber, which was just above my own.

'She's ill,' I told Sir Magnus.

'Her moon is influenced by Saturn,' he mumbled tapping his cheek. Then he went back to his crow's nest to consult his charts. Great help he was.

Cook tempted us with roast peacock, with jellies, and sweets.

'Eat,' urged Mother across the table, her platter as untouched as mine. 'You should be a plump and healthy bride.'

Bride. A sour word. I had no heart for Henry now. My heart had sailed away.

Still I was grateful at first when Mother found new occupation, readying the gowns for my wedding. She seemed to take some solace in the work. But soon she was stitching day and night. So what I'd hoped to be a cure only seemed to worsen her condition.

'Mother, slow your pace,' I said. She would not. As soon as the stars aligned we'd sail for Wales and meet the holy man who'd healed the girl with the severed arm. Once my claw was cured, we'd set out for Empress Matilda's court. Mother would have me wed by summer and her plan was all-consuming.

April ended, a fool's month for those foolish enough to love. Still, on the first of May, the maypoles were raised on the wide field atop Twisters Hill, as they were every year. Mother laid a new blue gown across my bed.

'Look what I have for you,' she said proudly. 'It's blue as a spring sky. Now all the islanders are to see how well you look before your wedding day.'

I kept my cheek to the pillow. 'My ankle aches.'

Mother slipped a glass vial in a pouch. 'Tuck this in your cloak,' she said. 'Sir Magnus made you your own honeyed poppy for the pain.'

'I'll stay here.'

'It's May Day, Rosalind!'

'You're ill, Mother,' I said as calmly as I could. 'Stay with me.'

'A queen performs her duties,' she insisted breathlessly, then fled into the hall.

I felt like a spent bloom in the heat of her wind. I went, and not because she ordered me, but because she was becoming more and more frayed each day. I would keep her in my sight.

In the high meadow atop Twisters Hill, I watched the villagers gobbling their May Day feast. Mother and a small group of elderly knights presided at the high table with Sir Magnus and Father Hugh, but I'd refused to join them, having no stomach for it. From my place on the hill, Mother seemed to be her old self, but she was always proper in public.

The maidens came round the maypole. All bedecked in flowers, they clung to their ribbons, their hair a-tousle with the wind as they wove in and out to the piper's song, 'Here We Go A-Maying'. Each girl whispered her lover's name into the other's ear as she passed by weaving her ribbon in and out. I held my chair whispering the name I'd say if I grasped the ribbon in my glove. I'd call my lover's name with such a force the maypole would crash down and set all the maids to weeping.

Cook brought me wine. I poured some honeyed poppy in and drank to ease my throbbing foot and aching head, all the while watching the grass blow about my feet. I'd had my chair set where the wind was stirring, and the grass was twisting round, knowing it was in this very place long ago that Lady Aster was whisked away to heaven.

'The lady flew upward like a leaf in a whirlwind,' Marn once said. 'And didn't the people hear angels singing as she spun up to the clouds? Ah,' she said. 'And still today if ye stand in that blessed spot, ye can feel a waft from heaven.'

Indeed, there was a soft breeze blowing on the hill. As the merry piper's tunes wrapped chains about my heart I longed for a wheeling wind to come to Twisters Hill and sweep me up to heaven, but the wind was too weak to lift me.

I did not know then how strangely my wish would be answered. That I would be swept into the sky before the twilight fires on the hill were lit.

But it was not God's hand that lifted me.

21
Taken

NONE SEEMED TO NOTE THE SUDDEN WARMTH IN the air, nor think the redness in the sky above was any more than the tracings of the setting sun. But swift the dragon came and from behind, the terrible stench of him and the pounding of his wings too late a warning for us. Soon all were howling 'Dragon!' and running in his forewind.

I stumbled from my chair as the beast spat a line of fire before the scattering villagers. A group of dragonslayers, bellies full of beer, reeled for their stack of weapons, but the dragon hurled the swords and shields over the cliff where they clattered to the rocks. The castle guard and a handful of elderly knights stood then and drew their swords, but their weapons seemed little more than prick-pins to the beast, and before the knights could rush up the hill, the dragon swooped down, grabbed me in his talons and lifted me above the crowd.

I tried to scream but the dragon's talons encircled me like prison bars. I sucked in a sickened breath and yelped, 'Mother!', kicking the air like a mouse in a cat's claw.

Below, Mother stood fast with her small escort of castle guards, hobbling knights, and drunken slayers.

Mother screamed, 'Release her!' The knights about her held their swords higher.

'I've come for what is mine!' growled the dragon, pounding the rocks with his great tail. He wheeled about, took a step and swung me over the cliff. Far below, waves crashed on the rocks. Pain tore my chest. My ankle throbbed. Piss ran down my legs.

'Ah, God!' I cried, my feet swimming in air, my soiled bandage blowing like a battle flag.

'Shall I release her now?' called the dragon.

'Don't toy with her!' commanded Mother, looking small as a poppet from where I hung. 'She's a princess! Take another girl to eat!'

Hearing this, the village maidens howled and smeared dirt across their faces to look less appealing.

The dragon drew me closer in. The cliff edge below me now, I flailed and kicked against his golden belly with my unbroken foot. It was hard as the garden wall I'd once kicked in a bad temper.

'I choose this one,' said the dragon holding me above the revellers.

Mother stood like a willow, her green gown billowing. 'If it's royal blood you want,' she called, 'take me!'

I felt the dragon shudder, the whole of him like a quaking mountain.

'No, Mother,' I screamed. He squeezed me tighter. Mother held out her hands as if to lift a babe.

'Leave her be,' she begged. 'You cannot take the twenty-first princess! She's the one prophesied!'

'More stink of human prophecy!' roared the dragon. 'She's mine by rights. Shall I show these people why?'

Mother's jaw fell. She raised her arm to caution her knights who stood ready with their swords. How I longed for her to scream, 'Show all!' I was ready to remove my glove and bare my claw to the stricken revellers on the hill if it would save my life, but Mother stood aloof, and my arms were pinned to my sides by the dragon's grip.

Ah, Judas, I saw the war across my mother's features then. She would have given her own life, or let the dragon feast upon the villagers one by one to spare me, but she could not move against this threat. A cold wave of shame swept through me as I saw my mother's eyes go hard before the dragon.

The beast reared back and laughed. All stood still below me. The queen with her assorted knights, villagers, maidens smeared with soil, and the only thing that moved was the wall of fire crackling behind.

The dragon pivoted, leaped from the high cliff and plummeted to the sea. My screams were lost in the breaking of the waves, then, lifting like a kestrel, he drew me skyward. Salt wind washed over me chill and thick as water. I bit my lips against it and turned for one last look at Wilde Island.

None had moved from their places. They were fixed as threaded cloth in a loom, and I thought of them so –

caught in time as tightly as I was in the dragon's grip.

My death was soon and certain; theirs still a shadow stalking. And, strangely, as the dragon rushed me from my life, I pitied those left on the hill whose death day still crouched in some unknown place, biding until the hour it would spring out and devour.

The island grew smaller as we sped over the sea, the wind tearing at my face and blowing my legs backward. But, jailed in the dragon's claw, I was strangely hot. I could feel the heat pounding in his blood, and his scales were like the warming stones Marn used to lay beneath my quilt in winter.

The dragon's grip had loosened some, and it pained me less to breathe. Still my back and hipbones ached in his rough hold. And my broken ankle throbbed as my legs swam in the abyss.

I worked to free a hand and grip my cross. 'Saint George, deliver me,' I called. 'Send your angels armed with heaven's swords.'

The creature lifted higher to the clouds. My ears filled with the thunder of his wings. I swam the sky like a wee fish caught and dragged under a galleon in a deep red sea.

At dawn we reached the isle of Dragon's Keep. Ruby light spilled across the shore as the dragon soared over the cliffs. Pine trees and rowan swayed beneath his pumping wings, then, circling, he landed near a waterfall, entered a cave, and flung me down. I lay on the sandy floor panting and cradling my broken ankle.

The dragon lit the fire in the centre of the cave. Towering over me, his head swaying to some inner breeze, he flapped the green skin ruffles that grew from the sides of his head.

'Why bring me here to eat?' I choked.

'Did your father not bring his hunt home?'

I shuddered. Marn had taught me to breathe deep in times of trouble. But with each breath, pain shot through my bruised chest. Clumsy as a drunkard, I wrapped my soiled bandage around my ankle splint.

'How did you break yourself?' asked the dragon, his voice deep and grinding as the miller's wheel.

'A fall from my horse.'

'And the gashes down your arm?'

'Wolves.'

'Ah, then you have known the feel of teeth!' said the dragon.

My flesh went hot-and-cold to what seemed a smile across the dragon's snout. And I saw how yellow his sharp teeth were.

A swirl of smoke rose above his twitching nostrils. 'Tasty,' he said closing his eyes and flicking out his tongue.

I crawled into the shadows near a large sand mound.

'You cannot hide from me,' laughed the dragon, his eyes still closed. 'I can smell human flesh from a hundred wingspans.'

He licked his jaws and sniffed.

Blood sang in my ears. My head was empty as a beggar's bowl. Was there no way out? Quickly, I patted about in the shadows, feeling the coldness of the sand through my gloves. If there were a sharp stone, or . . . here was something; heart pounding, I pulled it closer: a fish spine.

The dragon's laughter rang like the stonemason's hammer. 'There are no weapons here,' he said, 'but the one you were born with.'

He inched closer, his golden belly glinting in the firelight.

I crept backwards past a great tall mound. 'How do you know of my mark?'

'I saw the gash beneath Lady Charsha's eye the night you met on Morgesh Mountain. She told me of your sign.'

Sign? I'd never heard my curse called that before. But Marn warned me that dragons twisted everything. I could say it was a lie, there was no sign, but all he had to do was strip my glove to see the claw. And if there had been nothing but a maiden's hand under the gold, would my mother have let him abduct me? The dragon knew. And this was why he had delayed in eating me. He planned to gloat on my affliction first.

Now my flesh burned. I interlocked my fingers. He'd have to tear the gloves off and my flesh with them if he had a mind to gloat.

'Remove your gloves,' said the dragon, flexing his claws in the sand.

I said no word but looked into the fire.

'Show me your sign.'

'All those who have seen what lies beneath my glove have died,' I said.

'I have no fear of that,' he growled. 'Your mother is not here.'

I looked into his eyes, which seethed like molten honey. He was twisting things again. 'She has nothing to do with death,' I said.

He blinked. 'Twice when I hunted in the night my prey was murdered by another's hand. I smelled the one who stole my meal, and I never forget a smell.'

'What murders?' I choked.

'The first? Midsummer's eve. I like to taste human flesh after some fool stuffs himself at the fair. It adds a certain sweetness.' He flicked out his tongue. 'So I crouched in Witch's Hollow where a drunkard was sure to pass, when a red-haired woman came up the path. She was nearly in my jaws when the queen leaped out from behind a willow and knifed her in the —'

'Stop! You lie!'

'Why lie when the truth is sharper?'

I hugged my knees and shuddered, remembering Bram's words concerning Tess. 'There were dragon signs there. Aye, the beast had come to Witch's Hollow, but this killing was not his.'

The dragon shook his head, the ruffles behind his ears rattling like a leper's clapper. 'So I waited for dawn and made do with a drunkard.' He flicked a stray log into the fire. 'Again your mother took my meal: an old woman walking near the moat. Bony-armed, but plump about the middle —'

'No more!' I screamed.

The wall I'd built between myself and the truth about

my mother crumbled. I threw myself against the one who'd told me, howling like a death wraith. My screams echoed through the cave as I bashed my fists against the dragon's belly. I would beat the devil until he swallowed me!

22

Burningstone

SAND STUNG MY FACE. I AWOKE FROM MY FAINT, brushed the grit away and looked about. The smell of rotting hide, and the earthy smoke of burningstone filled my nose.

Spitting grit and blinking in the firelight, I ducked as another clawful of sand flew over. The dragon turned and snatched a piece of burningstone from the flames, pinching the glowing orb in his black talons then dropping it in a small pit by the sand mound. Covering it with sand, he patted here and there the way a mother pats a babe. Crouching low, he dug again.

Dark outside. I'd been unconscious a long while. Seeing me awake, the dragon assessed my huddled form, his slit eyes like uplifted swords at sunset.

'Fetch more burningstones while I dig.'

'I cannot lift a glowing stone,' I said hoarsely.

'Such weak flesh,' he sneered. 'And nails flimsy as rose

petals. Dig, then!' he snorted, his flaring nostrils sending out twirls of smoke.

Beneath his towering shadow, I crawled over to the sand mound and looked about for a stick.

'With your hands! And over there next to my last pit!'

'But my gloves will be torn if I –'

'Dig!' roared the beast.

I dug like a bone-lusting dog.

'Deeper!' said the dragon, holding the burningstone so close to me I could feel the heat of it at the base of my neck. I scooped out the sand and reached in again.

'Stop now,' he ordered and dropped the burningstone down as I pulled my hand away. 'Cover it and begin a new pit there!'

'What ritual is this?' I asked, but knew before the asking. Here was a mound of sand warming to the task of sacrifice. He would not eat me quickly as a creature in the wild, but truss me as Cook would a peacock on Saint Crispin's day. It was my own slaughter-mound I was warming.

My fingers, tender to the task, ached beneath my gloves, but I dug the pits.

The dragon dropped a burningstone into my pit. 'Cover it,' he growled. 'And start another.'

I buried the red-hot stone, feeling its warmth through my gloves as I patted the sand down. The heat spread out beneath me, burning my knees through my soiled May Day gown. I crawled to the next spot, cupped my gloved hand, scooped, and tossed the sand behind me.

We had encircled the sand mound with burningstone.

Now, damp with sweat, I rubbed my pounding ankle and checked my gloves. The right one was torn. How Mother would have scolded me if she'd seen the tear, shutting me in my solar, and ordering the weaver to make another pair. I brushed away the flecks of sand embedded in the golden weave.

'You will remove the gloves now,' said the dragon, his hot and smelly breath washing over me.

I was on my knees, unable to stand and bear weight on my splint. It was clear he wished the gloves removed before devouring me.

'It is the gold of them you seek?' I said.

'I have gold of my own,' he growled.

'Aye, stolen from Queen Evaine.'

The dragon blinked, his tongue slid out and in, bright red as the ribbon on the maypole.

'Let me die as I am, with my pride,' I said with chattering teeth. 'My family would wish it so.'

The dragon lifted his head and breathed a line of silk-blue fire. The top of the cave turned the blue of a summer's day. And as the heat of the flames spread across my flesh, sweat rolled down my neck and back and soaked into my gown.

I rocked and prayed and held the cross my Father gave me. The glittering threads of my gloves shone blue in the strange light. The beast lowered his great head. 'Take them off,' he ordered.

My heart pounded in my throat. So many years I'd longed to bury my gloves, throw them from the cliff, cut them thread-by-thread, burn them, but never had I thought I'd give them to a dragon.

The beast was not used to waiting. He opened his jaw, the more to show the sharpness of his teeth. Trembling, I pulled the right glove off. Beneath the gold, my hand was pale as milk. The fingers were raw and pink as cherry blossoms from digging in the sand.

The dragon licked his jaws but did not move from his place. He hung over me like a great cliff rock over the shore, as finger by finger I tugged on my left glove.

The fire popped and sparks flew up. They cascaded all around me as I dropped the gold glove and held out my naked hand, the fourth finger cursed as ever. The scales on my claw shone in the firelight, and my clipped black talon reflected the flames, as a shiny rook's wing will answer to the sun.

I saw the dragon's eyes soften as he looked on it the way a candle softens when there's no wind about. He did not blink, nor move as I held up my hand. I'd seen this trance before when I'd bared my hand to the female dragon on the cliff, though at the time I'd thought my hand wielded some magic power against her. Now I saw the moment stripped of wizardry. The dragon gazed at my talon, small, but in all other ways, very like his own. And he saw it with delight.

'Lovely,' he said.

Tears stung my eyes. He loved my hideous claw. He thought it beautiful! It had always been my secret hope that my hand would one day be looked upon with love. And by that one look, my curse would be broken.

I shook there in his gaze, like a small shadow under a

great lamp. Outside the waterfall tumbled, and my ears rang with the sound.

'Pity,' said the dragon.

A cold blade split me with the word.

'A thing so beautiful growing from a putrid form. Like a flower growing from a crippled branch.'

'A crippled branch?' I said. 'This is how I look to you?'

'All humans are detestable to dragons. Soft-skinned, colourless, snoutless, flat-toothed, hairy, wingless, tailless, graceless, and foul-smelling.'

'I disgust you then.'

The dragon's nostrils twitched. 'Not all of you.'

He started for the cave entrance then turned to look back, 'You will call me Lord Faul. All your life you have been Rose, but here your thorn's exposed so I will call you Briar.' He snorted at his little joke, then added, 'Crawl outside to relieve yourself, Briar. I keep my dwelling clean.' With a flick of his tail, he left me in the cave, the roaring of the waterfall outside echoing against the rocks.

I was not to die straight away as I had thought, but stay on Dragon's Keep awhile and live with one who scorned me. Lord Faul had delayed his kill, though his reasons were a shadow-game to me.

After a time, I crawled outside the cave to relieve myself in the grass. Squatting in the dark woods, I heard the evergreens blowing in the night's wind. Before me the waterfall tumbled black as ink.

There was no sign of Lord Faul, but I did not try escape. Even if I could crawl mile on mile through roots, stones and bracken to the sea, there would be no ship there yet to rescue me. Mother would send her knights, I knew. I must stay alive till then.

I eased onto my knees, helpless as a creeping babe. Lord Faul could scoop me up, toss me in his mouth and down me whenever he had a mind. It would take the knights three days at least to sail across the ocean to Dragon's Keep, and I might be in the dragon's belly by then.

I crawled towards the water, bent to drink and saw my face reflected there. In the night's pool shone the beauty of my mother's high forehead, her cheekbones and her firm chin. Mother killed to keep my beauty and hide my beast mark from men's eyes. But here, all was widdershins to Mother's world. I examined my claw gleaming green in the starry pool. If I'd been born here, hatched from an egg, suckled by Faul's lady, would they have covered me in golden sacking? In secret and disgust, would they have wrapped all but my claw against their dark-slit eyes?

I sobbed and laughed in turn until the night's chill brought me back to the fire in the cave. In came Lord Faul not long after, with a trout impaled upon a stick.

'Eat,' he growled. I sat up, took the stick he offered, and held the trout above the fire till the flesh was scorched.

Lord Faul looked on all approving of my meal. He had not offered me a knife to pick the flesh away, so I supped like a wild beast, whilst he flicked his tail.

Morning brought a ray of sunlight to my sandy bed. I crawled outside and saw Lord Faul sunning himself on the hill beside the cave. From there he watched me creeping round the forest floor. Finding a pine bough, I stripped the foliage from it, fashioning a cruel crutch.

Hopping like a one-legged beggar, and in full view of the dragon, I set out on a hunger-hunt. I must have looked a sight in my rose cloak and torn blue gown, hobbling about the forest, using Marn's woodland lore to forage food. But I found a patch of wild onions near a twisted willow. Digging plump-white bulbs from the soil, I feasted on them raw. My breath would stink, but not as much as the dragon's.

Later in the day, I gathered mushrooms in a shadowy place. Still, after a full day's foraging, I limped to the cave hungry and was grateful for the trout the dragon tossed. With the falling of the dark, I sought my sleep, but found little. Lord Faul shook me awake and bid me dig more pits for his burningstones. I worked the sand, my flesh rubbed raw with digging, but Faul would not let me rest until the mound was encircled with hot stones again.

While I dug the pits, I came up with a plan. If the dragon should try to eat me before my rescue came, I would use my father's cross to cut my way out of his belly, as brave Saint Margaret had in times of old. I shuddered thinking on this. To achieve the feat, I must avoid his fire and sharp teeth and leap down his throat. The dragon must swallow me whole.

23
The Breaking

I T RAINED MY THIRD DAY ON DRAGON'S KEEP AND LORD Faul kept well inside the cave. I knew dragons hated rain. Never had we heard of dragon attacks in the rainy months, and some said it was because the water downed them. I hoped that this was true as I planned my escape.

I waited until the dragon fell asleep, his snores rattling my ears like a hundred sawyers in the forest. Heart pounding in my mouth, I slipped into my rose-coloured cloak and pulled on my golden gloves. Here was my chance to try for the shore. The knights might well arrive this day, and if they were delayed, I could find a cave to hide in till they came.

In stealth, I crept past the sleeping beast. Outside the cold wind splashed rain across my face. Marn's cloak tight about me, crutch wedged in my armpit, I hobbled on the soggy ground, following the trail that ran beside the river.

I must somehow make it to the shore and win my freedom.

God's Bones, my progress was slow! I fought against the wind, hobbling on the narrow trail, battling mud and roots with every step. My cloak and gown fluttered behind me as the trail climbed higher, a steep ravine extending from the edge down to the rushing river. I pressed on, knowing I would at some time meet the shore. Soaked and worn, I reached the top of the trail at last and spied the shore a half-mile away.

The sea was grey as hag's hair, and the river was a grey strand flowing into it. I saw no rescue ship, but took heart. Cold gusts pushed me now backward, now forward, but I didn't care a bit, for there was the sea! And if the rain kept up, and if I made it to the shore, I might be rescued!

Handy with my crutch, I scurried down the trail, my heart clattering in my chest like Cook's spoon in a kettle. Then making a sharp turn, I tripped on a jutting root, lost my footing, and tumbled headlong down the gorge. I shut my mouth against my screams as I slid and grabbed for roots to stop my fall. I had nearly plunged into the river when I came to a sudden stop between two jutting rocks. Scratched and torn, ankle throbbing, crutch gone, I wept.

Wedged between two stones, I lay filthy and crumpled. I cursed the dragon, cursed my broken self, and curled up there a long while weeping.

With great care, so as not to tumble in the river, I pulled myself free from the stones. Little by little, I clambered up the steep ravine, swearing through my teeth each time I slid back in the frothy mud. I was stranded as a flea in a beer mug, unable to get out on my own. After an hour of struggle, I felt the sun come out above. Droplets on the leaves and ferns sparkled all round me, like the fairy's tears, and my spirits rose. I would escape after all.

Yet as soon as the sun was master again, I heard the pounding of great wings and felt his shadow come. The creature flared out fire, wheeling above as a hawk sighting its kill. Swooping down, he caught me in his claws and darted skyward.

Across the isle he flew and did not bring me to the cave but landed on a high hill dressed in purple milk thistle and yellow mustard blooms. The smell of the day's rain was still tender in the grass.

'Pluck the thistle,' said Faul tossing me my crutch.

I stood shaking in the damp grass gazing at the purple flowers whose leaves and stems were armoured with long, sharp prickles. 'Ah,' Marn used to say. 'Pluck thistles if you be of a mind to enrage a dragon, for they go mad around them. There's nothing like a dragon's rage once around a thistle.'

'Why thistles?' I asked.

'Uproot them now, Briar!' he ordered. 'And lay them at my feet!'

Lord Faul glowered as I dug around the thistle stems, the thorns too sharp to pull from higher up. The growl coming from deep within his throat shot shivers through my bones. I felt his anger like a thing upon my back as I garnered thistles, so I turned my head a bit and kept the corner of my eye on him. The thistles' spiny stems cut into my hands even through my golden gloves, and I saw a spot of blood between the weave. Still I laboured hour on hour

in the dragon's glare, sure the work was some strange punishment for trying to escape.

When the sun sank behind the hills, I laid another load
of four-and-twenty thistles at the dragon's feet. The day's
hunger, and the hours of gathering, hollowed me. I leaned
on my crutch and wiped the sweat from my forehead. The
thistle pile was by now waist-high. If this were my punishment, I'd had my fill of it.

'Is it enough?' I asked.

Faul gave a rumble like the lowering of a drawbridge,
and pointed to the thistles with his tail. Back I went.

The purpose of the task struck me then, and I reeled
with the knowledge of it. How many times I'd watched
Cook chopping onions, parsnips and mustard greens
whilst a fat pig roasted over the flames? I was to be the centre of the dragon's feast, and with my own hands, he had
me plucking the garnish! God's bones! I faced Lord Faul
and threw my last handful to the ground.

'I'll pluck no more!'

He laughed and gripped me in one claw, took up the
thistles in the other, and flew above the trees.

Wheeling over the tumbling falls, Faul swooped down,
landed on the shore, and plunged my head into the water.
The coldness of it and the shock set me to thrashing. I
held my breath, kicked and kicked until he pulled me up.

'Drown me?' I choked. 'Is this the way you prepare your
meal?

'Drink!' ordered Faul, and he lowered me down again.
This time my cheeks touched against the water, and I sucked.

In the dragon's den, Lord Faul left me by the fire and

returned, dragging a black cauldron behind him. He set the cauldron on the burning logs and said, 'Toss in the thistles, Briar.'

When the water came to a boil, Lord Faul pulled some stems out and dropped them on a flat stone. 'Sup on these,' he said roughly.

The boiled milk thistle curled my tongue and my teeth went to powder over it. Still I ate more leaves and stems, weeping with hunger as I chewed for the bitterness of it.

Lord Faul took the cauldron off the fire and set it on the sand, roaring, 'The time has come!'

I leaped up on one foot, grabbed my damp crutch and started for the entrance. Lord Faul whacked me flat with his tail and wrapped it around me.

Swathed tight in scaly flesh, I could not press my palms in prayer, nor could I kneel. 'God, you formed me in my mother's womb, you know each hair upon my head. Surely I'm more to you than the sparrows?'

As I prayed, Lord Faul dug in the sand mound, his tail wrapped about me as roots around a stone. I readied myself. I knew I must leap down his throat and be swallowed whole. If he cooked me in his fire or tore me open with his teeth, I could not live to cut myself out of his belly.

The dragon lowered his great head, and with a soft breath, blew the sand away. Four dragon's eggs appeared. All were robin's-egg blue, and grey-flecked, like the shell I'd seen inside the cave. I ceased my petitions and took in the sight.

The eggs jostled in the sand, showing some life

beneath. I felt such sudden joy at seeing them, understanding for the first time the purpose of the mound. Each egg was the length of an eagle's wingspan from narrow tip to broader bottom, and all were rattling softly. I remembered how Kye had knelt beside the broken dragon's egg like a father to a cradle. How he'd looked at me and whispered, 'Do you like it?' And I'd said, 'It is the blue of cornflowers.' Now here were the other four Faul rescued from his mate. He hovered over them, anxious, his future there before him.

An egg cracked. Lord Faul growled, not in anger as before, but like the purring of a feral cat. The first egg broke. After some jostling, a snout poked through the crack, sniffing and snorting.

'Make ready,' ordered Lord Faul, and quick he placed me by the cauldron. 'Be sure this brew is cooled,' he said to me as if I could do a thing to cool the water.

Another crack and the first pip was out. It crept onto the sand and flicked its red tongue at its father. I laughed though Faul gave me an angered look. The dragon was nose to tail the length of me. The scales, all shining wet, were more blue than green and near translucent. The wings mashed to its side were small. There would be no flight for a long while.

The pip scratched the sand with its claws and cried, 'Wah, wah,' with a voice like a newborn lamb.

'Chawl!' said Lord Faul. 'Mighty claw.' And so the first of the four pips was named. After the first, the hatchlings came on quicker, two, three, four, and with the eggs all broken, the pips tripped about inside the pit.

Faul named each as they broke into the world, and with the naming said its meaning. Second hatched was the female, Eetha – ruler of the air. Then came a male, Kadmi – great fire. Last hatched was female, Ore – precious one.

The males could be distinguished by their colours, a darker green at the edges of the blue scales. The females were a paler hue. All were golden-eyed excepting Ore who was smaller than the rest and blue-eyed.

'Is the water cool?' asked Faul.

'Still hot.'

'Add five thistles to it.'

I did so, then hobbled closer to the pit to watch the brood. Chawl, first broken to the world, was frolicsome. Tumbling across the pit, he crashed into Kadmi. Kadmi answered this with fire that flared from his jaws like the spilling of a lantern. Just a bit of flame, but from the snout of one so young, it was enough to warn me of his future ways. Chawl, thus scorched, left his angry brother and began to bat his tail.

Eetha, ruler of the air, sought solitude. When she found a private place in the far end of the pit, her sister, Ore, stumbled on behind. Eetha moved. Ore followed. She moved again. Ore came, nuzzling her and giving her a lick. At last, Eetha gave up and let her blue-eyed sister nestle in with her.

All this I watched as Lord Faul hovered beside me. Anon the dragon tapped my crutch and bid me test the water.

'Tepid,' I called back.

'Scoop the broth into a broken shell,' he ordered. 'Then

let the pips have drink.'

Faul shoved me a bit of shell, which, broken, was the rough shape of a great feast bowl.

'The pips are new to the world,' I said. 'This water's bitter, and the thistle brew will anger them.' I tipped the shell to dump the drink, but Faul shoved me to the ground hard and dragged the shell to his pips.

'It's bitter,' I warned. But the pips dipped their snouts in the brew and drank. In years gone by, I'd seen young calves suckle their mother's milk and watched Bram's wiggling piglets. All were anxious before the feed, and calmed when at the teats. But it was topsy-turvy with the pips. They'd seemed innocent as lambkins before the feed, but the brew enraged them. Soon they were growling, biting and clawing each other. Chawl bit Kadmi. Kadmi spewed fire, and Chawl leaped again. Ore scratched Kadmi's belly, opening a raw wound. Eetha bit Chawl's tail. Sand flew. Pips hissed and snarled. I put my hand in to stop them and Eetha bit my wrist.

'Ow! Evil creatures!' I screamed cradling my wrist. 'Why give them a bitter drink when there's sweet water just outside?'

'Bitterness is dragon's milk,' growled Faul. 'And it's your race that made it so.' He flicked his tail and snapped his jaws as if eating the very shadows that twitched along the walls.

The pips licked their wounds at last, and curled up tail to snout. Hatchlings a-slumber, I wrapped my wound with the edge of Marn's cloak, crawled to a warm place near the fire, and gave myself to rest.

I thought how the pips had been born on the feast day of Saint Florian who for his faith was set on fire and cast into the River Enns with a rock tied to him. And I fell asleep weighted with the strangeness of the world.

24

Knights' Folly

THE NIGHT AFTER THE PIPS WERE BORN, I DREAMED Kye rode his dark horse to the isle. Lifting me to his saddle he rode across the sea on a bridge of bones and feathers. On Wilde Island, he sparked a flame and burned the bridge. Heat rose over the sea and my hand grew hot. I awoke, found a burningstone glowing near my fingertips, and flicked it back toward the fire with my talon.

It was my fifth morn on Dragon's Keep and Lord Faul's purpose was clear now. Brood hatched, mother dead, I was to be their nursemaid. The task had my arms and back aching. I'd spent the day before cleaning piss and scat from the dragon's cave, plucking wild thistle, and boiling a bitter brew. And what was my reward for this? A trout flung to me at dawn, another at eventide, and all the boiled thistle leaves I could bear to stomach.

My hair was tangled, my clothing torn and filthy. And,

worse, I reeked of dragon smell. I longed for rescue, for knights brave enough to come ashore and take me home. How I wanted to stand at Dentsmore Harbour when Father returned victorious from war with news of his heroic deeds and Kye's mastery in battle.

I arose and brushed clumps of moss from my person. I slept now as a mockingbird in a nest of stolen forestry. Moss, rushes and leaves were my bower. Lord Faul flicked his tail and left the cave. I knew my task. Searching in the half-light, I scooped up pips' scat with a bit of broken shell. The sharp smell knifed my nose. Three of the pips were good about their leavings, burying them in the sand as cats will do, but Chawl shat wherever he had a mind to squat and never buried his, so the piss and scat were everywhere.

The pips slept on as I cleaned. The piss was bright orange and easy to see on the sand even in the morning's dark. I cleaned the cave with care but I still spilled orange sand on my flesh and on my May Day gown. The stain rose up the skirt like a stinking sun in a tattered sky.

Chore done, I hobbled to the mouth of the cave, took my sorry gift outside and dumped it in the woods. I was crutch-free now, a bit of dragon skin sloughed from Lord Faul's tail wrapped around my ankle. It was sound and strong as thick leather and he gave it to me so I could toss my crutch and work all the harder. My gait was graceful as a rooster's as I made my way to the river.

The falls sang nearby as I ate the trout left for me on the river stones and drank.

Lord Faul came up from behind, his scales turning the

water green-blue. Yet the centre of the pool, which reflected his chest, was like a golden hill. 'Come, Briar,' he said. 'It's time to harvest.'

'What is this river called?' I asked coming to a stand.

'The trees call it Ashath,' said Faul.

'The trees?' I said with a laugh. 'Am I to believe the trees can speak?'

'Believe what you like. Your race has been deaf ever since it learned to speak.'

He gripped me round the middle, though not harshly, and lifted me to the air. I knew dragons spoke many languages, those of men and even those of beasts, but I'd never heard trees speak. Wind rushed through the boughs below. Was this a kind of speech? I wanted to ask Lord Faul but he set me by the thistle patch and flew skyward. The dragon left me alone to work having little fear of my escape. How far could I hobble? And since no ship had come, even if I reached the water's edge, how many leagues could I swim?

I slipped on my gloves to protect against the thistles. The hills and the sloping valley were much the same as Wilde Island yet no people had come here to cut trees, plough fields and build their villages. Near the thistle patch, wild mustard swayed, and closer to the greenwood in the damper soil, cornflowers, wild iris and angelica grew. I gave a crooked smile at that. How many times I'd seen Sir Magnus sprinkle angelica in the doorways whispering, 'Step not across, thou evil beast,' to ward off the dragon. Yet it grew wild here and did not bother him at all. What a lackwit Magnus was.

Picking a posy, I tucked the stems under Kit's brooch, and went to work again. When Mother first saw the brooch, she'd been troubled by it. 'Where did you get that?' she'd asked, hurt and suspicious, as if the brooch were *hers*. Indeed, thinking more on it and knowing it came from Aliss, I asked myself if it had indeed been Mother's once. Had she given it to Aliss long ago when they were friends? Or had she slipped it to her before sending her away to Demetra? If not, how could a lady's maid, or worse, a hag's serving woman come by such fine silver?

I uprooted another thistle. The brooch was surely Mother's. What message did Aliss send my mother by giving it to Kit? This I could not puzzle out.

More hours passed. My back, legs, and arms ached, but I feared Faul's anger if I didn't pick a passel of the weeds.

When the sun spread its noontide gold upon the grass, I stood to ease my shoulders and saw a glint of metal crest the hill. Next I spied a helmet, armour, and the full form of a knight.

'You've come!' I cried, flinging down the thistles. Then another knight appeared behind the first, and behind him seven slayers. Knights and slayers to my rescue! I hobbled to the men. All knelt down on the grass.

'God be praised!' said Niles Broderick.

I crossed myself in hasty joy. 'The dragon will return anon. He's by the waterfall a mile from here. And we must away before he picks up your scent.'

'Sir Niles will take you to our skiff,' said Sir Kimball.

'No,' argued Niles. 'I'll slay the beast who killed my father!'

'You will use your sword to defend the princess,' ordered Sir Kimball. 'We'll kill the dragon and retrieve Evaine's sceptre.'

The slayers raised their swords.

'Don't go. Swords and wolf's-bane are useless. The dragon will eat you all before you ever have a chance to fight. We have to leave at once!'

'Our quest is set,' said Sir Kimball.

I pleaded more but Sir Kimball turned to go. 'You will tell her the news,' he said to Niles. Then clearing his throat he asked me, 'Do you know where the golden sceptre's hid?'

'I've not seen it. Come with us now!' But he led the seven slayers to the woodland.

Down the hill I hobbled. First Niles gave aid with his arm, then seeing my pained face, he swung me up and carried me, his nose wrinkling as he smelled my dragon stench. My weight and his heavy armour made our progress slow. Here we were exposed as docile field mice in the grass.

'Hurry,' I urged, and later still, 'I'll walk.' But Niles did not put me down until we reached the rocks. He helped me inch down the slippery boulders then brought me into a watery cave where the small sailing ship hid in the shallows.

'It's madness to try and kill the dragon.'

'It was our pledge. And by God if they fail, I'll wet my sword with his blood!' How he'd loved his father who'd lost his life to the dragon. I saw it in his fierce look. Heard it in his voice.

I grabbed the boat. 'Help me pull it outside. We have to get away!'

'We stay and wait for the others.'

'They'll all die,' I shouted, tugging hard. The ship moved a few inches in the shallow water. 'Help me, knave, if you want to live!'

Niles seemed amused as I strained against the skiff. He crossed his arms and looked at the dragon skin wrapped about my foot. Lowering my gown in modesty, I stopped pulling and tried to reason with the man.

'Niles. The dragon's all power. Already Sir Kimball and his host of slayers are lost, I swear, and once Lord Faul has feasted on them –'

'Lord who?'

'The dragon will come after us. Will you not help me?'

'We stay on.'

I lunged for him. 'God's bones,' I shouted, shaking him. 'I'm queen here, and I order you to help me shift this boat!'

Niles gently pulled away and held out his palm. 'Do you see this?' he asked, tracing a scar across his flesh. 'I pledged blood upon this quest as did the good Sir Kimball. We swore before our sovereign queen, we would kill the dragon, and bring you home along with the Pendragon sceptre.'

'Mother and her wants,' I shouted. 'Does she wish me rescued or the sceptre?'

'Both.'

'If she still thinks I'll wave the magic sceptre and restore Wilde Island to England's bosom, she's a knave!'

'Don't talk like that about the queen!'

'I'll say what I like. Ignore my mother's greed for once and obey me! The queen is . . .' I searched for the right word here. 'Unwell.'

Niles frowned.

'Think,' I urged. 'The sceptre isn't worth your life, is it? Think of all the dragonslayers we've lost, Niles.' I caught myself before saying his father's name, but we both thought of him. I saw it in his eyes.

'Your father was the best of our knights,' I said more gently now. 'I don't want Mother adding your name to the Dragonstone.'

Niles stood back, rubbing the scar on his hand, considering Mother's blood oath as I struggled with the ship. My muscles strained. 'Help me get this outside. Do as I say. Or if you will, obey my father the king. He would say to take me now! He'd order you to pull –'

'The king's dead.'

I fell back against the ship. So this was the news Sir Kimball bid Niles to tell me. If he'd crushed my chest with a mallet, it would have felt the same.

The cave echoed with the soft sound of lapping water. Niles lowered me to a sitting stone. 'I shouldn't have told you,' he said. 'I should have waited for Sir Kimball.'

'How?' I said.

'In battle against the usurper King Stephen.'

'And Kye?'

'No news of him.

'Did . . . they win?'

'Lost, but the king fought with honour, princess.'

I put my head on his shoulder and sobbed. Niles held me close. Wind whistled through the cave and cold washed over me as if I'd been swept out to sea.

25
The Bargain

ALREADY THE DRAGON WAS LANDING ON THE BEACH. How swift he'd come and silently, the sound of flight covered by the tide. Beside me, Niles drew his sword.

'Give me your knife,' I said. Niles unsheathed his blade and gave it me as Faul crept closer. The cave was small for the great dragon, but kneeling low, he entered.

Niles rushed forward, shouting. But the dragon snatched him up and drew him from the cave. I hobbled outside.

'Kill him, and I'll slit my throat!' I held the dagger to my neck. It seemed a strange thing to do. But if I died the pips would be left without their nursemaid. Faul needed me.

The dragon blinked, then shook his head like a wet dog, his dinner flailing in his talons. 'I'll turn my back to spare you of the meal,' he growled.

'You'll find me dead when you turn round.'

'Why do you care so much for my supper?' he roared, shaking his dinner like a poppet. Niles let out a fearful yelp.

'I'm done with death. The measure of the blood spilled for my life is on me like a river. I cannot bear another drop.' This I screamed out all at once and without forethought, but the truth of it swept through me in a flood.

Niles shouted and swung his sword, but Lord Faul removed the weapon like a twig and tossed it to the tide. Then with his claw he flicked the knight's head. Niles flopped over, and was still.

I cut my neck. My flesh stung.

'Stop!' warned Faul. 'The morsel lives.' He held Niles close so I might hear his breathing. 'It doesn't matter,' I said. 'This boy or another. My mother will send you another supper with her heart set on my rescue, and on Evaine's sceptre.'

It was true enough. Lord Faul would be pleased with the meals, peeling off their armour and swallowing knights whole, as a man would shuck an oyster. There'd be no end to the blood upon my head. The sickness of these deaths made the knife at my throat seem sweet. I would end it here.

'These men are pests,' said Faul. Towering above me, he shook Niles till his armour rattled. 'I must get rid of them. No putrid man will endanger the lives of my pips!'

The sea crashed behind us and pulled back, leaving silver carpets on the shore. There seemed no answer here. If I slit my throat too soon, Lord Faul would eat Niles after. We were locked together, the three of us on the sunlit sand.

'I won't let any more people die for me,' I said again.

'Cast away your knife,' said Faul, smoke pouring from his nostrils. 'And I will spare this knight.'

I held my ground. 'I'll discard it,' I said, 'if the knight is returned to Wilde Island with the message not to send out any more.'

'No message will stop the queen from sending out more slayers.'

'It will if I toss her my glove.'

The dragon blinked. 'Does your pretty part bring her that much shame?'

The answer stuck inside my throat. I nodded.

Sunlight played across Faul's scales. The sea pulled back, and in that hush before another wave, the dragon said, 'Humans cannot be trusted with my brood. The pips must grow up in secret.' He breathed smoke, the greyness of it shrouding his eyes. 'Swear you'll stay here, Briar, to be the pips' nursemaid. And for their protection, you must not speak to human folk again.'

'Not a word?' I asked. Faul tipped his jaws heavenward and breathed blue fire. A wave swept up, encircling his feet. 'Nursemaid the pips, keeping silence with your kind,' he said, 'and I'll return the knight alive. I'll deliver you myself to drop the gloves at your mother's feet.'

I looked on my left glove, stained and filthy. Knowing if my curse were exposed, Mother would send no more knights. This way no more would die.

'I'll will my life over to you and keep your pips secret as long as you stay clear of my people. Swear never to eat human flesh as long as I'm silent before all men.'

Lord Faul considered this as wind swept along the shore. I knew how he enjoyed his human meals, how sweet he thought man's meat above all others.

'A human fast.' The dragon looked hungrily at Niles, a silver glob of drool hanging from his mouth. He flicked his tongue, the more to catch the drool. 'Aye.' He shuddered. 'To keep my pips from trouble. But speak one word to a human ear,' he said, 'and they are mine to eat.'

'Done!' I dropped the bloody knife. I was dragon's keep now. The daring oath stripped me of my past, my heritage, my very humanness.

Lord Faul laid Niles down, dragged the boat outside and set fire to it on the sea. I shook as the sails and rigging burned, imagining what he'd done to the other knights. Beside me Faul hummed a tune.

Ashes winged upward and fell back in the sea. I tore a bit of gown and tied a blindfold around Niles. He would wake to the stink of the cloth, but I hoped not for a while.

'Climb on my back,' said Faul, unfurling his tail like a spiral stair. I clambered up straddling his neck like a tree trunk and gripped the horned flesh for support. The neck flaps at my backside pressed against me like a saddle. I leaned into them as Faul lifted the sleeping knight and took to the air.

He tipped his wing to turn and I held on tight as he sped over the sea. I wished my father could have ridden like this in life, for he was a man that loved speed. He rode Crispin faster than any man on horseback and jumped him over fallen trees. How strong he was on the hunt, how quiet when we rode to the lake. Tears stung my cheeks in the sharp wind, as I remembered how we'd watched the yarrow moths fly upward and how he'd picked up a stone, calling, 'Come by the water and make a wish, my girl.'

We flew all day until the sun was lost. In twilight the water had a way of mocking the heavens, and both sea and sky seemed tossed with stars. The moon rose full, which seemed fitting. Hadn't Marn said long ago that a vow made at the time of the full moon was three times binding? I'd sworn, and so had the dragon. Now we were three times bound to our vows and all for the good. I'd won Niles Broderick's life. More, I'd won the lives of my people. As long as I kept my promise to Lord Faul, guarded the pips, and kept silence with my fellow men, all the folk of Wilde Island would be safe from dragons.

Death was in a jaw-strap and I held the tether. What did it matter that my own life was over? The vow would be my amends for the lives lost over me. For Mother's murders, for Sir Kimball and the slayers.

As we flew over Pendragon Castle, I begged Lord Faul to land first near the tomb so I could pay my respects to Father. I was surprised when he granted me this, but I'd seen him sorrow over the body of his lady, and death of a loved one was still within his memory. There was a speck of kindness in him to let me go.

Torches burned about the Pendragon tomb to light my father's way to heaven. And as we landed, I spied lavender and wild roses scattered on the ground. All who'd come to honour the king had left their blossoms. I crossed myself and took the stairs to the lower vault.

Standing near the secret tunnel door, I wavered. I could follow it to the castle and leave Faul in the graveyard. But I'd made a solemn vow – and what would happen to Niles if I did escape?

I knelt to pray.

Candle glow lit the rubies on my cross and spilled across my father's raised stone casket whereon his effigy was carved. In such light his stone face seemed only to be dreaming. I'd seen that look many times as a child when I'd worn my father out in the walled garden. After playing my horse and trotting along the narrow paths, he'd lie back in the shade to sleep. His face looked just so, as if he'd just jostled me from his back. My throat tightened. Tears darkened the grey stone and the words of Saint Columba whispered in my mind:

> Day of the king most righteous,
> The day is nigh at hand,
> The day of wrath and vengeance,
> And darkness on the land.

Had I understood these lines when first I'd read them with Kit? They played a knell through my hollow soul now. The echoes were still resounding when I heard the dragon's growl above.

Voices outside – and one of them my mother's. What would Faul do to her if I escaped down the tunnel? *Veritas*

Dei! I had to keep the vow!

I hobbled up the stairs. Just down the hill, Mother passed the lilac bushes, a line of knights raising torches to light her way. She was coming to pray for her husband's soul. Seeing the dragon lying in wait beside the tomb, she stopped and stepped back.

'Stand away!' ordered Lord Faul. 'Dismiss your knights. We have business here with your daughter.'

'Go!' ordered Mother, and her knights obeyed. Niles began to moan and roll his head about in the dragon's claws. Mother saw me as I stepped out of the tomb.

'Rosalind!' she cried, rushing up to hold me. I caught the rose oil in her hair that was always a part of Mother's scent. At last she pulled away, saw my wet face, and took displeased acquaintance with my stinking gown and tousled hair. All this passed between us with our eyes, for she had not spoken yet except to call my name, and I could not speak at all if I did not want her in the dragon's jaws.

'Send no more knights to Dragon's Keep,' said Lord Faul. 'Your daughter is mine, as you know from the sign on her hand. I'll not kill the girl, but you must swear to keep all men away.'

'Do you think I'd swear to that?' said Mother, brushing back my tangled hair. 'The princess is mine. I bore her.'

'And you stole an egg from my nest to quicken your womb!'

'That was Demetra. I didn't know when she took it that it was –'

'Still you drank!' roared the dragon.

Mother started, and a strange silence fell around the

tomb until she found her strength again. Raising her chin, she said, 'Rosalind is going to marry Prince Henry. Nothing can stop the purpose of a Pendragon queen!'

Fire spilled over the dragon's teeth like molten metal. 'You should have thought of that before your people killed my mate. The girl is mine by blood. This ransom is fair. It cannot be undone any more than the sun can be stopped from circling the earth.'

'What do you say, Rosalind?' asked Mother, touching my cheek. 'I'll call my knights forward, and we'll have this creature's head!'

Lord Faul took me in his talons and roared at Mother. The hem of her gown caught fire. She jumped away, screaming and stomping till the flames were out. The knights started for the queen.

'Stay back!' warned Faul.

'Do as he says,' Mother ordered. The smoke from her gown rose up to greet her cheeks. She gazed up at Faul, 'Let my daughter speak,' she demanded, 'Or have you put her under a spell?'

I was under a promise, not a spell, and the wish to speak was great. But speech would endanger all. Only one thing would still my mother's wandering knights, and this was in my hands to do. Peeling off my gloves, I tossed them at my mother's feet and held my hand out, talon forward.

Mother screamed – a wail full of such rage and power, it was like the sound Lord Faul made when he saw the body of his lady on the sand.

How I wanted to tell her the gloves were a flag of peace:

that there would be no more deaths from the dragon's jaws. She looked up at me with condemnation and moaned, her eyes twisting the truth of what I'd done to an evil purpose.

In that moment Mother's dreams of a Pendragon queen sitting on the English throne were lost. The murders she'd committed, useless; Father's death for Empress Matilda's cause, a waste. She sobbed and fell on her knees. It seemed to me then it would have been a kinder thing to plunge a knife into her heart than to have tossed her my golden gloves. This her eyes told me, even as her cries awoke Niles.

Faul dropped the knight on the grass with a clatter, placed me on his scaly back and took flight above the graveyard. I held his neck as the knights below rushed uphill to Mother.

We soared over field and orchard, then above Pendragon Castle wherein my childhood hid.

The moat seemed nothing more than a strip of dark ribbon as we flew over, and the walled garden looked no more than a broken bowl. To the dark sky and my new life the dragon sped, his great wings pounding the sky.

PART THREE

Briar Rose

26
A Language Lesson

IF A GIRL WERE ASKED WHICH PART OF A PLANT SHE would be, would any choose the root? Blindly clutching the dark earth; never seeing sun nor feeling wind? Toiling there to feed the stem and flower with never a thank-you from them? And which would choose to be the thorn? Thorns protect the plant from pluckers, but who gives honour to them? Nay, any girl would choose to be the bud, opening to the sun, fragrant and beautiful, tickled by bees and butterflies, and looked upon with love.

So, like a rose, in my first years, I'd been sought out and loved. I was the flower of Wilde Island, fair as the day, honoured, cherished, admired and protected as any rose. But here on Dragon's Keep, I'd gone from Rose to Briar, and since I could not speak my bitterness, I wept it into the bitter broth each night as I stirred the pot. And each morning as the pips lapped up the brew, they drank my salty tears.

It's well-known that dragons cannot cry. Tears put out their inner fire, and death follows soon after. So Lord Faul tipped his head and watched me with some curiosity.

Spring gave way to summer, and I was at work each dawn, pulling thistle. I was glad enough Lord Faul was moulting, though he scratched himself endlessly. Hadn't his shed scales saved my ankle? I'd use strips of hide to spare my hands while in the field. Thistles still stabbed my fingers, but my palms were freed from blood blisters. The only part of my hands that did not suffer was my talon. I wondered as I plucked the thorny stems if the she-dragon would have been so enslaved to the thistle? Or did dragons have teats to suckle their young as other creatures had? I could not ask Lord Faul this. I knew better than to mention his lady. It had been three months since her death, yet I still saw him leave the cave some nights when he thought all were asleep. Outside he'd roar her name into the rushing waterfall, the fire from his jaws reflecting in the water like a giant torch.

My body grew leaner as I toiled. My hips once hinting towards the round were straight now as barley stalks, and my breasts small as crab apples. Indeed no man would have me now, and I would have hid in shame if my lover had come across the grassy hill to see me in the thistles. It gave me some comfort to know that Kye had chosen war. He would not come to rescue a sweet rose only to find a spindly weed.

In the heat of the day I worked to please Lord Faul but he was never content. If I harvested too little, he'd spew fire at me. Once he set a fallen pine alight. He had to stomp it out before it set the woods ablaze.

I feared his anger and piled the thistle higher, learning to work with such speed that I managed to pick enough to give myself a free hour before Faul returned. I used this secret hour to begin carving a boat from the log he'd scorched. I'd once seen a boat carved from a burnt log floating in Kaydon River: an odd ship, but water worthy. I'd use one like it for my escape.

Day on day when my harvesting was done, I used a sharp stone and hacked away at the charred wood. Faul would not harm me while his pips were small, but I knew the time would come when my usefulness would be over. I must have a way to leave the isle or die.

I was stirring the bitter broth late one afternoon when Faul entered the lair and tossed six wriggling trout on the sandy floor.

'This night the pips will feast on fish,' he said.

I was glad to hear it, already at just four months old, all the pips, except for little Ore, were the size of full-grown oxen. There were six trout on the floor. I had hopes I'd sup on one myself. But I waited by my cauldron. Lord Faul was not to be rushed.

'And for this prize,' he said, 'they'll say the word in DragonTongue.'

When he called the pips from their pit, they stumbled sleepy toward the fish. The dragon held out his claw and made them sit. They knew many words already for Lord

Faul spoke to them primarily in DragonTongue, naming things in their everyday world, and telling tales at night, so that even I'd begun to understand it a little. Still some words were difficult even for the pips, so Faul would reward their efforts.

He held up a trout and made a strange noise, 'Auruggullittht!'

The sound he made was like a strangled trumpet, a goose with a knotted neck, a man shouting under water.

'Auruggullitthhh,' said Eetha and she was tossed her trout. Cooking the fish in her small fire, she tore the flesh with her talons, sniffed then tasted. Chawl snuffed over to his sister. Lord Faul batted his rump and he rolled across the floor. The lesson continued. Each pip, on saying the word, was tossed a fish. Ore, the youngest and none too bright, was the last to sup.

The pips finished their feast, lapped tepid bitter broth, fought half-heartedly, and tumbled into sleep.

Two fish still lay in the sand. Their scales sparkled in the firelight as if they were swimming in the sun.

'Am I to eat?' I asked, hunger having driven me to words.

'Speak and you shall sup,' said Lord Faul.

'Please may I have my meal?' I said as sweetly as I could.

'Say the word,' said Faul.

'Word?'

'In DragonTongue.'

'Surely not!'

'You will be using our language with the pips, so you must learn it, Briar.'

'Aurug . . .' I growled. My stomach pitched. The only

time I'd ever made a sister sound to this was when Marn had my head over a bowl for me to wretch. I tried again, '. . . ruggullit . . .' Spittle dribbled down my chin.

Hopeless. My teeth and tongue were not made for such sounds, and I told Faul so. He pierced a trout with his talon and blew his fire on it. The cave filled with its rich smell. The sweetness of it taunted my nose.

'Not fair!' I cried. 'I'd never ask the simpkin Mouser to spout Latin, nor would I ask a dog to give a speech in French! It is beyond my mouth!'

'Then so's the auruggullittht,' said Faul.

On my knees already, I barked out the sounds till my throat was sore and my tongue was raw with rubbing on my teeth. After more struggle, I vomited the word, 'Auruggullittht!' and was given a roasted fish.

In the days ahead, I came to dread Lord Faul's language lessons. Restricting my speech with the pips to the twisting and growling of DragonTongue turned me to a fool. But Faul would have his pips trained up right, learning DragonTongue before other languages. In truth many of the words began somewhere in the gut as a belch does, and most were low of pitch. These sounds were well suited to dragon's bellies, and the pips took to them as a ladle to the soup. But my belly had neither the roundness nor the breadth of my blue-scaled fellows, and my soundings showed it.

At home Mother and Father took pride in my agile tongue. I'd learned a goodly bit of Latin and mastered French with ease. Yet here, as Lord Faul spoke to us all in a row before the fire, I looked for all the world as dumb as a mushroom.

27

Hissstory

AUTUMN BROUGHT POUNDING RAIN TO DRAGON'S Keep. I was expected to harvest even in the heavy weather, though Faul would not fly me there in the rain. So, wet and stinking as a cur, I hiked the hills to pull thistles. When rain ceased and the air was damp and chill, I took Mother's small round mirror from my cloak pocket, caught what ray of sun I could, and by reflection, lit myself a fire. When she'd first given it to me, I'd held it up to her face, saying, 'See the angel in the glass?'

I did not seek an angel now, but the fire there to warm a ragged body. In the flames I'd cook the bit of raw meat Faul had given me. Some days fish, others fowl. After this spare meal, I was back to harvesting.

When Faul first found me near a little fire, he huffed out smoke. 'How did you make this?' I did not answer straight but said, 'By fuel and heat.'

'And a tinderbox,' he scoffed.

I would protect Mother's gift if I could. It was all I had of her here. 'No tinderbox. I have none.' This was true enough.

A strange look came to his eyes and lowering his great head he sniffed the fire as if to assure himself it was real.

'So, Briar,' he said. 'You have a fire in your belly.'

I started. It was the selfsame thing his lady dragon said to me when first we met. Faul misread my surprise and took it to mean that like his pips, I too was gifted with fire. I should have disclaimed it, but liked his admiration.

Near day's end, if the piles were of good height, I stayed on to carve the boat. Even in the storm I'd stay gutting the charred wood while lightning lit the devil's banners in the sky. The slowness of the work angered me. How I longed for hammer and chisel! Even now, the boat was only a quarter done.

The pips had long since grown out of the need to use the cave as their privy, so the hated chore of cleaning up the piss and scat was at an end. But they hungered all the time now and when I was not harvesting, Faul made me hunt and forage with his brood.

Dark clouds hung over the greenwood, and thunder rumbled in the distance. Chawl snuffed around the tree roots. 'Dig here for the truffles,' he said in DragonTongue.

'If you help me,' I answered in English. 'You have the sharper claws.'

He batted my backside for not using proper speech, though not hard enough to harm me. I said it again in DragonTongue. It made no difference. Chawl roared and tumbled down the hill with Kadmi. They slapped each other's tails, chanting the rhyme from Merlin's prophecy I'd translated into DragonTongue for them. 'Bright fire. Dragon's fire. Broken sword. One black talon ends the war!' They bashed each other in earnest, finishing the game with words that twisted Merlin's peace prediction, 'Turn them into mincemeat! Bake them in the flame! Cut them up! Spit them out! Start the war again!'

They rattled the words off well enough in DragonTongue, could spew the rhyme in English and more recently, in French. Lord Faul allowed some schooling in human tongues after they'd come to master their own, which they'd done at great speed already. I was proud of their progress. They were great mimics. No words or sounds troubled them, and no wonder. DragonTongue was the most difficult language ever devised; so all others came easily once the pips wrapped their slit tongues around that.

I put my reed basket by the roots, a roughly woven thing I'd made myself. 'Will no one help dig?'

Eetha chased Ore around a tree. Truffles were a favourite with Lord Faul and I'd be blamed if we came up short. I knelt, unearthed a truffle and threw it in my basket. How tired my bones were. Never did I treat my mother the way the pips treated me. Did I enslave her? Ignore her? Bat her behind? Order her about? Never!

There was some pleasantness here digging up truffles. Once Kye challenged me to shed my gloves and feel the daffodils. His words had touched an old wound. Hadn't I longed all my life to feel the plants with both hands? Ah, and not only the plants but also the soil. This earth was rich and damp and it clung to my fingers.

Eetha brought Ore over to help and we added more truffles to the basket. Some were the size of walnuts, but a few were as large as a man's fist. Ore found the largest one and her blue eyes went nearly round as she dug it out.

'For Father,' she said.

'He'll like it best of all,' I answered.

Eetha fell into a hush, lifting her head and listening to the breeze the way I'd seen Faul do sometimes. She breathed out a breeze sound; a kind of wind talk, then listened again. Of all the pips, she had a way of sensing the future. How, I could not tell, but I'd learned to take notice when she spoke in creature tongues or answered the wind as she was doing now.

'A hailstorm comes,' she said. I wiped my hands and stood. Dark clouds moved across the sky, but it wasn't chill enough for hail.

'Are you sure?'

Lightning flashed. Thunder, and the hail fell so suddenly, Ore squealed and sidled up to me.

'It's all right, little one. The hail won't hurt you.'

Chawl bounded up the hill with Kadmi. Sliding to a halt in a spray of mud, they twitched their ears, opened their jaws and roared out thunder. There seemed no sound the pips could not make, from the buzzing of a bee to thunderclaps. The pips' imitation was so close, that Ore put her head on my shoulder. She was the runt and not much bigger than myself; any smaller, I think and she would have crawled under my skirts to hide just then.

We waited out the storm under the pine boughs. Great hailstones pelted the ground like a wealthy king emptying a treasure chest of pearls. A two-inch pile of hail covered the forest floor before the storm was over. The clouds retreated and the wind sighed in the trees.

'How did you know the hail was coming?' I asked Eetha.

She answered with a shrug.

I envied her skill. In truth she had truer divining powers than Sir Magnus who could never predict weather or tell the future with all his star charts, scattered bones and books, though he claimed to do both.

Chawl snorted then ran down the hail-covered path calling, 'Wild goat!'

I knocked over the truffle basket, leaping onto Kadmi's back and we were off. The pips could not yet fly, but that didn't keep them from the hunt.

That night we supped on roast goat, wild onions and truffles. Faul beamed at his family as proud as any father. The pips ate heartily now, but they still wanted thistle broth. I was often left alone to harvest on the hill. I hated pulling thistles but the gouge in my boat grew deeper.

Throughout autumn my chores seemed never-ending. I was a servant, living in a cave, harvesting, cooking and cleaning, and sleeping on a pile of moss and rushes. One rainy afternoon I returned exhausted with my thistle pile. No sooner was I in the cave than I was pushed outside again.

'Gather more kindling,' ordered Faul.

In the greenwood, I piled up the branches, my back and arms aching. God's bones! Would Faul never let me rest? Besides, the kindling was only an excuse to send me out.

While I was away harvesting, Lord Faul had been teaching the pips his dragon history. The lessons proclaimed the treachery of humans. I'd seen contempt in Chawl's eyes when I'd entered the cave earlier in the midst of Faul's litany. Even little Ore had looked angry, so I knew it to be true.

In the windswept forest, I slipped through the mud in my threadbare shoes, cursing Faul and his kind through my chattering teeth. Weighted down with wood, I hurried back to the lair and was about to duck inside, when the shouts from within halted me.

' . . . their deceit,' roared Faul in DragonTongue. 'All humans are liars!'

Why must he teach the pips to hate man so? I hid in the shadows at the cave's edge and peered inside. Smoke rose from the central fire. A cash of wood at Kadmi's side – more proof kindling wasn't needed. I would wait here where the drifting wood smoke covered my scent.

'I tell you this,' said Faul. 'In our great race, those of us who did not have their own inner fire, died off in the age of ice. The human race would have frozen then. They would have been scoured from the face of the earth if the DragonLord hadn't given them his fire.'

Given his fire? No one had ever told me this. I held my tongue against my teeth, listening.

'Then why did he give it?' asked Eetha, always the cleverest and most attentive to her lessons. Lord Faul raised his head and hissed, a sound I'd never heard from him before. I shuddered in my hiding place.

'Pity!' spat the dragon. He eyed the pips one after the

other, his slit pupils shining like hammered copper in the fire. I gripped the kindling tighter, rain pounding on my back.

'No pelts to keep them warm, the cold was killing mankind. A clawful of deaths would have wiped them out for ever. It was then a lone man staggered through the snow to beg the DragonLord for mercy.'

Lord Faul whipped his tail. The cracking sound made me jump and nearly drop my kindling.

'Mercy,' he growled. 'And the DragonLord took pity on the man! And with the gift of fire blazing on a wooden staff, the man fought his way back through the snow, lit a fire in his cave, and lived!' spat Faul. 'Lived, bred, thrived, and stole our land from us!'

Here, Lord Faul shouted fire to the roof. A canopy of flame spread out above the pips. And even from my hiding place, my face stung with the heat of it.

'Then we'll take it back!' roared Chawl.

'Take it back!' roared Kadmi. 'With wings and teeth and claws and fire!'

'We'll hold a Dragon Council and call for war!' shouted Eetha, leaping to a stand. I trembled at her fervour most of all, for Eetha had always been the kindest to me.

I thought to leave and traipse back through the storm where I'd wait out their war cries. But Faul warned his pips.

'Stop your shouting, pips, or the man-child will hear. Come summer, when you've found your wings, we'll fly to meet the others.'

'And begin the war!' called Chawl.

'Not yet,' said Faul.

'Why?' asked Kadmi.

I peered inside and saw the dragon narrowing his golden eyes. 'Now this secret must be kept from Briar.' The pips gathered closer, and Faul lowered his voice. I strained to hear from my hiding place.

'There are too few of us left to fight. Man has killed our kind. Aside from us there may be only five or six.'

'In the world?' cried Eetha.

'In all the world,' said Faul.

Little Ore let out a strange sound, which I took to be a sob.

'Stop now!' roared Faul. 'I've told you before. Tears will kill!' His roar was deafening, but he put his arm about Ore and said more quietly, 'Turn it into anger, Ore. Lift your jaw and roar it out.' And so she roared blue fire to the ceiling as I'd seen her father and siblings do, but this was the first time I'd seen her do it.

'We must bow to Merlin's vision and make peace or we'll die out,' said Eetha.

'Peace?' Faul batted Eetha across the cave. 'Merlin's vision was a lie! A dragon giving king and queen his talon? A king breaking his sword and laying it at a dragon's feet? No one believed Merlin six hundred years ago when he told the DragonLord he'd seen this written in the stars. And any dragon that believes such lies now should be clawed and thrashed until he finds his sense.' With that he bashed Chawl, who'd begun chanting, 'Bright fire. Dragon's fire –'

'Lie down!' Faul roared and all the pips curled up on the floor.

'Make as if to sleep,' he said. 'Before the servant girl returns.'

Servant girl! Rain rattled the rowan trees across the river and I shivered in my place. But fear kept me leaning on the rock and I waited in the cold outside the cave as long as I could bear. When at last the dragon's breathing settled into sleep, I tiptoed in. Lord Faul opened one eye as I placed the kindling on the coals. And swift he had me in his claw.

'Where were you, Briar? The pips grow cold!'

'I . . . fell in the mud,' I sputtered. He shook me once and tossed me in the corner. I crawled, sore and freezing, to my moss pile. Flames licked the fresh wood. I curled as close to the fire as I could without completely crawling in, and shivered as the steam rose from my wet cloak.

Outside the dragon's lair, trees wrestled in the windstorm. I felt unsettled as the waving branches. I'd never heard the tale of dragons saving men with fire, but this news had not undone me as much as Merlin's prophecy. Kye had spoken of it and his eyes were full of wonder as he told me the dream, yet even Kye's own father wore a claw cut from the she-dragon to show his victory over her as men had done in the dragon wars. Knowing men did this, what dragon would cut off his own claw for the sake of peace? And even if a dragon made such a sacrifice, what king would toss his broken sword to a dragon's feet when year on year the beasts had set fire to his villages and feasted on his countrymen? No, Lord Faul was right in this; the prophecy was an old wizard's parting dream and nothing more.

I turned on my side and listened to the wind moan outside the cave. If reading the heavens was anything like translating Latin, I could forgive Merlin for misconstruing the stars. It may be the heavenly script is written in some unknown celestial tongue. Or God writes from right to left, and the wizard read the sky from left to right.

Shivering, I watched the steam rising from my damp gown and worked to swallow down the dread rising up my throat. If Merlin's prophecy was wrong concerning dragons, how had he misread my fate?

28
Strange Treasure

I STARTED IN THE WINTER MONTHS MORE AND MORE to think of myself as Briar. Lord Faul had named me well, for I was more the leavings of a princess than the stout of her by then. Knowing he planned to leave the isle when the pips were strong enough to fly made me work all the harder on my boat, but my hours in the hills were shortened. By autumn's end, I'd harvested the last of the wild thistles.

Faul made me cook the batches down to a bitter syrup. This, mixed with river water, was to be the pips' winter drink. Snow soon covered my harvest hill, cloaking the woods all round till nothing but the waterfall would speak. Harvesting done, I thought myself in more danger than ever, but Faul gave me more tasks and I worked hard to prove my usefulness, hoping to delay my death.

How strange the island seemed in winter when a sombre magic came over the world. Ice formed in sweeping shapes along the edges of the waterfall, and early in the day, when the sun shone down, the ice glittered like great angel wings clinging to the black cliff rocks. I saw this one morning as I shivered on the shore, and broke a hole in the ice to fill a dragon shell with water.

Struggling under the water's weight, I carried the shell to the cave. But before I set it on the floor, I tripped and broke the shell. Freezing water splashed across Chawl's back. He leaped up with an angry hiss, for it's an insult to wet a dragon. I stood, half-drenched myself, and stammered, there being no words like 'sorry' or 'forgive me' in DragonTongue.

Angry at the insult to his pip, Lord Faul stomped over and lifted his great foot to crush me. I cowered at the edge of the cave as Faul opened his black talons, his naked green foot larger than myself. Then with a tumble and a stumble, Eetha and Kadmi rushed to me like scale-clad soldiers.

'Spare her!' Eetha cried in DragonTongue. 'She cannot help her blood! Mind her pretty part!'

Kadmi bravely grabbed my arm and showed my talon to his father. Lord Faul spilled impassioned fire to the roof, then turned and left the den. Beyond the booming of the waterfall, I heard bellowing and crashing that was like the thunder. The roars and crashes made my flesh sweat, for here was Lord Faul's anger fully exposed. I knew beyond doubt that without my claw and my caring for the pips, he would have had me between his teeth long since. And my screams and pleadings would have been to him a pleasure song.

I sucked in a shuddering breath and picked up the broken shell as the pips gathered round to comfort their wet sibling. Then I poked my head outside and saw the dragon's tail disappear behind the waterfall. There must be a cave behind the falls, though I'd not detected it before. Soon Faul emerged from behind the falls again, treading through the snow with a large copper pot to replace the shell I'd broken. My heart quickened. Was this where he hid his treasure? I vanished back inside the lair before he caught me looking on.

Late on that same day, Lord Faul flew off to hunt. While the pips were curled up tail to snout and snoring, I left the cave and headed for the waterfall.

A light snow laced the ground. Dragging a fallen branch behind me I managed to cover my tracks to the waterfall. The rocks were icy where I entered the hidden cave. Behind the falls, the crashing of the water sounded thunder in my ears, and once inside, the dark accosted me. Yet a little ray of sun cut through the water as a good knife cuts through butter, and I let that slash of sun guide my way.

The cave was filled with all manner of things, and copper pots were the least of it. In the very middle of the sandy cave was a pile of gold, which sank in at the top, as if it had been laid upon. And coming closer, I saw the shape of Lord Faul there. Marn told me once that dragons loved to sleep upon their gold, and I had not believed her, but here was the impression of his leg, a curl where his tail had been, and the gold held his bitter smell.

Such a treasure trove! Queen Evaine's sceptre must be

here. I looked about and dug into the mound, stopping once to hold a coin in my little slice of light. How it shone like a torn piece of sun in my dirty hand. Such riches I'd never seen before even in our castle strongroom. Here was the gold of kingdoms upon kingdoms, and all of it hidden in a cave. I dropped the coin with a clink, and the pile shifted where I'd been digging. More coins tumbled down, covering my feet till I stood like a small tree that was rooted in riches. No sceptre still. It must be in another hiding place. I stepped from the coins and built up the pile again, lest the dragon should know I'd come.

Behind the gold was a smaller mound of jewels. Even in the dim light, the jewels glittered with their own brightness. Emeralds shone the green of dewy leaves. Rubies were tossed about like blood after a battle. Oh, and there were sapphires too, and diamonds broken over all like shattered glass.

I blinked against the jewels. Belts, bracelets, necklaces and crowns lay about like so much fodder, but it was my little ray of light that brought me to the ring. The gold ring was set with a single sapphire. It was more beautiful than all the jewels in the room, yet it was too large for a woman's hand. It would have slipped off my mother's finger, and off all of mine but one.

Here I stole a moment, my heart pounding and my breath coming on like a runner's as I did what I never should have done. Slow and with a single twist, I slipped the ring over my claw and held it in the light. It shone like a caught river dancing over a gnarled branch. And the pity of its beauty encircling my claw sickened me. I tore it off,

237

threw it aside and ran.

I would have rushed from the cave, but a strange glint coming from a smaller chamber made me pull back. The glint was not from gold or jewels, but from a tumble of armour. I set my jaw. Here was the room my mother made and the Queens and Kings before her. All hungry for revenge, for the dragon's treasure, and the Pendragon sceptre that would prove our royal lineage, they'd sent their knights and slayers out year on year to die on Dragon's Keep. And the dragon knew it, for as I stepped into the alcove I saw Queen Evaine's sceptre hanging high above the stone arch at the entry.

Here was the very sceptre Evaine took from her father, King Uther Pendragon, six hundred years ago. The staff was the length of a man's forearm. A fist-sized golden dragon perched atop with diamond teeth and ruby eyes.

The dragon had hung it like a teasing poppet just out of reach of the dead knights' armour, which was piled nearly to the ceiling. The armour was tossed one upon the other in an easy manner as if each were no more than a clamshell with all the meat sucked out. All were empty even of their bones. So the armour was just the metal leavings of the dragon's feast.

The names of the knights I'd known washed over me then. Sir Robert, who more than once bounced me on his knee as he sang a sour-noted tune. Sir Broadon, blond as a woman, long as a poker and seemingly brittle, but always one to laugh at his own jokes: and Sir Kimball, whose voice was dry as summer wind. But it was the sight of Sir John Broderick's herb pouch lying at my feet which hurt the most. I fell to the floor and ran my hand along the letters J B his lady had embroidered there in green. My throat ached. Tears warmed my cheeks. I hated Mother for sending Niles's father here, the best of all our knights. The pouch smelled of sweat and vervain as I pressed my blistered hand against the simple lettering. How proud he'd been marching off to meet the dragon, and how full of love his eyes were when he looked on his lady the last time.

As I tugged the dusty drawstring, vervain spilled out on my lap, the small blue flowers dried now and the leaves curled. Wolf's-bane seeds tumbled after, along with an inkbottle. I shoved the herbs back in the pouch along with the bottle and slid the pouch into the inner pocket of my cloak where it kept company with my round mirror.

Sir John Broderick was a fine poet and had no doubt brought this ink to write a verse to his lady, but the poem went down with him, and the waxen seal atop the bottle was never broken.

Water roared outside the cave entrance. Already, I had taken too long behind the falls. I must away before Lord Faul returned. Soon I was clinging to the slick wall behind the fall, then seeing no one about, I rushed outside, took up the branch I'd left, and walking backwards, swept all trace of footprints from the snow until I reached the pips' cave.

At twilight and under a half-moon, I hid the inkbottle in the hollow of a giant willow, the tree where I'd found wild onions growing my first day on the isle. Next, I fashioned three quills from Herring Gull feathers. After so many months alone, I'd grown sick with longing to speak to another human soul. This I could not do so I yearned to write as a beggar yearns for bread.

It took some weeks before I found a place to pen my words, though the answer was scattered all about the dragon's den. The pips were growing and thus they were moulting as lizards and other creatures of their kind do. With the exception of Ore, each pip was already twice my length in body, and longer than that if tails should be included in the measure. From morn to eventide the pips were scratching and stripping off their scales, and since I was nurse, housekeeper and scullery maid, it was my duty to take the sloughed skins from the cave.

I took them. Ah, did I! They were like gold to me. Translucent, they shimmered blue-green like a strip of sky. The scales were the size of my two hands open and placed together, and though they had a bitter stink about them, they were strong and supple as vellum. Arms full, I raced to my willow before Lord Faul returned from his hunt, and stuffed the skins inside.

I stood upright and smiled to myself, the sun on my back and the sound of the woodlark chirping above the roar of the waterfall. Then all about the stately tree, I gathered a posy of crocuses from the snowy ground to celebrate my victory. Who would have thought a princess would stoop to hoard dragon skin? And wouldn't all the kingdom wonder at a girl who was glad to write her thoughts on a dragon's back?

Between my serving chores and my stolen hours working on the boat, I could spend but little time writing on the skins I'd stitched together, but the book that grew from my days of silence and lonesomeness was as strange as the scales it was written on.

In the secret hollow of the tree, I penned in the story of Kye. How I met him at the pier. The strange soft words between us, that came even from the first. The dragon's egg he showed me hidden in the beach cave. I penned my love for him, but I could not write about what happened when he saved me from the wolves, not even on the dragon's skin. Instead I wrote of my abduction, the birthing of the pips, the coming of the dragonslayers, my vow of silence to Lord Faul.

After that, the scaly pages turned back to my early life. I wrote of my swan shadow, Kit, told tales of my nurse-maid Marn, and scratched stories of my father on the dragon skin. How he'd let me ride upon his back when I was small. How he always believed I would grow up to marry for love, and last how he'd bid me make a wish before I tossed my stone in Lake Ailleann. I wrote of Sir Magnus who served the stars and locked himself in the crow's nest, boiling strange brews and meddling with books. I even wrote on the pigboy, who swelled up with bee stings and who thanked me with a dried chicken's foot, 'which be for luck', Bram said, though I tossed his stinking treasure into the mews and the birds were flustered by it.

It was nearly a month before I could bear to scrawl the rest of my story. By then the ink was gone so I fashioned my own with strained blackberry juice and soot. I'd avoided up till then all mention of my mother. I knew writing her part of my twisted tale would be simple as spilling blood. So spring was nearly at its end before I could begin.

29

Flight

SNOW MELTED AND THE MARCH RAINS KEPT US IN
the cave. The pips were restless. Chawl was the
worst, frolic being in his blood. An hour would not
pass before he'd be slapping Kadmi's tail or biting little
Ore in the rump.

'Stop that,' I'd shout. Chawl would stop for two breaths,
mayhap three, then roll himself into a ball and tumble into
Eetha; more shouting from Eetha and roaring from Chawl.
How the pips tested me!

In the middle of March the sky cleared and we left the
cave for the sunlight. Lord Faul led us through the woods,
the pips running circles round me in their joy.

At first I thought Faul was taking us out hunting, but
he had another purpose. We climbed the hills and rounded
back toward the Ashath River. Our path ended at the top
of the waterfall. There the dragon spread his wings and
flew from the cliff. Skimming over the river, he sped above

pines, oaks and rowans. Then he seemed to disappear over the very edge of the world.

Indeed, standing on the rocks beside Eetha and Ore, I wondered why he'd brought us thither only to leave us high and lonely at the falls. But from behind he came again, his shadow swooping over us like a dark angel. I felt the cold of it on my shoulders, and the wind he stirred tousled my hair.

Landing nearby, Faul folded his wings neat as a lady folds a fan, then he motioned to his strongest pip. 'Chawl. The sky is yours to conquer.'

'Sire?' said Chawl, backing away from the edge.

'Do you think those things upon your back are for wiping your snout?' growled Faul.

'No.'

'Then find the use of them!'

'Lord Faul,' I said meekly. 'It's a high place to learn the skill.' The pips lined up behind me as I spoke, and I took courage from it. 'If we were to venture lower down, the pips could –'

'Stay clear of this,' shouted Faul, pulling Chawl out from behind me. Chawl fluttered his wings. A poor sight they were, flimsy as a virgin's sheets, and my stomach turned.

We were as high as the castle tower. I looked down at the churning water and my breath caught in my throat.

'The day is lengthening,' said Faul, his eyes never leaving Chawl.

'It's deadly far,' I said. 'He could be crushed and killed.'

'Climb down if you haven't the bowels to meet the day,' ordered Faul.

I stepped back, unsure if he was speaking to Chawl or me.

'I hunger,' said Chawl, and I did hear his belly growling.

'No supper till the lot of you have leaped.'

'Unfair,' I argued. Lord Faul knocked me on my back-side. I banged my head against a stone and lay there, arms outstretched. My head throbbed and my shoulder ached. Somewhere beyond my feet I heard the tumbling water. Oft times the many sounds of the Ashath had seemed like angel songs, but now I heard the addled rage of dragons in its roar. Rubbing my sore head, I came slowly to a stand and watched Faul pick up a stone.

'When I toss this over, jump,' he said.

'Eeeach!' cried Chawl, fear or anger stirring such a flame inside his belly that he poured fire from his mouth.

Lord Faul drew back his arm and tossed. Chawl didn't move, but with a whack from Lord Faul's claw, he was over the cliff and falling.

'Spread your wings!' shouted Faul. Out Chawl's wings went, slowing him to a spinning spiral. Still he was going down to death in the crashing water.

Lord Faul dived and caught him in his talons, and brought him screeching to the cliff.

'Again!' shouted Faul. Out flew the stone, out came the claw to knock Chawl over. Off fell the pip, down and spi-ralling again. And just at his wet death, Chawl's wings caught the air. Over the pool he sped, then crashed into a willow, where, stunned he fell onto his back, and lay feet upward in the air.

'Leave him to his dreams,' mumbled Faul. 'Eetha! Step

up! The edge awaits!'

So the lessons went as, one after another, Eetha and Kadmi fell close to death, were rescued, fell again, and took flight.

Day fled and the sun began to sink into the sea. Hungry and stinking with the drench of my own sweat, I watched Ore, last and smallest of the pips spill downward a third time. This time her wings unfurled, and she managed a bloodless landing in a brawl of blackberry bushes below.

'Done!' snorted Lord Faul, his sides heaving from his day of hurling and retrieving pips.

Below us, Chawl, Kadmi and Eetha were by the pool fishing for trout while Ore tried to disentangle her tail from the blackberry bush.

Lord Faul picked up a stone and turned to me.

'What? You would throw me over now?' I said this in English.

He blinked and answered in kind. 'Much as a caterpillar flies.'

I gripped my gown. 'Aye, after the growing of her wings.'

'Who's to say there aren't wings in her all along?' said Faul. 'And what if one who has the blood, with pretty claw and fire in her belly —'

'I have no fire,' I corrected.

'You have! I've seen it, Briar!' Anger drove the words through his sharp teeth. I shook. Too late to tell him the little flames he'd seen were the work of Mother's mirror.

The dragon closed his eyes then opened them slowly like curtains parting to a fiery chamber. 'Who is to say you don't have hidden wings?'

I huffed, but it made me wonder how grand it would have been to have a curse like that. Wings instead of my old claw. Then my mother would have said I had the blood of a kestrel, or perhaps a fairy. None would have died for me, but there would have been great pride in my gift.

The sunset sky was poppy coloured, and a cool wind chilled my damp back. Faul tossed the stone in the air and caught it much the way I'd seen the gamblers do with their coins at the fair.

'I'd have to be a simpkin to hurl myself from here,' I said. 'You dived for the pips and just in time. But you may not —' the words caught in my throat. Here was death coming uninvited as it ever does. I bit my lip considering the pips' new skill. With the mastery of their wings, their hunting skills would be fool-simple. And hadn't the pips nearly outgrown the need for bitter broth now? My usefulness was over.

I tried to run back from the edge, but Lord Faul blocked me with his tail. His eyes turned red as the sunset, and were all-devouring.

'We should go back to . . . to the cave,' I sputtered. 'I've got bitter drink to boil.'

Lord Faul kept me in his gaze. I saw my own reflection standing in his slit pupils. Hair matted as a crow's nest; face pale, slender as a boy.

'The thistle's all in a pile and I haven't sorted through it yet,' I said. I was trying not to tremble, but my body shook like a baby's rattle.

Lord Faul did not move, nor answer, and it seemed he

smiled. At last he said. 'Do you value your life, Briar?'

'I want to live!'

He knocked me from the cliff.

I fell screaming, thrashing in the air. The pips below howled along with me. Just before I hit the water, Faul's claw caught me, crushed my ribs, and plunged me in the churning pool. He pulled me to the surface. I sucked in air, the shore spinning like a top. Then he dunked me under again. Biting cold water swirled round my flesh. He held me under where I thrashed. Faul's golden belly above me, rocks below where my feet kicked, my breath left me in bubbles. No air to suck, my chest nearly burst. I tore at his claw like a prisoner would dungeon bars.

Then up! I hung sputtering and Faul tossed me on the shore saying, 'You've had your bath!'

Kadmi ambled over and sniffed my hair. 'She smells no better for it.'

My 'bath' transformed my gown. Held together so long by the grime, it tore in fourteen places as I dried myself by the fire that night. A maid with any pride does not show her nakedness to others, thus after our meal as the pips talked on about their first brave flight, I broke a bone from the fish, pulled a pink thread from my cloak, and tied it to the little rib.

Wrapped naked in my cloak, I laid my threadbare gown across my knees. The blue cloth, stained orange from pip piss, would be all a patchwork of pips' moulting. Patch on patch, I covered the tears with dragon scales.

Across from the mellow fire, Faul picked fish flesh from his teeth with the tip of his talon. 'See how Briar steals from others to ease her life,' he said. He scratched a tooth and spat. The fire hissed. 'Humans are born stripped. No pelt nor scales to cover them, they must steal another's skin to make their own.'

I said nothing but stitched and stitched, hoping Faul would not start another history lesson. He'd schooled the pips well when he thought I was away, but I'd gleaned bits of his teaching now and again. I'd not known until this year how many times human kings and queens had signed treaties protecting the dragons' ancient hunting lands, only to turn about, take up arms and drive them from their valleys and high mountain dwellings, so now the dragons hid in but a few small scattered islands.

Lord Faul's anger rose every time he spoke of men's betrayal, and in truth, I didn't blame him. I'd found small comfort knowing a few humans were trusted. Mages like Merlin and his followers who'd worked to keep the treaties binding, but they'd not won out.

Pink thread to blue scale, I mended my gown as the dragons talked, wishing I were invisible. The tears were many so I covered all the cloth with scales. I was sure there was nothing in the world like it.

'Tell us again how man misused our gift of fire to forge weapons,' grumbled Kadmi.

'No,' called Chawl. 'Tell us about the time man enslaved the DragonLord, pulled out all his teeth, and cut off every talon!'

Ore leaped up. 'And then how brave Kazrol burned all the castle guards to rescue him.'

'And ate the jailers!' added Eetha.

'We won that battle certainly,' said Faul. 'But in that year we lost more of our lands to men.'

'I hate all men!' said Chawl, adding his fire to the flames in the pit.

'And I!' said Kadmi, Eetha and Ore, till all were breathing flames. I backed away from the heat.

'Sit, Briar!' ordered Faul. Down I flopped, grasping my little log for support.

'It's good you hate all men,' said Faul proudly to the pips. 'Keep your bitterness towards them. Know them for what they are: liars, murderers and thieves.'

'What about her?' asked Chawl, pointing to me.

Faul's yellow eyes were like the lightening. 'Briar is kept honest by her dragon's blood,' he said.

'How did she come to be our kind?' asked Eetha.

'Egg stealing,' said Faul, his words so harsh I dropped my needle. 'And think on this, pips,' he said. 'If this had not been so, you would have had an older sister.'

'A sister?' said Eetha coming to a stand, her bright gold belly catching the light of the fire.

'Aye! But a witch stole our fertile egg for the queen to drink. Do you see what usurpers humans are? They steal another's pips if they cannot make their own!'

Now the pips were all around me, smoke spilling from their snouts.

'Hold out your claw!' said Eetha.

'No.' I hid my hand behind my back.

'Hold it out to me!'

'Why for? You've seen it often enough.'

'Bring it out!' said Ore, and the shock of the smallest

one speaking to me so made me draw it out.

I held out my scaly claw. Uncut by Mother's knife these long months, the black-nailed talon had grown out full and pointing, sharp as a blacksmith's nail.

Eetha flicked out her tongue and kissed my claw.

'This was our sister,' she said.

I awoke that night bathed in sweat, having dreamed of Kye. In my sleep I saw him standing on the dock, just as it was the first day we met. In life he had not cut the dragon's talon as his father had done, but in my dream, a claw hung at his side. Blood congealed about the edge where his sword had severed the dragon's claw. He looked at me, his eyes going from blue to gold, and there was blood upon his lip.

Lord Faul and the pips were all asleep. I stirred the fire and watched the wavering flames. I'd known long ago about the egg stealing, but never had I considered its full meaning. Mother and Father were human, yet Faul and Charsha's egg had prepared my mother's womb, else I would never have been born.

My skin flashed hot then cold as I stared across the fire at the great sleeping dragon, his scales burnished silver in the blaze.

I was human, but also in my veins, ran the blood of dragons.

33
The Scales

I T WAS NOT LONG AFTER THE PIPS' FIRST FLIGHT THAT I braved a leap. Not one from a high place, but one in my own heart, and I felt the falling just as much when I faced my hidden book. Filling my quill with ink, I wrote about my mother.

In the hollow tree my hand quaked as I wrote of Mother's early years with me. Her dream for me was my water and sunlight, my evening and my morn, and I grew under her constant gaze as a rose will in a gardener's care. But was it love? I could not answer this.

Was it love that drove Mother to drown my dear Marn?

Tears smeared the ink as I wrote of Marn's death; my heart ached with the memory of her. I'd shut my mind against the thought of murder when first we fished her from the moat, but even then a part of me had known.

Why so driven? Mother had to protect me. Marn had seen my claw, so the threat of witch burning might have driven her to violence. But Marn loved me with all her strength. Wouldn't my nursemaid have kept silent? Mother never waited to find out.

I wept many hours as I wrote, and held the skin away from the tears to keep the letters sound as I wrote how Mother knifed Tess, scrawled witchery in blood across her hut, and let the angry crowd rush to Morgesh Mountain to burn Demetra for the crime. Marn, Tess, Demetra. Three deaths I knew of to keep my claw secret — were there more I knew nothing of? Was it only a blizzard that killed the midwife on my birthing day?

My quill broke. I sharpened another. My ink-stained fingers moved across the scales, my naked claw had a two-inch talon now in plain sight. In the hollow tree, I watched my hand spill secrets my mouth could not admit.

Six years my mother had tried to have me. Facing barrenness, she'd gone to Demetra. She would not give in, but set two plans in motion — one, at least, would win out.

The queen would quicken her womb with Demetra's magic. If that should fail, Aliss would have a babe for her. A pillow wedged under Mother's gown would guise pregnancy while she waited for Aliss to give birth in Demetra's cave. Ah, but it never came to that. The dragon's egg sparked her womb and Father planted a sturdy seed that stayed and grew. So Aliss was abandoned, her girl raised as a bastard and a servant.

I'd kenned Mother's plan for Aliss using scraps of memory from things she'd said, from the pleas Aliss had made the day she'd begged us to take Kit. And lastly from Demetra's words regarding Kit, which had echoed long in my head. *Ah, she could have walked in your shoes.*

Indeed what a princess Kit would have made if I had not been born. Still, Mother had condemned her childhood friend to life with the hag, so I was glad that Kit and I had risked our lives to save Aliss.

Stiff from huddling in my hollow, I stood, stretched and made a little pile of sticks in the clearing for a fire. Mother's mirror was scratched but not broken. Pearls and emeralds still encircled the rim. Tipping the mirror up, the pearls like baby's teeth, I saw the dragon girl inside: this mirror now my source of fire. The day Mother gave it to me; her face had hardened when I'd held the mirror up to her face saying, 'Look. An angel in the glass.'

How her lip trembled then and she'd covered her reflection with her hand. 'Angels are innocent,' she'd whispered, 'And I'm . . . Oh, Rosie.'

She'd put me in the hall and though I heard her sobbing through the door, I did not go back inside. All her deeds were upon her that day. She'd seen them in the glass darkly. I had not known then what made her weep. But I knew now.

31
The Hunt

LORD FAUL MADE ME WORK THE PIPS EACH DAY until their wings were strengthened. I was to ensure they stayed within the wilds of Dragon's Keep, but keep them hours in the air to build the muscles in their wings. Neither Faul nor the pips knew I'd overheard their plan to meet the others on an isle across the sea, but I knew that by strengthening their wings, I was numbering my days on Dragon's Keep.

I had little time to work on my boat. It was nearly finished, but weeks went by when I could not even make it to the hill. From mid-March until early April, when the sky was clear of rain, we soared over Dragon's Keep, following the river through the hills, or visiting the cliffs on the far side of the island. On land, Ore was the least of the pips, but once lifted to the sky, she was queen to it. Ah, she was like the sparrow that swoops and twirls with easy grace, darting in and out of trees too tangled for the other pips.

I took to riding Kadmi's back, as I had in our hunting days on land. Once in the air I knew my childhood dreams were some strange chanting of my dragon's blood. A beast memory passed on from dragon to pip. I'd had the same flying dream so many times, though in them I'd thought myself an angel or a bird. Yet always I'd seen a great shadow on the earth below me, cast by my own mighty wingspan. I was full of power in these dreams and always happy. Now as I flew on dragon's back, the dream became flesh.

'Lower down,' I called up to Kadmi. We were trying a new trick. He was dangling me over a pinor tree where I was picking fruit. I had not seen this strange tree growing on Wilde Island, for it was come from the dragon lands of the east. The dragons of yesteryear had planted a small grove here, tending the orchard for its sour fruit which ripened quickly in the spring.

My hair hung down and my gown was askew. 'Lower still, I cannot reach them!'

Chawl swooped past and tore a branch from the top.

'Not like that!' I shouted. Chawl hissed and circled round us as Kadmi lowered me closer to the treetop. I plucked the egg-shaped fruit, which was larger than my fist and bright red. The fruit was bitter and sour all at once. It sickened me, but the pips adored it. I gathered twelve in my woven sack, dropped three as Kadmi bashed me into a branch and we counted it a victory.

On the ground Eetha and Ore joined us for the snack. They gobbled the fruit, their jaws blood-red. A robin sang from the high branch and it put me in mind of Kit. 'Did I tell you,' I asked, 'About the time Kit threw herself in the moat to rescue a robin?'

'More than once,' said Eetha, popping another pinor fruit in her mouth. Faul had his history lessons. I had my stories to combat them. These were not history lessons, but tales of my childhood told in English to ease my mouth from DragonTongue a while. I'd begun to share them with the pips when they rested between flights. The DragonLord was far away and he did not have to know. I'd sworn the pips to secrecy, though Eetha had taken some convincing.

'Tell a battle story,' said Chawl. These were the only tales he cared about and the more blood the better, but I didn't want to talk of war.

'I'll tell you what happened to Demetra.'

'The one who stole the egg?' asked Ore.

'Aye, the one who stole it long ago.'

Eetha blew out a flame. 'She should burn for that.'

'She did burn.' I twirled a stick as if I didn't care whether I should recount the tale or not.

'Tell us!' they cried in DragonTongue.

I twirled the stick again. 'Say it in English.'

They begged again and this time in my favoured tongue.

'Very well,' I sighed as if I cared little for the story. Now they were all within my power, begging me to tell. I recounted Demetra's death. The pips all cheered when the villagers threw their torches in the hag's cave and cocked their heads when I told them of the shadow wraith climbing out of Kit's mouth. In the weeks to come, this became their favourite story. In this way Demetra burned again and again as if she were caught in the devil's eternal fire. I liked that right well.

The pips and I were rich in sky that spring. And all of us were coming into our power. I looked the part of a dragon's maid by then. My one-time May Day gown had gone to so many holes that now it was completely patched with the pips' moultings. It shimmered blue-green as I soared over the isle. My hands round Kadmi's neck, we sped over the hills, my red hair blowing back, my face and hands brown from the sun, my talon full exposed.

I could no more play the part of the pretty princess then than a warty frog could sport a queen's bright crown. But the pips were not ashamed of me. Indeed, they seemed to tolerate me better now. It may be the familiar smell of my dragon gown appealed to their snouts. Even Faul seemed less sickened by my form, his broad green nostrils twitching less at my approach.

The pure joy of flying drove us on, as did our hunger. Spying a wild boar in the woods below, Kadmi circled above the trees. I could feel his body pulsing under mine as the boar raced for cover.

'Stay back, Chawl,' warned Eetha. 'I see your blood!'

Chawl wheeled lower, ignoring his sister's warning. Wind sang in my ears, and a fearsome cry rang throughout the wood as all the pips but Eetha dived for the prey. The attack was swift but the boar gored Chawl's back leg before Kadmi finished him off.

Chawl roared fire as his blood spattered the body of the boar. Eetha landed near me. I tore my cloak with her help and together we bound Chawl's leg.

'You should have listened, Chawl,' I scolded. 'Eetha has the sight.'

Chawl only bellowed more fire.

The pips ate roasted boar that night in the lair, but Faul was angry with me over Chawl's injury and would not let me eat of it. I nibbled bones after all were asleep, but it didn't touch my hunger.

In mid-April a rainstorm swept over Dragon's Keep. We ceased our flying lessons as Ashath River swelled beside our cave. I'd borne the closeness of the lair two days straight, staying within for warmth, but the dragons' chief occupation on rainy days was sleep, and the sounds of their heavy snoring fairly rattled my bones. At last I left the lair to brave the storm.

My teeth chattered as I scurried for my hollow tree and the comfort of my little book. Huddled in the cold, I stitched more scales to the booklet, took up my quill and penned my life with Faul and the pips, the joy of flight on Kadmi's back, and my discovery of treasure behind the falls. How I slipped the sapphire ring over my claw, found Evaine's sceptre, discovered Sir John's inkbottle.

I scripted all Lord Faul said about the dragon wars. It seemed fitting to write dragon history on dragon skin as I worried the scales with my ink over the dwindling of the dragons. If there were no more than three or four aside from Faul's brood, then the pips must live, fly across the sea and find their mates or dragons would be no more. A year ago I would have been glad of this, but not now.

Two pages filled, my thoughts turned to Kye. I wrote my love for him without shame. No eyes but mine would ever see the scales, so I let my fingers do all the weavings of my heart, and never did I leave a strand out. I wondered how Kye would see me if he returned just now. Could he love a girl wrapped in dragon's scales? It might be that fighting in a war would make him bother less with skin than soul. And like the threshers of the grain, he'd see the heart of wheat beneath the husk.

The wind was fierce and the trees all about were losing branches to it. I shivered in the belly of the tree and tried a new verse on Kye. But my scrawl did not conform to the beauty of my thoughts, so I washed the ink off the dragon scale with wet weeds, bit my tongue, and tried again.

Head bowed and eyes to the script, I did not attend the noise outside. But when a gust of wind shook my tree with violence, I looked up and saw a figure. At first she seemed an apparition, rain and fog befuddling my sight, but on she came, brown-caped and soaked with rain. The girl moved past the brambles, and closer still, I saw who it was.

32
The Messenger

KIT! MY KIT! SMALL AND WEAPONLESS. WEARING THE rough brown garb of a novice, she was wandering lost it seemed, but heading towards the curl of smoke that came from Lord Faul's lair.

Quick, I tore the scale I'd been writing on from my book, and wrapped it round my claw. She'd never seen my beast mark and I couldn't risk shocking her with it now. Silence was needed and haste. Bolting outside I grabbed her from behind and covered her mouth.

Kit screamed into my palm but when I turned Kit around we held each other weeping. Ah, to hold my dearest friend so close again. My body shook with joy. Fear for her life soon had me pulling her further from the dragon's cave. Faul said he would not eat human flesh, but his vow rested on my promise not to speak to my kind. If he should spy Kit here with me, wouldn't he think I'd broken my vow? And if I'd broken mine what was to stop him from eating Kit? These thoughts made me run all the faster.

Rain pelted our backs, and wind fought against us as we fled over the steep hill. To our right a great tree swayed low and lower in the singing gusts, then with a crack it broke in two and came crashing down. We slid down the muddy hill and reached a small cave beneath an overhanging rock. Lightning streaked the sky and thunder followed. We watched amazed as another tree toppled over in the gale.

'Rosie,' said Kit, and 'Rosie,' again as if she could not say my name enough. I knew I had to push her away from Dragon's Keep without speaking a word or she would be dragon's meat. Still, I couldn't let her go just yet. I'd longed so for her company.

We stayed close in our little cave. With luck the smoke from the fire in the dragon's den, mingled with the heavy rain, would befuddle Faul's nose and keep Kit's smell from his nostrils, if only for a time.

'I came to bring you home, Rosie,' said Kit. 'Things have gone wrong since you . . .' She bit her lip, her short cropped hair such as novices wear dripping rain down her cheek. I placed her hand on my pin, her pin, to encourage her. I could not say the message aloud but she knew well enough what was etched there.

Slowly she drew back. 'I wish,' she said. 'I don't want to . . .' She was fighting with her words. I could not help her.

Kit looked down at her lap. 'Rosie, your mother —'

I covered her lips with my fingers and shook my head.

Dead. I knew by Kit's look and I would not let her speak it. Kit took my hand away. 'Your mother mourned after you were taken, and worse still after your father's death. In her grief, she sent word to Saint Brigid's Abbey asking for my mother to come. They'd known each other when they were young,' she added.

I nodded. Mother would want her oldest and dearest friend with her, I knew.

'My mother arrived to find the queen slender as a stem and failing. Sir Magnus made her crave the poppy potion, and though my mother tried to keep the drug away, the queen took more and more. She dreamed though she did not sleep. Times she saw things that were not there, screamed and fought with shadows.' Kit frowned saying this. 'Other times she did not know what was before her. She was lost, Rosie, do you see? And then one day she took so much potion . . .'

Hot tears flowed down my cheeks. My breath came fast as a startled creature.

'My mother's sure it was the poppy potion killed her, and that this was Sir Magnus's intention, though she was clever enough not to say this to his face. But as soon as the queen was laid in the tomb, Magnus locked my mother in the dungeon.' Kit grabbed my arms. 'You have to come home, Rosie! You're the only one who can free my mother and stop Sir Magnus before he's crowned king.'

Kit said these last things panting, her words spilling out sharp and quick. And I heard them like the pelting of stones. Mother dead. Kit's mother locked away. The murderer, Sir Magnus, about to be crowned.

My head swirled.

My vow of silence had kept Faul from feasting on my

people, but I hadn't kept them safe at all. Treachery, murder and deceit. I could not let Magnus sit on my father's throne. Yet how could I go?

I wept on Kit's shoulder as quietly as I could, knowing Lord Faul slept less than a league away. I was bound as a hawk to the tether. Go with Kit, promise broken, and the dragon was released to kill again. Stay, send Kit away, and the kingdom was lost to Sir Magnus.

'Tell me,' said Kit softly. 'What will you do?'

I drew back and shook my head.

Kit frowned. 'A silence is upon you?'

I nodded.

She shivered. 'A shadow wraith . . . stuffed down your throat?'

A loud crack came from somewhere down the hill, and fearing Lord Faul's discovery, I pushed Kit from our little cave, grabbed her hand, and ran.

We raced through the waving grass. Rain soaked our backs as we clambered down the cliff rocks to the sandy beach. Kit had tied her small sailing vessel to a thick branch at the mouth of Ashath River. I marvelled that she could have made it to Dragon's Keep in such a small ship, but had little time to wonder at it. Kit untied the rope, leaped inside and held out her hand. 'Hurry, Rosie!'

I stepped back. Sir Magnus was not yet king.

Leave Dragon's Keep now and Lord Faul would surely find us. He'd feast on Kit. Then speeding to Wilde Island, he'd swallow man and maid alike, his hunger whetted by my deceit. There was no reason to risk Kit's life when I could escape in my boat later and alone.

I gripped the stern and pushed her skiff away. She rowed back to me, shouting, 'Get in, Rosie!'

Away I pushed her boat again, this time harder, and running fast I reached the cliff.

'Rosie! What's happened to you?' screamed Kit across the wind and waves. 'My mother rots inside her cell!' she screamed through the wall of rain. 'Won't you come save her?'

I kept climbing.

'Don't you love me any more?' she screamed. 'Do you love only dragons now?'

Halfway up the cliff I hung, her words wounding me so deep, I could not move. I clenched my jaw and screamed into my teeth.

'Rosie!' cried Kit. 'I come back for you!'

And turning round, I saw her rowing toward the shore. Would nothing turn this girl away? I scrambled down the cliff and threw a stone at her. Kit held her oar above the waves and stared, mouth agape, at me. The next stone struck her shoulder and she screamed, gazing on me now as if I were cursed. Another stone flew past her face, and another until Kit turned her small craft round.

Rain pounded the water, waves crashed, and mist blew grey between us. 'Live, sweet Kit,' I whispered, 'Live till you are old and your hair is the white of dandelions.' Curling the last stone tight inside my fingers, I watched Kit row away.

33

The Takings of the Storm

THE PATH ALONG THE RIVER WAS BROWN AND swollen with rain. Shedding the dragon skin I'd wrapped about my hand, I fought my way through the gusting wind, climbing over one downed tree after another. So many trees had fallen. Such a storm I'd never seen on Dragon's Keep. The pool at the base of the waterfall had risen higher in the past few hours. Muddy water lapped against the entrance of the dragon's lair, wetting my feet up to the ankles as I went in.

'Where have you been?' growled Faul, lifting his great head.

'Walking,' I said in DragonTongue.

'In this rain?' He scratched himself. 'Only fools walk on such a day.'

There was a bit of care in his saying that, but he was quick to cover it. 'The pips thirst for thistle brew. You are server here, or have you forgotten?'

I prepared the broth and poured the brew into the pips' drinking shells. As the pips lapped their drink, I drew up to the fire. Wind and weather warred outside. I wondered now, if in trying to save Kit, I'd condemned her to death.

The logs sent sparks to the ceiling, and I thought on how Mother used to sit with me beside the fire in my solar and sing 'Lady Come Ye Over' as she wove a purple ribbon in my hair. Now she was gone, lying dead beside Father, and I blamed her dream for it. It was the dream that had demanded my father's life in service to Empress Matilda. The dream that drove Mother to cover my flaw. The dream that twisted her to murder. Sir Magnus may have helped her dose herself with poppy potion, but the dream was Mother's poison.

I wrapped my arms about my legs and rocked. None bothered over me, the pips to their drink and Lord Faul curled up nose to tail. All were used to my tears; it was as much my task to weep on Dragon's Keep, as it was to gather thistles.

A loud crash outside gave me such a fright that I leaped up and raced to the mouth of the cave. A fallen pine spanned the river at the far edge of the pool. The water swelled about the tree as a mudslide rolled down, burying the roots.

'A tree's gone over,' I said with a shiver.

Lord Faul came up beside me. Just then a second pine crashed down the steep hill. It splashed into the river near the first, and a great wall of mud came tumbling after. The muscles on the dragon's back tensed. 'We have to move them,' he said, 'or soon our cave will be under water.'

Lord Faul was large, strong-backed and strong-legged, but the pines were as tall as citadels and broader round than his great neck. I hadn't faith that we could move them.

'Pips,' said Faul. 'Come quick.'

The pips gathered behind their father.

'Together we will move those trees damming up the river,' said Faul.

'I won't go in,' said Kadmi.

'You will!' roared Faul. 'We must dig the roots out of the mud, then roll the trees aside so the water can get through.'

'It's that or lose our cave,' I said to Kadmi. And so we ventured out.

In the freezing water, I dug beside the dragons, feeling small and useless as a beetle. Still, I'd seen many a sexton beetle do a deal of digging in the walled garden, when it was pleased to bury a dead mouse, so I worked as best I could in the muddy river.

Faul's great claws dug and tossed out heaps of mud. Rain pelted his strong back as he worked on the left side of the trees where the water was deepest. The rest of us dug to the right of the fallen pines.

Kadmi and Chawl hurled their mud hard and fast; more than once the mud landed square on Eetha's back, and once straight in my face. Fearing the flying mud would knock Eetha into the river, I called, 'Toss another way!' But they could not hear me over the rushing water and the howling wind.

Eetha and I moved closer to the tree where Ore was at

work freeing a tangle of roots. Ore was still half the size of the other pips, and being no larger than myself, she had to delve close to the river's edge. Eetha bent to help her wee sister with the roots. 'We'll never dig these out!' said Eetha in DragonTongue. 'There's too much danger here, Briar. We should get out now. Our cave is already lost.'

'Not lost yet,' I said. Ah, but I should have listened to Eetha who had the keenest mind of all the pips and she had the sight too. Time after time she'd proven her powers. But I turned away from Eetha's warning, licked my lips, spat mud in the river, and dug all the harder.

Would that we had stopped and backed away. The loss of the cave was nothing to the loss our staying on would bring. I worked another hour beside Eetha and Ore as the storm shouted thunder in my ears. When the sky went green with lightning, my lips quivered with prayer to Saint Scholastica who has power over storms. Trees above thrashed in the wind, bowing low as brooms to sweep the hill as Kadmi climbed over the log to dig beside his father.

I was groaning with the weight of mud, wet to the bone, and praying for Kit, when I heard the roaring from the hill above. The sound was like a mountain ripping in two. With it came another fallen tree and a wall of mud rushing down at us. Before we could escape, the sliding hill threw us all into the water.

I fought the heavy mud in the freezing river, then, choking and flailing, I came up and sputtered for air. Chawl, Eetha and Ore struggled at my side. We grabbed at roots and pulled ourselves out of the tumbling water. But to the other side of the tree, Faul and Kadmi were still buried.

Faul to his knees, Kadmi to his neck. The pine had rolled over him, and the river was rising.

'Help him!' shouted Faul. We rushed to Kadmi's side. 'We'll dig you out,' I screamed. Then each of us about his neck thrust claws and hands into the water. Faul dug himself out, and joined us, clawing mud all about the tree to free his pip.

All of us were ringed about Kadmi, thrusting arms into the mud as if in some frantic dance. We scooped and shouted, flinging mud in every direction. How we tried to free him, but even in the cold river, I felt the heat of fear burning in my veins as the water swirled near Kadmi's mouth.

'Sing your favourite rhyme,' ordered Faul. He hated the English rhyme, but even Faul would shed DragonTongue to help us drive away our fears. Kadmi raised his jaws, so close to the water's edge by now, he had to spit before he chanted.

'Bright fire. Dragon's fire. Broken sword. One black talon ends the war.' The rest of us joined in as we worked to unearth him.

'Turn them into mincemeat. Bake them in the flame. Cut them up! Spit them out! Start the war again!'

High up on the hill as we chanted and dug to free Kadmi, I spotted Kit. She'd made her way back to shore! Drenched and clinging to a tree above us, I saw her take us in, the buried pip, our frenzied digging. Faul's back to her, she could have turned then and slipped away unnoticed, but seeing me at work beside the dragon's claws, and hearing the quaver in my voice as I tried to comfort Kadmi with the silly chant, Kit rushed down the hill and splashed into the churning river.

'Turn them into mincemeat! Bake them in the flame!' she chanted right beside me, thrusting her hands into the mud and tossing it behind. Lord Faul's eyes hardened as she dug near him, but he could not spare the time to question her.

We toiled against the rising water, while Kadmi struggled to free himself from the weight of the pine tree. Digging hard, back bent, hands flailing, I saw all in a moment how Kit's eyes grew wide at the sight of my naked hand. The blue-green scales of my dragon's claw were shining in the water, and my long black talon was blotched with river mud.

'Dig!' screamed Eetha, and we went to work again. Kit did not speak a word of condemnation, but dug all the harder beside me. How I loved her for that.

Working as one, Kit and I nearly freed Kadmi's foreleg. Kadmi raised his snout, trying hard to lift his head higher, but now the water was in his mouth. He blew out. Heaved in a choking breath. Blew out again.

'Faster!' shouted Faul. And in his haste to free Kadmi, he knocked Ore into the water. Over the logs she washed.

'Ah, God!' I cried. 'The wee one cannot swim!'

Swiftly, Kit leaped in the water after Ore. She gave no more thought for herself than she had the day she'd leaped into the moat to save the robin. And together they tumbled down the rushing river. 'Kit!' I screamed. 'Ore!' But I could not go after them. My hands were deep in mud, clawing like a dog to save Kadmi. Now his head was underwater, but life was in his eyes.

I was still digging beside Kadmi's golden chest when I saw him die. Faul lifted his head and screamed, 'Kadmi!'

Yellow flames hissed in the rain, and above us, grey steam rose. I screamed beside the dragons, my throat burning as theirs did, though no fire came.

In our haste to find Ore and Kit, we left Kadmi's body in the water and sped along the riverbank. Drenched in muck I ran mile after mile, my heart pounding, my breath coming in gulps.

Racing with the dragons, my eyes were fixed upon the river, which was now a stranger to me. The storm had turned the glassy water of our sweet Ashath into a brown and heaving thing, filled with swirling branches, dead rabbits, squirrels, and in one place, a drowned fawn.

Further down the Ashath, Faul shouted, 'There!' And I saw Ore, caught against a row of rocks in the rushing water. We could not see if she were dead. Faul and I waded in, Chawl and Eetha behind. Lord Faul stooped and gathered Ore to himself. Gashed and bloody, she moaned, her head rolling back against her father's shoulder.

'Alive!' I screamed to the others. Ah, but there was loss here. In the place where Ore had lain, I saw what had kept her from drowning. Not river stones or branches wedged beneath, but Kit.

Her death came over me in a roaring silence. All sound was the river, all movement the water. Faul took Kit up and laid her on the ground. I was still in the river. It was Chawl who brought me to shore and set me beside her. There was an aspen leaf in Kit's fair hair, gold entangled in the gold. Rain poured over us and the wind howled all around. I kissed her stone-cold cheek and took her in my arms.

The sky was clear the next day, but the wind still blew strong with the sharp smell of storm on it. Gusts swept across our backs as we dug two graves on the high hill. A large hole at the very top, and further down, a smaller one.

Faul laid Kadmi in the deep pit. Stepping back, he lit him with his fire. Chawl, Eetha and Ore joined in till Kadmi was ablaze in yellow flames.

Long did he burn, and long did Faul and the pips send more fire on him, their grief being more like burning rage than sorrow, since for their lives they could not cry. Standing beside the pips, I added to the roar, screaming high and piercing like a hawk. Wind drove the flames higher. And the smoke tumbled in waves above our heads.

When Kadmi was full-burned, we covered him with soil, the heat of his bones making the very earth hiss and steam. Then the dragons turned and followed me to the smaller grave. I stood over Kit who lay sweet as sleep in the ground. Even the grave could not dim Kit's brightness; her damp hair lacing over her cheek, her face pale against the brown earth. She looked like a summer bloom fallen from its stem, yet with all the petals kept.

I wished I could scream for Kit as I'd done for Kadmi.

But the sorrow that impaled my heart could never be undone with screaming. Chawl started a blue flare but I held up my hand. I need only give my say and all would spill their fire on her. But I couldn't say farewell with fire. It would have killed me sure to watch Kit burn, so against those gathered there, I went on with the service.

With Father's golden cross held high above Kit's grave, I sang, 'His Banner is Love' and said the releasing prayer, which ends with 'and to bright heaven I'll follow Thee'.

From my threadbare cloak, I unclasped Kit's silver brooch and saying, 'Omnia vincit amor,' I placed it on her sodden chest.

'What is the meaning?' asked Eetha. Chawl flicked her with his tail for asking so.

I answered, 'Love conquers all.'

Lord Faul shivered with the words, his scales rattling above the grave like dried leaves in the wind.

34

Lord Faul

THE RAIN CEASED AND THE RIVER FELL. WHEN THE
water came down and was thigh-deep just past the
fallen trees, we set to work digging out the pines.
This we did in silence, having no heart for the task. All
dug together, careful to step around the place where
Kadmi died, and when we cleared the fallen pines, the
water rushed past in a great sigh.

Next we cleaned out the den. The flood had filled it to
the very top, leaving ring on ring of mud across the stones.
We shivered with the damp as we scraped away the rings
with sticks, and swept the thick mud from the floor with
pine brooms.

At day's end, cold and tired, we burned our brooms.
Chawl lit a fire, and seeing his father worn from work, left
the cave to hunt. Some time after, he returned with trout
and tossed each of us a fish. All ate but Faul, who turned
away to sleep.

The river's cold had marked us, every one. We'd spent too many hours clearing the trees from the water, and it took a roaring fire to touch the chill. I lay shivering, listening to Lord Faul as he slept. The rattle of his breathing was like the clacking bones our jester waved on All Hallow's Eve to frighten off the dead.

I'd not heard him breathe this way before, and it troubled me so I lay half-awake while the others slept. Eyes closed, I saw the golden fire through my eyelids and in the glow the very image of Kit. In her bright company at last, I fell asleep.

Near dawn Eetha shook me awake. 'We must go to your thistle hill,' she said. 'Father's breath is rough. He needs bitter broth.'

I sat up, hearing myself that his breathing had worsened. Little Magda's breathing had been that rough when she'd suffered from the croup. Marn had treated her with a poultice of mustard plaster. Wild mustard grew on the hill. I would garner some.

A soft red light gowned the woods outside where I climbed on Eetha's back. Unused to my weight, she pumped her wings hard as she skimmed above the treetops, dipping too low now and again. We reached the hill where she skidded down and landed with a thud, which sent me headlong into the thistle.

'Oof!' I cried. But Eetha stood up and shook herself. 'Pluck,' she said. 'And swift!'

The thistle stalks were still green, and sported purple blooms. I knew the dragons liked it better later in the season when the plants were drier, but I gathered what I could in the rising sun, paying no mind to the thistles that scratched and cut my palms. Eetha pulled alongside me in a patch where I'd never known another's help.

When the thistle pile was waist-high, I climbed the hill to harvest mustard.

'No time for flowers,' called Eetha with contempt.

'Wild mustard holds a cure for chest ailments.'

Eetha fluttered her wings. 'Hurry then, Briar.'

I pulled great handfuls of the mustard plants. I'd lost one father. I would not lose another. Eetha took our morning's harvest in her claws, and we flew back over the green hills.

I could hear Lord Faul's rough breathing as we entered the cave. Behind his enormous back, Chawl and Ore were digging.

'Bring another stone from the fire!' called Chawl. Eetha dropped her bundles and brought Chawl a burningstone. Digging a small hole, he placed it behind Faul's back.

I'd not seen burningstones placed in a half-circle like that since Faul and I tended the pips' nest before their hatching day.

'Nothing warms him,' said Chawl. 'His front is to the fire and we've pitted hot stones behind him as he told us to, but feel his scales,' Eetha ran the soft upper part of her claw over her father's shoulder.

'Briar will heal him with bitter broth,' she said, a mix of hope and fear in her eyes.

Already I was throwing thistles in the pot. And while I waited for the brew to boil, I gathered all the seeds from the mustard plants. So tiny and so few! And I needed flour to make a paste for a poultice as I'd seen Marn do. No flour here. What then? I crushed the seeds between two stones then added dirt, dampening it with my spit to make a paste. Demetra had used mustard on my claw. The burning paste could heal or harm. My intent was healing.

Lord Faul opened his eyes. 'Come by me, pips,' he said in a rasping voice. The pips gathered by him as I mixed the mustard plaster.

'Have you felt the stirrings yet?' he asked.

'Aye,' said Chawl. 'A strange itching in my wings.'

'That's the calling,' said Faul. 'Soon you'll fly south to meet your fellows.'

'Our kith,' said Eetha. 'I've wanted to go there so long, but with Kadmi drowned and –'

'Go still.' Faul coughed. The rough and rattle of great fists banging down a door. He wheezed another breath. 'You have to go. Promise me.'

'You'll take us there,' said Chawl nodding.

'You'll find your way.' Faul closed his eyes.

I stepped up. 'Here is hot mustard paste to ease your cough.'

'Hot?' said Lord Faul. 'It can be nothing to a dragon's fire.'

'Aye, you're right there.' It was good to hear him boasting. With stinging nose and watering eyes, I coated his neck and chest, my own hands burning as I spread it. 'The heat will grow,' I said. Then wiping my hands on the sandy floor, I went back to the cooking pot.

'Thistle milk will be ready soon, Father,' said Eetha. 'The bitter taste will restore your guile, and your fire will come on strong again.'

'No,' said Faul. 'This death has stolen my fire.'

My breath caught in my throat. I dropped my stirring stick and went to Faul. 'Don't let Kadmi's death take away your will to live,' I said. 'You still have your daughters and a son.'

'It's not only Kadmi's death that haunts me,' said Faul. His slit eyes opened and he looked so long on me I felt a coldness wrap around my bones.

'The manchild who gave her life for Ore.' He heaved a breath. The sound of his coughing echoed in the cave. 'Never did I think . . .' He closed his eyes. I leaned my head against his side and put my clawed hand on his great neck.

'Kit never thought of herself when a fellow creature was in trouble.' I told him then of Kit's love for wild creatures. How a fox once came to her in the wood and how she'd thrown herself in the moat to save a robin.

Faul shuddered and I felt the tremble beneath my hand. Under his breath he said, 'How can I not be changed by this?'

And then I saw them. The shining drops so small and clear that had chilled Lord Faul to the core and doused his inner fire.

'Don't cry, Father!' I begged and as the pips saw the tears they joined me pleading, 'Don't cry, Father! Stop now! It will kill you!'

More tears rolled down Faul's blue-green flesh and puddled in the sand beside his talons.

35

Voice in the Falls

THE PIPS DUG A GRAVE BESIDE KADMI'S AND SET Lord Faul ablaze. The flames burned bright all that day and into the deep of night. We stayed beside the dragon's death-fire, lifting our screams to the sky, stinging heat and bitter smoke shawling the moon grey.

At dawn, we filled the pit until the grave became a mound of steaming sod. I laid my father's cross atop, then sat in the long wild grass facing clouds and sun. Covered in dirt and smoke, I was too worn to walk back to the cave. My joints ached, my throat was parched and sore. I was like Job in his grieving pit, having lost all that mattered to me in life, and seeing nothing but sickness and sores ahead. Looking out over the sea, the words of Saint Columba came as if on the wind whispering:

Day of thick clouds and voices,
Of mighty thundering,
A day of narrow anguish
And bitter sorrowing.

These words described the storm that had come and left us shaken.

Two nights passed. We ate little and spoke less. On the morn of the third day, the pips began to plan their southern flight across the sea. I went to the water's edge and washed the tears and mud from my cheeks. The woman looking back at me from the quickened pool seemed aged beyond her seventeen years. There was something of Marn in me now, all bone and sinew and stooped with life – though, at seventeen, I was half an arm span taller than Marn.

The pips would leave this day or the next. I'd thought to stay on Dragon's Keep and like a sexton tend the three graves here. But in the night, Kit's spirit hovered over in a dream, and whispered a single word, *Alissandra*.

'Ali,' I said to the woman in the water, 'Aliss.' And I felt the smallest echo in my chest: a sign of one last fleck of love. Mother's dearest friend. She'd borne a girl child out of wedlock for the queen. She'd lived in Demetra's cave because of it. Now Magnus had her jailed in the dungeon.

I stirred the water, distorting my reflection. My mouth widened in the pool, my eyes floated outward. I could not go. I felt all but dead.

Do you love only dragons now? Kit shouted from her boat.

She was right. I was more dragon than a princess now. I'd grown into my dragon's part more fully in the past year, and castle life seemed foreign.

I brought my head down to the earth, no heart left, my soul and body wanting ease. 'God, release me,' I whispered. Still, I felt the grip of Kit's song, and the waterfall above seemed to take up her mother's name, till all the tumbling water sang, *Alissandra*.

At dawn, Chawl took me on his back, and together with Eetha and Ore, we left Dragon's Keep. As we sped across the water, Dragon's Keep grew small as a dust mote in the great eye of the sea. Between sky and water we flew, the stinging wind blowing back my cloak. The early sun spilled across the water. And far across the sea, I thought a show of white might be a ship sailing for Dragon's Keep. Looking again, I lost the image in a spray of mist.

It was nightfall by the time we neared Wilde Island, I saw the land ahead as I clung to Chawl's broad neck. The heavy sound of his pumping wings was nothing to my heartbeat as I saw Pendragon Castle. Suddenly I wanted to scream 'Turn back!' but thoughts of Aliss curled up in the dungeon straw – dirty, hungry, and left to the dark – kept me to my course.

By the Pendragon tomb we landed. All was dark about us, and the wind-blown birches accompanied the rustling of dragon wings. Climbing from Chawl's back, I said goodbye to the pips.

'You will rule in power,' said Eetha. I smiled at this, thinking how little she knew of humankind.

'Don't forget your inner fire,' said Chawl, breathing a bit of flame to me. And I used his fire to light a candle from Sexton's box near the tomb. Then I kissed the pips, which they did not like but took with dignity. Last, Ore licked my cheek with her rough tongue and said, 'Briar.'

They rose into the night. My candle flickered in their wings' wind. Turning for the musty tomb, I crossed myself and entered, descending the narrow steps. The chamber to the right housed Mother's parents and brother who had all died the same week from the pox. How small Prince Bion's effigy seemed as I passed by. He was younger than myself when he died. Mother must have come here, and alone as a girl – released from Saint Brigid's to mourn her family and be crowned queen all within a month. Now I would kneel before my parents as she had done. How the world turns back on itself and we travel on the byways our parents strove along whether we wish it or no.

An hour passed – two. As I prayed, I saw through tears, a yarrow moth fly in and flit about my candle. I minded the day Father and I rode to the lake and watched the moths' birth from their waxen tombs. 'Look ye, Rosie,' he'd said. 'Out of death to life.'

I gave thanks for the sending of the moth, for in the darkest times it is the small things, a bit of bread or a flitting moth, that can bring a body hope.

Night was passing. I descended the twisting steps that led to the underground passage and prised open the wall. As I raised my candle and stepped into the damp tunnel, I was greeted by scores of spiders. I bit my lip and journeyed on, taking the full length of the passage under yard and moat. My plan was simple as a sailor's knot. I would present myself on the morrow, acting the part of queen. With regal bearing as my mother had of old, I'd order Sir Magnus to the dungeon, free sweet Aliss, and claim my rightful throne.

At the far end of the tunnel, I opened the hidden door and slipped into the wine cellar. Up the servants' stairs I fled, crept down the narrow hall and stole round the corner. Seeing Mother's door unchallenged, I went in.

Her scent greeted me as I entered the solar. It came across me in a ripplet as if my entrance had disturbed the very pool of air inside. I closed my eyes and took in the sweet odour.

In the flickering candlelight, I sought the washing bowl and, finding it empty, tiptoed to the laver to fill it. Back in Mother's chamber, I stripped away my dragon skin, and washed a year of dragon smell from my person. I'd grown used to the scent on Dragon's Keep, but I thought my fellows would think it rank. The soap ball, which Mother had especially made for her, smelled of rose oil. It brought to mind her soft cheek when she kissed me, the brush of her cool fingers, when, alone, she'd taken off her gloves. My eyes welled up.

I wrapped up in a coverlet, and stood before the wardrobe. My naked fingers wandered across a stiff lace, a gathered sleeve. The red velvet was soft as a petal. Mother had worn this gown the night we celebrated Kye's victory over the dragon at the great banquet on the shore. And kneeling down I found still some grains of sand about the hem.

I donned the gown, slipped on my mother's shoes, and took up her comb to battle my tangled hair.

A war ensued which left my head aching with a thousand pricks. When my scalp felt needled as a pincushion, I gave in to the tangles, twisted my hair into a mass and pinned it on top of my head. 'Done!' I said. Now and only now did I turn for the mirror on the inside of the wardrobe door.

Before the glass I took in the slender woman dressed in red. Mother used to bring me here. Ah, she opened her wardrobe door for me when I was six and nine, ten and fourteen. But always we viewed the glass together gloved so she could face me smiling, willing with her heart that I was whole, then she'd say, 'Queen Rosalind Pendragon. Know who you are.'

'Know who you are,' I whispered. 'Rosalind.' I held up my naked hands, 'Queen Briar.'

The talon had grown a full two inches on Dragon's Keep, the blue-green scales had brightened in the fresh air. Never had I seen my claw in Mother's glass. I could hold my naked hands out now and take in all I saw without shame. The dragons had given me that. I marvelled at the gift.

Lord Faul would have roared out fire if he'd seen me prune my 'pretty part,' as he had called it. Still, I knew the people here would burn me for a witch if they saw it so I knifed the talon, peeling it slowly as a carver whittles wood. Black pieces clattered to the floor, smoke curled warming me with a familiar dragon smell. When the talon was cut down to the nub, I hid the shavings behind the logs in the hearth. No fire to burn the leavings as Mother used to do. I knew better than to light one and announce my presence here. In the chill room I sheathed the knife, shuddered and donned a pair of Mother's golden gloves.

Stars still burned outside the castle walls, so I said a prayer to Saint Brigid, asking for her blessing of witty speech against Sir Magnus on the morrow, then I lay on Mother's bed where sleep encompassed me.

36
Discovered

AFTER DAWN THE CHAMBERMAID CAME IN, SAW ME abed in Mother's gown and fled screaming, 'The queen's ghost! God save us!' Quick the castle guard clattered up the stairs, tore me from my bed and led me down the hall.

'Let go!' I said. 'I order you!'

Servants peeked around doors, eyes wide, mouths agape. In the Great Hall, the sight of Sir Magnus at his breakfast fairly twisted my spleen. The mage sat in crimson robes with soft fur slippers on his feet and golden gloves upon his hands! Mary and Joseph! Nothing I'd seen on Dragon's Keep had insulted me as much as this! I was used to the women of high rank wearing gloves, though never golden as Mother's and mine. But for *him* to don golden gloves, wearing them as a sign of power as a whore wears silk, this offended me more than Lord Faul's power, which had been real and his anger pure.

'Bring her forward,' he ordered. The guard shoved me to the floor. I tried to stand but Sir Kent, whom I knew well from childhood, booted my spine. Thus I lay in supplication to the mage.

'Who are you that you creep into the queen's chamber in the middle of the night?'

'I am Princess Rosalind.'

'Rosalind is dead,' said Sir Magnus.

'No, I live. Let me stand, and you'll see for yourself.'

Sir Magnus nodded. Boot removed, I stood, rubbed the small of my spine and brushed the straw from Mother's gown. Fire filled me now. Sir Magnus would be punished for this.

'There is some likeness,' admitted Magnus. 'But a witch can guise herself.'

'I'm no witch!'

Sir Magnus speared his sausage and held it up. 'If you are Rosalind, tell us how you entered the castle unnoticed by the guards? I know myself the drawbridge was not lowered yestereve.'

'There is another way inside,' I offered, but I said no more, having promised Father I would never show the tunnel to another soul.

'A way into Pendragon Castle? Not unless you swam the moat or used a spell to fly across on crow's back.'

'I did nothing of the sort. I heard about my mother's death and came home to claim my crown.'

'Your crown?' he scoffed.

'And,' I continued, 'my first command is to send you to the dungeon for poisoning my —'

'Make commands?' shouted Sir Magnus coming to a stand. The sausage dropped to the floor to the delight of the dogs, but the breadth of his belt showed how little Magnus needed meat. 'You may call yourself Rosalind, but we all know it cannot be so. We saw the dragon swoop her away last May Day.'

The guards' faces were stone, the servants, all but Mouser who was dumb to the proceedings, cowered at my stare. Cook, cheeks red and chin a-quiver, crushed the corners of her smeared apron.

'The dragon spared me.'

'The dragon showed you mercy? Never. But entertain us with more lies.' He sat and speared another sausage. 'And tell us why he did not eat you.' He jammed the sausage in his mouth. The room rang with laughter.

This I could not answer. Sir Magnus smacked his lips loudly as I looked at the floor. I'd vowed to keep the pips secret. The last of the world's dragons must have their chance at life.

'Answer,' demanded Magnus.

'I cannot,' I said. 'But I can say this! My mother died because you filled her with –'

'Sorcery!' shouted Magnus. 'It must be by the devil's sorcery you lived with the dragon.'

'No!'

'I say he spared you because you are a witch, and the dragon your kith-beast.'

I screamed and rushed for the mage. Before I reached the table, I was caught by two guards and held at bay like a wild cur.

'My lord, a word,' called Sir Winston from behind. Sir Magnus waved him forward. The knight's grey hair fell across his brow as he whispered in the mage's ear.

I looked about the room for help and found none. Indeed, my mother's gown and shoes could not hide the wild girl I'd become on Dragon's Keep. And though I'd bathed, I knew there was a stench about my person and everyone seemed afraid to look at me. Another thing I saw as I looked about for help: all the women were wearing gloves woven of the best material each could find. In years past only women of high standing donned gloves, now I saw my mother's fashion had extended even to the servants.

At the high table, Sir Winston hissed in Sir Magnus's ear. The mage stood then and frowned. 'As I suspected, we have evidence of witchery here,' he said. 'We'll hold a trial in three days' time. Take her to the dungeon.'

'Poisoner!' I screamed, but the crowd paid my words no more mind than they would the ravings of a mad woman. 'Let me go!' I shouted. 'I'm your queen!' The guards dragged me from the room. All along the halls the servants covered their noses and looked away. Down the steps we went, the sounds of our feet like the clatter of spilled pebbles. Sir Winston threw me in a cell and slammed the metal door.

37

Witch Trial

THE CELL WAS DARK BUT FOR A NARROW STREAM OF light from a high slit in the stone wall. I crept to it fearing what might lurk in the shadows.

'Aliss?'

No answer. The dungeon had more than one cell. Kit's mother should not be far off. 'Aliss?'

What light I had showed me two dead things: a crow and a rat. Black feathers were neatly arranged in a pattern of spreading circles. Small to large, they rayed outward like a sun. It seemed a woman's hand had done this. Beside the crow's bones lay the half-eaten body of the rat. I wrapped my arms about my knees and rocked, the foul smell and the chill making me long for the clean spill of my waterfall on Dragon's Keep.

Late in the day the cell door opened.

I leaped to a stand. 'Sir. Have you come to free me?' The old man flung a bit of bread on the floor and left slamming the heavy door shut. Two rats from the dark corner raced for my meal.

'Stay back!' I grabbed my bit of bread and ate standing, the rats at my feet making do with their brother's carcass.

Black flies buzzed about my head. I swatted and planned what I would say at my witch-trial. I must shield myself from the sharp words meant to cut me from the throne, and use them to condemn the mage.

The dawn of my fourth day, as the cell door opened and the guard came in with the rushlight, I awoke to find the rats nibbling on my hair. I was still screaming when the guard pulled me from the cell and bound my hands behind my back. In the Great Hall a crowd awaited. It seemed Sir Magnus, who sat above all dressed in blue velvet and wearing golden gloves, had called forth all of Dentsmore and other villages besides, for the hall was full and the younger children clung to their mothers.

All were gathered as if for a great celebration and the dogs roved about slobbering in anticipation of a feast. I was led to the centre of the room. Sitting on either side of Sir Magnus were Sheriff William and Father Hugh. It gave my heart a tug of hope. Both men were sound, and just.

To my right Jossie Brummer stood with Niles, wearing a hardened look. It was the same proud glance she'd given me aged twelve when she beat me at apple crowdie. My heart panged to see how Niles had chosen her after Kit was sent away. Near Jossie stood her father, Keith the miller, and his plump wife Kate.

Among the heads, long-haired and shorn, stood Marn's son, the blacksmith. Mother's band of lady's maids, including the nib-nosed Lady Beech, stood in assembly. And idling about here or there as if they had not a jot of work to do this day, were the castle servants. Nowhere in the throng could I see Sister Anne. Her presence would have strengthened me, but she must have left the castle long ago for the abbey.

Sir Magnus stood. The crowd murmured excitedly. Yet in all the faces besmeared with dirt or clean, none had a smile for me but Cook. I gave her round face a nod, but she took a sudden interest in the rushes at her feet and tidied up her skirts.

'We are bound today,' began Sir Magnus, 'to try this Rosalind who disappeared a year ago to abide with the beast on Dragon's Keep. I've called all present here to give witness to her witch-crimes which are many as all shall see.' He lifted his finger in the air. 'But we are a civilized people and do not condemn on hearsay.'

With this he nodded to the sheriff and acknowledged Father Hugh. The good Father gazed back, his heavy brows discontent. 'Has this woman Rosalind done any crimes that she be here?' he asked.

'Well,' said Sir Magnus with a shake of the head. 'Many may be counted against her if all I hear is true. I call Sir Niles Broderick first to testify.'

Niles stepped from the crowd proudly wearing his knight's garb, his sunny hair combed back. He was an arm's length away so I caught the smell of hay and horses, a welcome scent.

Magnus eyed him encouragingly. 'Tell us what you know, Sir Niles.'

Niles's shoulders slumped. It may have been his chain mail vest, but I thought the weight of what he had to say was heavy on him. 'A year ago we sailed to Dragon's Keep to rescue the princess.'

'This I know well,' said Magnus, proudly. 'I equipped you at your knight's fitting.' He leaned forward. 'What happened there?'

'We found the princess. I brought her to the ship where we awaited Sir Kimball and the slayers' return,' said Niles. 'But all the while the lady here challenged me to launch the ship and escape the island. I stood firm for waiting. But she didn't care about the others, she –'

'I cared about them all!'

'The accused is not allowed to speak until all witnesses are heard!' warned Sir Magnus. 'That is the law.'

I clenched my teeth as he motioned for Niles to continue. Indeed it was the law, but I'd be hard pressed not to break it with all this truth-twisting.

'Go on, sir,' urged Magnus.

'The others did not come back.' Niles paused and crossed himself as did many in the throng.

'And then the dragon –' He frowned and looked askance at me.

'Fear nothing here,' said Sir Magnus.

'The dragon landed near us, cutting off escape. I charged him but he captured me.'

A moan from the crowd.

'As he held me high in the air, I swung my sword to slice his throat and shouted for the princess to attack him from below. She had a knife, but she . . .' He shook his head. 'She would not attack. Instead she . . . drew the blade against her own throat.'

I worked to slow my breathing as a series of gasps and murmurs crossed the room.

'What threat would this be to the dragon?' said Sir Magnus. 'Unless the beast had a special feeling for the girl.' He said these words to the air as if they were his thoughts, yet all about heard him clearly.

'What then?' asked Magnus.

'The dragon cracked my skull. I remember nothing more until I awoke near the tomb in the arms of our good queen, God rest her soul.' Niles crossed himself again.

'Were any present there to witness this knight's return from Dragon's Keep?' asked Sir Magnus.

'I was there,' said Sir Allweyn. The falconer emerged from the crowd, his long neck stooped forward. The baldness had increased across his pate in the time I'd been away. Three grey tufts remained. These he'd combed outward like a jester's cap, but there was no joy in his face or in his dark-ringed eyes.

'I saw the dragon throw young Sir Niles on the turf by the tomb. Then the princess tossed her gloves at the queen and cursed her mother before she flew off on the dragon's back.'

More gasps.

'I did not curse her!'

'The accused will be silent or be gagged!' warned Sir Magnus.

'Indeed,' continued Sir Allweyn, 'I was not close enough to hear the curse, but the queen spoke of it straight away.

"Cursed," she cried when I led her to the castle. She was weeping and all undone by her daughter.'

'Hmm,' said Sir Magnus. 'This tells us much. The girl tossed her gloves to the ground – and this before the dragon when we all know a high-born woman does not remove her gloves to any but her husband.'

He shook his head. My blood fairly boiled. I withheld a hiss.

Magnus went on. 'I tended the queen after that strange night. How twisted her bowels were, and how morbid her liver.' He looked up at the ceiling as if to consult the chandelier. 'Neither toadflax nor bloodletting nor St John's-wort cured her. Indeed she muttered strangely to herself often in the months ahead, and many times called out from her fevered sleep, "The curse!" He raised his voice when he said the words to mimic Mother's tone. This pleased and stunned the crowd, who always liked a show.

'I wondered what the queen meant,' said Magnus. 'Now I begin to see.'

Waves of body heat wafted from the close-knit crowd. I tried to swallow, my throat dry as stale bread. 'And you *poisoned* her with poppy potion!'

'Gag her!' ordered Sir Magnus.

'Wait. I'll not speak again.'

Too late. The gag was across my mouth. Sir Magnus looked down at me. 'Who but a witch would curse her mother so,' he said, 'and choose a dragon's company over her own kin?'

I screamed into the gag. How the mage twisted everything!

'It would kill me if my daughter chose a dragon over me,' said Kate Brummer with a nod. And Jossie, who now stood arm in arm with Niles, held her chin up proudly.

'You may step back, Sir Allweyn,' said Sir Magnus.

'If I may . . .' said Sir Allweyn with a cough.

'What more have you to say?'

''Tis a thing I fear to speak.' He turned his three-tufted head to the crowd. 'A strange sight I saw long ago still troubles me.'

A smile twitched the mage's lip. 'Speak,' he offered.

'It concerns an old friend, once a servant to the princess, who died unnaturally, and whose soul weighs on me. Some here remember the princess's nursemaid, Marn?'

'Aye! A kindly sort!' cried Cook.

'My mother,' called the blacksmith.

'I say this with some dread,' he went on. 'I knew Marn well, and never would she throw herself into the moat.'

'Aye! That's God's truth!' The blacksmith's voice was deep and fairly echoed in the hall.

Sir Allweyn sighed. 'I was the man that fished Marn from the water,' he said. 'And as I lay the lady by the moat, I saw the marks about her throat, too small for a man's hands to make.'

More stirrings from the crowd behind.

Sir Magnus leaned forward. 'What are you saying, sir?'

'Marks, I say.' Sir Allweyn pointed to me, stretching out his forefinger the way I'd seen him coax a small bird from the cage. 'I remembered how many times Marn ran to the mews when the princess was having one of her fits. The poor woman lived in fear of her. So I wondered at the

296

marks the morn I fished her from the moat.'

'I told ye!' shouted the blacksmith raising his fist in the air at Father Hugh. 'I told ye she'd never killed herself. It was never in her!'

'Hush!' warned Sir Magnus. 'This trial shall be orderly.' He faced Sheriff William. 'Why did you not see these marks?'

The sheriff turned stiffly, sucking in his belly. 'I was still attending to the murder of Chandler's wife, Tess.'

Sir Magnus nodded knowingly.

'And the dragon attacked that same morning!' called out a villager.

'After the Midsummer Fair!' called another.

'Demetra died,' added a third.

Magnus didn't silence them this time. 'Well,' he said at last, giving a sober look about the room. 'If murder is suspected here, we should dig the nursemaid up and look into the matter.'

'There'll be no flesh left on those bones by now,' said the sheriff. He exhaled and his belly rounded for a moment before his next breath. I closed my eyes. The thought of my dear Marn all gone to bones brought vomit up my throat. I worked to swallow it, recalling my lady training. Ah, if Marn were at this trial, she'd defend me. And if I felt faint, she'd tell me to lean on her, though she'd whisper, 'Thimbles, how my back aches,' if I rested for too long.

Marks on her neck? I hadn't seen them on her drowning day. Sir Allweyn said the bruises were too small for a man's hands – Mother's last farewell.

Bram was called to testify next. He shook as he spoke. I'd never seen him tremble so.

'You may speak plainly,' said Sir Magnus.

'I do,' said Bram. 'That is, I always have, being a pigboy, thou knowest.'

This brought a snort from Sheriff William.

'Tell us what you came to say.'

'Pigs are my pride and duty so I should have been more watchful, but I let the princess touch a sow one spring, and that sow birthed a two-headed piglet within the hour!'

A story, I thought, for he had never told me this. Still the villagers moaned, the sound crossing the Great Hall like wind in a thicket.

'Two heads, I say. And I knew it were a witch-sign. But her being the princess and all, I kilt the piglet swift, and buried it behind the barn.'

The crowd was murmuring now with stories of strange beasts.

' . . . born without a leg after she saw my sheep at the fair,' said a man's voice from behind, 'and the lamb had to sport about on three.'

' . . . and the dog hadn't any tail,' said a woman's voice. 'So it was all rump and no wag. Have ye ever heard of such?'

Cook rushed forward. 'I have some things to say in defence of the princess!' she called.

'Wait your turn, Cook!'

'Bram's done, aren't you, pigboy?' said Cook bustling to the front of the Great Hall.

'I be done, sir, unless you want to hear her spell.'

Sir Magnus's bushy brow went up. 'Don't hold back, boy.'

'I was all over stung with bees and that was bad enough, but she,' he pointed to me to make it clear whom he was accusing, 'She held me down and rubbed a potion on me and said a spell that went, 'Sting, sting of the bee. Remove thy sword –'

'Don't repeat it here, lackwit,' shouted Magnus, as if he feared the words when he knew as well as I that he'd shown me the healing charm in his own book when Bram was stung.

'Oh,' said Bram, eyes wide. 'Sorry, Sir Magnus.'

Many were crossing themselves against the charm, though Bram didn't seem to feel the need to.

Cook nudged the pigboy aside. 'I've known the princess longest here. Haven't I worked over the kitchen fire at Pendragon Castle since before the queen's wedding day? Aye, so I was here for the princess's birth and all. Ah, what a storm there was! Wind and snow so's a body couldn't see a foot ahead, and the poor midwife died in it!'

'Hmm,' said Sir Magnus. 'A bad sign.'

'Aye! And the poor babe with none to attend her but her mother and she wouldn't let anyone near, keeping the babe to herself as if in mourning, but some women take on that way. Anywise, what a rosy babe she was! And didn't I serve up a mighty table at her christening! The roast was tender as churned butter, and the pan puffs light as clouds –'

'Menu not needed here,' said Magnus. 'We look to the state of the girl's soul.'

'My head's always at the table,' laughed Cook.

I bit my lip, praying to Saint Brigid for Cook's kind words to heal the wounds made here. Thus far, she'd only added more weight to the witching scale.

'Who could blame her nursemaid Marn for loving the child so?' said Cook. 'How she fussed over the princess! How worn she was, yet she'd work and work to serve the girl's every whim. Ah! The child had her nurse in such a love-spell. Marn would have died for her! I say it now and I say it again, the woman would have died!' Cook dabbed her eyes with the corner of her apron. I prayed she had no more words of help for me, but she heaved a sigh and went on.

'And her lady's maid, Katinka. Never was there such attending. Didn't she come to my kitchen early each morn to bring sweet milk and bread to the princess? Ah, she was up with the dawn to serve her. Ah, they had a bond. I once saw the princess help the girl from the moat. Didn't Rosalind bravely go into the water when all know only witches can swim?'

By this time I was praying to Saint Balbulus to inflict his stammer on Cook. Still Cook went on, 'I often wondered why the princess shunned Katinka. A pretty girl like that shouldna' waste away in a nunnery!'

'Ah!' she went on. 'But we all loved the princess! When she was but a poppet, she rode her father the king like a horse and ordered him about the castle gardens, the precious little thing. And sure it was her mother loved her so! She'd never hear my complaints of the princess stealing food from my pantry, not even when she took whole rounds of cheese and meat besides!'

Cook raised her eyes. 'And when the dragon took the princess that last time, the queen's heart broke! I say it now though I've no doctoring sense. It wasn't her bowels nor her liver that twisted her to her end, Sir Magnus. I'm bold to say the princess kilt her!'

'With her curse,' said Magnus, driving in the final blow.

'Aye,' sobbed Cook, 'You could say that, love's curse it was, for she'd not touch her food and withered away in mourning for the girl.'

Cook lifted her apron to her face, and wept mightily into it, her shoulders quaking. All stood befuddled by her display, unsure of what to do. Sir Magnus waved his hand and had her whisked away.

'We have strange evidence still to come,' announced Sir Magnus over Cook's loud bawling, which still filled the room though she was far down the hall by now. 'There may be some here,' he said, 'who would swoon at what Sir Winston is about to show. Remove yourself if you have a weak stomach.'

None moved. No man protected his good wife. No mother took her child from the room.

'Step up, Sir Winston, and show what you found on the floor hidden under the queen's bed the very morning you discovered Rosalind there.'

Sir Winston came forth with a simple cloth bag such as the castle laundress used. He paused to run his fingers through his thinning hair, looked first this way, then that, and pulled out my dragon-skin gown.

'Oh! Ah!' crooned the ladies.

'Um,' said the men.

'Would you call this lizard skin?' asked Sir Magnus.

'Aye,' said Sir Winston, 'if it be a giant lizard like a dragon.' He held it higher, the shape of it still showing my form that once lay under it, like the hollow of a wasp husk.

'Here is her dragon skin!' said Sir Magnus, 'and there's no denying it is hers, to view the shape. Here is how she used dark magic to enter Pendragon Castle unseen.'

'Look away,' said Miller's wife to her children. 'Don't gaze into her witch's eyes!'

This was too much! I squirmed in my bonds, shouting in my gag.

'Grab her lest she cast her spell on us!' ordered Sir Magnus. I fought the guard, but he held me tight and from behind.

Sir Magnus stood. 'Here before us all is the woman who wafted into Pendragon Castle. Logic tells us she used witchery to float above the moat, for we all know the bridge was up. Thus, she came wrapped in dragon skin, invisible to mortal man. Coming home, as she said, after she was sure her mother was dead. Returning to Wilde Island to claim the Pendragon crown. Think now,' he said leaning toward the crowd. 'Are you safe with the queen's crown on this woman's head? She who chooses dragons over kin? A spell caster and a murderess?'

He let the word 'murderess' fall across the crowd like silk.

'Nay!' shouted the crowd. 'Hang her!'

'Is this sure proof she is a witch or murderess?' asked the sheriff cautiously.

'Proof a-plenty!' said Magnus.

'Trial by water,' said Father Hugh padding across the rush-strewn floor to my defence.

'No,' said Magnus. 'For one such as her it must be trial by fire. She'll walk the coals, and if her wounds don't heal in three days' time, we'll know her to be guilty.'

'God have mercy,' said Father Hugh shaking his head in good sadness, and so all were agreed.

38

The Devil's Footpath

I WAS THROWN INTO MY RAT-INFESTED CELL TO contemplate my sins before my torture trial. Stale bread and brown water were brought to me each day. I battled the rats for my food, relieved myself in the bucket, went down on my knees in the narrow bit of sunlight, and called out to God.

When at last the guards came for me, I was taken to the castle foreyard where an audience could watch my torture in the bright, good, morning air. Sir Allweyn leaned over the bed of coals, taking special care to keep them hot with his bellows.

The air above the coals wavered glassy with the heat. I was sick with fear as the guardsmen brought me forward and made me sit down on a stool. There I was gagged and blindfolded and someone, a man I think by his awkwardness, removed my shoes and hose. I felt the shame of my bare legs and ankles exposed to the onlookers. Thus with naked feet, I was hauled to a stand.

'Check her for herb charms and sniff her for salves!' ordered Sir Magnus. More shame as large hands felt me up and down, touching even my breasts for hidden witch cures. Next the sound of sniffing, a man's face at my neck, and at my feet a dog's wet nose. The cur sniffed up my legs and down, licked my foot and yelped. The man no doubt had kicked him.

'See how the beasts love her,' noted Magnus.

'There is a stink!' the man reported. 'But no witch herbs or salves here, sir!'

'Good!' said Sir Magnus. I heard a strange low muttering in Latin, which I took to be Father Hugh close by. What prayer he said, I could not tell, but I knew he was good-hearted. In this entire crowd, it seemed he and Cook were the only ones who hoped my burns would heal and prove my innocence.

'Take her!' ordered Magnus. I felt the growing warmth as I was led to the edge of the coals. Before the burning path, my mother's gown was twisted to a knot above the knee. Standing near my torture bed, I thought on the last thing Chawl had said before we parted, 'Don't forget your inner fire.'

The heat from the coals washed upward from the ground. I prayed to the Holy Spirit who lives inside the wind, to blow an inner fire in me such as the dragons have. Thus stoked, I hoped to meet fire with fire as I stepped out.

Ah, God the pain of that first step! The searing heat! I could smell my flesh burning as I hastened across the cruel bed. Stumbling sideways, I was righted and placed firmly on the coals again. I screamed into my gag, the sounds coming from my throat like a strangled hen. I walked forward. More agony. The rhythm in my head chanting: Fire. God. Fire. God, and the crowd about me moaning like a sea wind.

When I'd walked the devil's road, I collapsed and was dragged before Sir Magnus who ordered my gag and blindfold removed. Unable to stand on my burnt feet, I stayed on my knees, breathing hard as a runner. Sir Magnus bedecked in blue robes and wearing golden gloves, took out a small phial and held it under my right eye, then under my left.

'See,' he said lifting the phial for all to view. 'Not a single tear!'

'Ah!' called the miller's wife. 'It's a sign for witches and dragons who never cry!'

'Aye, all know it!' called Jossie.

I swayed under the searing pain burning up my feet. 'The b . . . blindfold,' I stuttered. 'It soaked up –' I couldn't finish.

Father Hugh rushed forward. 'We should wrap her wounds.' He bent over me and touched the back of my neck with his cool hand. 'She's in God's hands now, Sir Magnus, and in three days' time her wounds will show her guilt or innocence.'

Sir Magnus paid little mind to Father Hugh, but held the glass phial up to the sunlight as if the dryness of my eyes were proof enough.

'Wrap her!' insisted the good Father.

Still on my knees, I cringed as my feet were bound and the cloths knotted tight. With aid I stood on the binding-cloth, pain sharp as hot pokers searing up my legs as I was led away.

After two days in the cell, I was still in pain. Sweat covered me, and bouts of trembling. I sipped brown water, but could not touch my crusts. The rats were joyful over it. More fever-dreams came, and now they were of Kye. My lover called me and I tried to come, but my feet were wrapped in molten metal. With a will to my legs, I walked into his arms. Kye lifted me close and I could smell the sweetness of his skin. But as I leaned in for his kiss, he threw me under a table as a feast-goer would a gnawed bone, and in the dream he shouted, 'Dragon-filth. I've seen your claw!'

I screamed, awaking to the smell of my own foul sweat. I wept and crawled about in the dark as one gone mad. If Sir Magnus held his phial in the corner of my eye then, I would have overflowed it.

On the third morning, I awoke to a tingling in my feet and felt hope stirring in my breast.

This would be my testing day where innocence or guilt was proved. I ate a bit of bread for strength and stood on my bandaged feet, counting up to thirteen before falling to the straw again.

At midday, joy-songs drifted into the dungeon. I crawled to the wall, and pulled myself up to the barred window. Outside I spied two men marching to the draw-bridge with a maypole. In a flutter of red and yellow ribbons, three musicians played 'Will Ye Come A-Maying' on their pipes.

So it was May Day. I took this to be a good sign. The window slit was too small to see the fullness of the fore-yard, though I could hear hammering as workmen built the selling stalls for the fair. Pipes played and I saw a crowd moving about in the foreyard. All were signs of May Day preparations.

The cell door opened. Two guards gagged me and led me up the narrow steps. I walked to prove my healing, though there was still some pain. The sight that greeted me in the bright-lit foreyard hit me with such violence I dry-retched in my gag. Apart from a crowd of hooded Benedictine monks on the edge of the crowd, all the people in the foreyard encircled a gallows.

Villagers parted and grew silent as I was led to the stage beside the gallows where Sir Magnus sat dressed in velvet robes, and wearing a great gold chain that ended in my mother's jewelled cross. On either side of him, sweating in the midday sun, were Father Hugh, and Sheriff William.

Directly, I was brought to an empty stool before them and made to sit, which eased my feet but not my heart. Father Hugh was called forward to unwrap my bandages for all to see. The good father's hands shook as he unbound my right foot. The wrapping came away to my flesh, discoloured, but untorn. With care, Father Hugh inspected it, pressing first the soles then pinching hard each toe. 'It's healed!' he said. Cook cheered, but was alone in her cheering.

In heavy silence, Father Hugh unbound my left foot. As he tore the final wrap away, my skin tore with it. Fresh blood dripped from the wound. Father Hugh frowned as he watched the blood flow down, and began a prayer in Latin for he could not declare me healed.

'Ah! Ye can all see!' called Kate the miller's wife.

'This proves her witchery!' announced Sir Magnus, tapping the cross on his breast.

'No!' I cried under my gag but none could hear with the crowd shouting, 'Hang her! Hang the witch!' I fought the guard, who had me in his grip, but he was the stronger, and he dragged me step-on-step up to the gallows.

The rope swung in the May breeze and my knees went all to water as Cook lifted her hands in the air, crying, 'Ah, she was such a pretty thing! Such a love-charm she had over all of us!'

The villagers bustled forward as I struggled with the guard and screamed into my gag for mercy. Sir Magnus raised his arms. 'See how the witch calls upon the devil!' he shouted to the crowd. Then he held my mother's cross before him and spewed Latin verses to shield his soul against Satan.

The village folk were all jostling each other, fighting for a good view of the gallows, like rats to a meat-bone. Cook was knocked over and trodden on, then I saw Jossie fall down screaming and flailing against the steps.

Before she was crushed, the guard who held me reached out to her, and in that moment I leaped from the gallows, landed on my bleeding feet and rushed into the crowd.

Screams of 'Catch her!' and 'Hold her fast!' resounded as I plunged into the gathering, pushing, pounding, kicking my way through.

'Grab her!' called the guards while the tanner's wife screamed, 'Ah! She touched me! Now I'm cursed!'

Sheb Kottle captured me, but I knocked him down and rushed right over the top of the old man. Breaking free, I ran along the curtain wall until a strong-armed Benedictine caught me round the middle.

I screamed and beat against the monk's chest, but he lifted me so my feet were flailing in the air, and under the cowl I saw his blue eyes glaring down. He grimaced as he held me up, his strong chin clamped shut with the labour of it, but I knew the man and suddenly ceased my struggling. Kye, older, taller, and gowned as a holy man. I drank in his face. I thought he'd come to protect me from the hanging rope, but Kye turned and carried me back to the gallows to the cheering of the crowd.

I flailed against him then, but he hauled me up the steps with ease and with one arm tight around me, Kye threw back his hood. The crowd gasped.

'You see that I am Kye Godrick!

'The dragonslayer!' called a villager.

'He's taken holy orders!' cried another.

'I have a thing to show the nature of this woman's blood before justice is done!' Kye shouted.

My bones fluted hollow then, and it seemed an eastern wind rushed through them. Kye had seen my claw and he meant to prove my witch-blood now by tearing off my glove.

39

Blood Proof

STILL TIGHT IN KYE'S GRIP, I CLENCHED MY FISTS. Here was the thing I'd dreaded most, the day when all Wilde Island would see my beast-part and call me devil's spawn. Ah, I feared it more than the witch-trial or walking on the coals, for I'd had the full of my life to imagine the horror of that moment.

As I struggled in Kye's arms, Sir Magnus came to a stand by the gallows shouting, 'Unhand the witch! We'll take no orders from a bandit in monk's guise!'

'I'll keep the wench a while,' called Kye. 'I have all rights. I fought alongside your king. My ship's crew is here with me,' he said, nodding to the group of brown-clad men who tossed back their cowls, and not a single head was tonsured.

'I know more about this woman than any man here,' continued Kye. 'I say hear me out before the noose is fitted!'

'Give him his chance to boast,' agreed Sheriff William coming to Sir Magnus's side. 'He's honoured as our dragonslayer and the poor man missed the witch-trial.'

I thrashed and screamed into my gag.

'Be still!' Kye warned. He brought me to his front, wrapped his strong arms about my chest, and the hold was like a dragon's grip.

'On promise to your king,' called Kye, 'I returned to Wilde Island after the war, and hearing his daughter had been stolen, I sailed to Dragon's Keep.'

There before all, Kye told of coming to the isle with his crew, how he sought me on Dragon's Keep and found all abandoned. As he spoke, my claw pounded and I curled my fingers inward. Kye was coming to the moment of showing my dragon's mark to all, and I swore to myself he'd have to cut the gloves off first.

'And now,' he said, 'I have something to show that will give to all sure proof of this woman's blood!'

I moaned into my gag.

Kye gripped me hard with one hand. I bent my knees and shoved my gloved hands between my legs as he reached into his monk's robe. Sure he was going for a knife, I plunged my hands in deeper. He'd have to prise my legs apart to reach my hands. But a knife did not appear.

From beneath his monk's robe Kye drew out a golden rod with the dragon's head atop. The dragon's ruby eyes shone blood-red in the sun.

'Queen Evaine's sceptre!' shouted Cook, for all knew by descriptive tales what it should look like.

'God be praised!' called Father Hugh, crossing himself.

Kye held it aloft. 'Here's final proof,' he called, 'that Princess Rosalind is of true and royal Pendragon blood.'

I stopped my struggling. Kye smiled down at me. 'You see?' he whispered.

Rumblings from the crowd. 'But she was found to be a witch!' called one disappointed villager, no doubt still wanting to see a hanging.

'Was she?' said Kye as if surprised. 'A storm made me take shelter in a hollow tree on Dragon's Keep. And there I found a book written by the princess. In its pages I learned she served her time as captive there to free you all from the dragon.'

How I blushed, knowing my love confessions written in that book, but the crowd was a-whisper. Kye went on, 'Were there any dragon attacks the year your princess was away?'

More mumbling. Then a villager called, 'None sir.'

'Ah,' said Kye. 'Now you begin to see. The princess traded her freedom to keep the beast away. And if you accuse her of witchery because she healed the sick, I ask who among you hasn't said their share of healing charms when the herbs fell short?'

Silence; a few coughs.

'We saw her dragon's gown!' called another. These villagers were a stubborn lot.

'Made for modesty when her own gown was too threadbare.'

The noose was slipping from the astrologer's grip. 'Step away from her,' ordered Sir Magnus.

Kye went on. 'Give honour to your princess.' He placed the sceptre in my hand. I held it up. Under the sway of Kye's words and the golden sceptre the crowd cheered. A few at first, then many voices came all in a rush, the sound washed through the foreyard like a great wave covering Magnus's protests. Even the sheriff and good Father Hugh were cheering.

It was then I called for Alissandra's release and she climbed from the darkened dungeon, as the sun will rise up shaking off the night.

40
Talon

BY JUNE MAGNUS WAS TRIED, FOUND GUILTY, AND
hanged. He swung from the very gallows he'd had
built for me. It seemed for his young wife's murder
in years past and for my mother's poisoning, the Fates had
spun this rope to noose his neck alone. In the following
month on the feast day of Saint Felicity, Kye and I were
wed in Saint John's chapel and Father Hugh presided over
sacred vows. I'd learned it was the good father who'd
housed Kye and his men and given them monk's garb – the
more to aid me if my wounds were not yet healed – for
soiled and stinking as I was, he still believed me innocent.

On our wedding night, I came trembling to our bed. I
feared the moment when I must peel away my gloves. But
in this my lover proved himself true beyond any other.
He'd seen my claw before in the company of wolves, he'd
read about my shame in my little book, and so he was tender to my fears.

Under the soft rain of his kisses, I took off crown and jewels, gown and shift. And like the yarrow moth who frees itself from its death shroud, I shed my gloves to Kye. He did not turn away, but lifted my hand to the candlelight. It was like the moment we'd shared long ago in the little cave beside the sea, when Kye called the dragon's egg beautiful. He stared at my claw in awe. He did not call it beautiful, the man could not lie, but he held the mystery of it to him, not as a separate curse, but as a part of me, his wife.

In part Merlin's vision had come to pass. I'd saved Wilde Island from Sir Magnus, but this seemed a small thing. I'd not yet ended war, redeemed our good name, or restored the glory of Wilde Island. The tapestry on my wall, aged by the sun, held a prophecy that was still uncertain. Yet Empress Matilda ended her war with Stephen though it took a few more years for her son to become Henry II, ruler of all England. He was married to Eleanor of Aquitaine and I wished them all joy.

In the sway of Merlin's vision Mother dreamed I'd win honour for the Pendragons, ruling England and Wilde Island. But I looked at the starry vision with another eye. Merlin said I was to restore Wilde Island's glory. Would the fairies return to Wilde Island to play in the meadow grass?

Would the spirits sleeping in the trees awake and speak to us again? This would indeed bring glory – a kind I understood, and Kye also. For he'd heard the pine trees whispering this vision the night he'd spent on God's Eye.

We held the Midsummer Eve Fair on Twisters Hill the following year. As the villagers danced about the bonfires that roared high and golden on the cliffs, I felt such a rush of pleasure that I lifted little Tess, daughter of Sir Niles Broderick and Jossie, and took her dancing near the fire while the villagers sang. I was full of joy because I'd just learned I was with child.

I'd worried from the day we wed that I would be like Mother – unable to conceive without sorcery. But my worries fell away and my joy grew as I felt a new life growing in my womb. Only Kye and my worthy queen's counsellor, Alissandra, knew my secret. Still I danced with little Tess to celebrate, as the sun set and the sky blushed pink.

On the high blowing cliffs before twilight it seemed the russet-coloured sky was no more than the last kiss of the day, so I did not read it as a sign until I heard the pounding of the wings high above the cliffs.

Seven dragons swooped down from the clouds and landed in a half circle around the revellers. In the cool midsummer wind, the dragons stood, their golden chests heaving from their long flight over the sea. I heard a familiar rustling sound as they folded back their wings, then all stood stiff as great stone columns, glaring down at me.

It had been a year since I'd seen the pips but I recognized all, who apart from Ore had grown nearly as large as their father, but the other four were strange to me.

With our backs to the cliffs and the dragons stationed all around the crowd, everyone was cut off from escape. I feared for my people.

The pips might not risk speaking to me in the presence of their mates. Still, I handed Tess to Alissandra, and stepped forward. Kye, brave man, came up beside me and together we faced the dragons.

We were on the hill above, the villagers below cowered on the grass, mumbling prayers or covering their mouths to weep into their hands. I waited under the first showing of stars. I should greet them in DragonTongue, but how before these people?

My mouth went dry as a barley husk in the power of the dragons' gaze, their eyes bright as an enchanter's balls. And when Chawl opened his great jaws and roared blue fire as he'd done when he bid me farewell that last time by the tomb, my flesh crawled in the heat.

Then Eetha and Ore stepped through the blowing grass, doing what must be done, and so quickly, I could not stop them. With swift and single motion, Eetha tore off my golden gloves.

I screamed, stepping back, but as I tried to hide my cursed part, Eetha gripped my wrist.

'For your service to us, Briar,' she said in DragonTongue. Then she licked my talon.

With my hand exposed, the dragons all stepped closer. Ore lifted my hand, 'For Kit,' she said, her blue eyes shining then she too kissed my claw.

Kye, seeing what the dragons offered by the kiss, turned, broke his sword upon the stones, and laid it at the dragons' feet.

It took a mind simpler than mine to understand what Kye had done.

Cook pointed to the sword and shouted, 'It's come to pass just as the old rhyme said! Look ye! The dragon has given our queen a talon, and the king has broken his sword!'

Then, with my heart pounding in my breast, I held my

talon up for all to see.

'A peace gift from the dragons,' called Father Hugh.

'Ah, see how it clings to her hand!' called Marn's son. 'As if she were born so!'

I dropped my other glove and held my hands high, feeling the wind rush through my fingers.

Ah, the freedom of this nakedness. That which I'd hidden so long from all, transformed by a kiss and held in reverence. Merlin had said the twenty-first queen would end war with the wave of her hand. But I'd not known till now the mage meant the war between men and dragons.

The talon had, all in a moment, become a sign of peace between us.

Stars came out showing the deep of heaven as the dragons all went down on their knees and bowed to me, their scales shimmering in the moonlight like wind-blown water. And a sigh of pleasure rose from the crowd on Twisters Hill.

And there, with the dragons bowing, the bonfires crackling, and the sea churning far below, the people chanted:

Bright fire.
Dragon's fire.
Broken sword.
One black talon ends the war!

I raised my kissed claw higher.
My curse a blessing.
From that sweet night and on.

Acknowledgements

Many thanks and roses to my editor, Julia Wells, who is both keen-eyed and kind. To the members of Artemis: Katherine Grace Bond, Heidi Pettit, Margaret D. Smith, Jill Trepp Sahlstrom and Dawn Knight, for their artistic prowess and unabridged imaginations. Thanks also to my encouraging husband who says I should say he's nothing like the dragon.